THE
SECOND
MRS
STROM

THE SECOND MRS STROM

KAIRA ROUDA

bookouture

Published by Bookouture in 2024

An imprint of Storyfire Ltd.
Carmelite House
50 Victoria Embankment
London EC4Y 0DZ

www.bookouture.com

ISBN: 978-1-83525-448-6
eBook ISBN: 978-1-83525-447-9

To the readers and the dreamers, thank you for keeping stories alive.
I hope you enjoy this one.

ONE

Paul

There she is, the Iron Lady, the sparkling centerpiece of Paris, the Eiffel Tower. She makes my heart flutter with excitement, or maybe it's the anticipation of the evening ahead. I turn toward my date, my beautiful young wife, Cecilia, to be sure she's sharing my enthusiasm. I want this night to be the best night ever.

"That's our pillar, Pilier Est," I say, pointing to the base of the tower. The structure is held erect by four such pillars, but only one, the east entrance, is for those with dinner reservations up above. "VIP for us, darling."

"How special," she says. She's wearing a red dress that complements her figure, and a big smile. Her blonde hair sparkles in the twinkling lights of the tower like fireworks on the Fourth of July. She squeezes my hand as a huge group of tourists descend on us like a swarm of flies.

"Shoo," I say, walking through the middle of the group, using my elbows when I need to. We have places to be. These people are just aimlessly milling about, headphones in, listening to their tour guide, clueless. I have half a mind to confront their tour leader, the one holding the red flag and clogging up my passage.

We finally plow through the last of the heedless, drifting tourists and reach the restaurant's check-in center. I've read all about Madame Brasserie, the elegant setting, the panoramic views of the city from the first floor of the tower, 190 feet up. Everything on the menu is supposed to be amazing, created by a famous chef. But with my sensitivity to the food over here, well, we'll see if I can enjoy my meal. I pull out the email I printed before we left home and hand it to the woman behind the reception desk.

"*Bonsoir*. Welcome," she says as she examines my paper-work. She's elegant, VIP, just like us. Her very demeanor makes me glad I chose this spot for our final evening.

"Paul, they need to have you empty your pockets so we can go through security," Cecilia says slightly impatiently, as if she has said it before, and perhaps she has.

I smile and toss my pocket contents into the plastic dish next to Cecilia's. Her phone is face up. Evan Dorsey is calling and his photo pops onto my wife's screen: his smug, too-white smile, his rippling blond hair, his plastic-surgery-perfect nose. He looks like every other actor wannabe in LA, truth be told. How unacceptable for him to bother us tonight. Cecilia is ahead of me, already through the metal detector. I grab her phone, answer it.

"Stop calling my wife on our last evening in Paris for our anniversary," I say. "Do you not have any manners?"

"Paul, is that you? I need to speak with Cecilia," Evan says. I hang up on him. I imagine his snooty face, pinched with self-importance, as he rushes around some event venue in Miami Beach, acting like he's somebody, much like he does when he's catering events at our home in Malibu. He has quite an air about him, but he's not an heir. Ha. He's a servant. He serves food to important people. There is quite a difference in the hierarchy of life, as you no doubt understand. There are the servers, and the servees. My wife will not be a server.

"Monsieur, s'il vous plaît?" The security guard is motioning for me to walk through. I toss Cecilia's phone back into the bucket. As I go through the security scanner, I notice Cecilia waiting on the other side, hand on hip.

She won't be pleased about my little phone chat with Evan. I'm certain of that.

"Paul, do not answer my phone," Cecilia says with an edge to her voice as she grabs her phone out of the security tray. "Did you speak to Evan?"

"Just trying to help," I say, enchanted by the view from under the tower. "Wow, look up at that beautiful sight."

Cecilia can't help but follow my gaze. The tower is enchanting, despite the throngs.

"It is lovely, Paul, but I'm not sure I can handle going up there. I'm afraid of heights," Cecilia says.

A ping of anger throbs at my temples. She will not ruin my plans. "Darling, you've never told me that before. But not to worry, the restaurant is on the first platform. You'll be fine. After dinner, we'll head to the top. Once you've gotten acclimated."

Cecilia's face scrunches as she looks up at the tower. "We'll see."

Yes, we will. She'll do exactly as I've planned. No more taking phone calls from random men, no more spending money without my permission, no more oppositional behavior. We're celebrating our first anniversary, not our twentieth. Life should be good, and easy. We are in Paris, for heaven's sake. But you know what they say, vacations won't help you escape your problems, especially not if you bring them along with you. I look at Cecilia and I wonder what she's thinking.

"OK, I'll try it. But just up to the restaurant. No higher," she says.

I chuckle. "Sure," I say to appease her, and wrap my arm around her waist to escort her to the elevator.

But I'm lying. We will go to the top of the tower tonight. It's part of the plan.

TWO

PARIS, TWELVE HOURS EARLIER

Paul

I glance at my wife as she sleeps like a little angel, snuggled in the dense thread count sheets of The Peninsula Hotel, sunlight bouncing off her shiny blonde hair in the same way light bounces off a fine crystal chandelier, and I am bursting with confidence. Everything is as it should be.

Well, almost.

I close the door to the bathroom—I don't want to disturb her peaceful slumber—and hurry to my side of the sink, open a drawer and rummage for another antacid. The food in this town is killing me. I mean, it tastes spectacular at the time, but I pay for those rich sauces almost immediately with a stomachache, followed by worse. That's what woke me up again in the early hours of the morning. Intense abdominal pain. But it's almost subsided now. I should climb back into bed, savor our last full day in Paris beginning with an extravagant sleep in. Something I'd never allow myself to do back home.

I look in the mirror. I'm pale. I splash some cold water on my face. Better. The white marble floor is cold on my bare feet.

I must face the fact: I'm awake. Perhaps Cecilia is as well. This vacation to the City of Light, my first, Cecilia's as well, hasn't been as perfect as I could have hoped for, and the inhospitable tone of the locals hasn't helped. Parisians are as advertised, at least to Americans, in my experience, despite the fact we are here, spending significant dollars at their hotels and restaurants. It's a shame we are underappreciated.

I am unaccustomed to this feeling, of course. At home, in Malibu, everyone appreciates me.

I place my new watch on my wrist. Patek Philippe. Purchased yesterday in an extravagant impulse buy. I love it: the elegance, the simplicity, the sophistication it implies. It's just so nice to be rich, it really is. My new watch tells me it's nine o'clock in the morning. Cecilia should wake up. I feel like I've been awake, hiding in this bathroom, forever. It's Friday, the city is waiting for us.

Truth be told, this could quite possibly be our last carefree vacation together. Cecilia and I want to start a family, and we've been trying. I'm certain that particular dream of ours will come true. We both want it so much. We've been married a year now. This little trip to Paris is our anniversary celebration, and tonight we'll have a special dinner at the Eiffel Tower. A perfect evening in May, for a perfect couple. What could be better?

I look at my reflection in the mirror again. I'm holding up well, as they say, despite the fact I've been baking in the South Florida sunshine for the past five years. It's not hard to look good there, all things considered. My age, almost fifty, is young for down there where everyone moves once they retire, and my Ohio-raised skin, relatively unlined. I lean in, check the small crow's feet fanning out from my blue eyes. They give me an air of dignity, a certain gravitas. A successful man enjoying the spoils of life. I'll Botox them if they start to turn anything but complimentary.

With a wife twenty years my junior, I have learned over the

past year that I must stay on my toes in the looks category, among other things. I slide the bathroom door open and step silently into the bedroom. Mrs. Strom still slumbers.

I glance to my left and notice the walk-in closet filled with my beloved's rather excessive travel *trousseau*. She packed like there were no clothing stores in Paris. She packed as if we were to be here for a month, not five nights. But I love her, despite the added weight we had to haul to the airport, fetch from the baggage claim, roll through customs. We're here now, and that's all that matters. My second wife always dresses well. Shopping is her superpower, turns out. My first wife, Mia, was too focused on being a good mom, too selfless, really, until the end when she betrayed me for another man.

I shake away those thoughts. This is our last day in Paris. With lightning speed I cross the room and sit on the bed, using my finger to smooth an errant hair away from Cecilia's porcelain, heart-shaped face. She is exquisite to look at, even without makeup. In my experience, women need a lot of help to look flawless. But not my Cecilia. She's a natural beauty. I lean down and kiss her full lips.

"Good morning, darling," I whisper softly. "It's time to rise and shine."

Cecilia's eyes pop open with a start, and her hands push against me. "What? What's happening?"

"Nothing, nothing at all. Just another fun day of you and me exploring the city," I say.

"You startled me," she says, taking in a big breath.

"I had to wake my sleeping beauty with a kiss," I say.

"OK, well, your sleeping beauty needs her beauty rest. But, never mind that now. What time is it anyway?" she asks, a smile replacing the startled look from a moment ago.

"It's a little after nine," I say. "Time for the *petit dejeuner, n'est-ce pas?*"

"Oh Paul, you're so cute when you try to speak French to

me," she says, pushing the covers back and climbing out of bed. She seems to think she's a natural in picking up the French language these past five days. Perhaps she is. As for me, well, I'm trying.

"I think I've got it down now," I say, pleased with myself. I've been working to get the darn pronunciation right. I like to impress my lady.

"Well, your pronunciation is, well, it's not right, but I appreciate the effort," she says. "So sweet the way you're trying so hard."

I smile. How nice to wake up with such a sunny disposition. "Well, thank you. You know I'd do anything for you."

She taps the tip of my nose with her finger before walking past me on the way to the bathroom, a grin on her face.

We love each other so much. In a year we've managed to grow extremely close. We know each other's best qualities, and we know each other's darker sides, I suppose. Although newlyweds don't really have dark sides, right? There's just too much romance going on, or at least there had been, until a few months ago. This trip was to remedy that, take us out of the pressure cooker environment of LA. But since we've arrived, I've had a stomachache, or she's had a jet lag headache every evening. It's a shame.

Tonight, everything will be perfect. Tonight will change it all.

THREE

Paul

Cecilia has been in the bathroom of our suite getting "ready" for almost a half hour now. In desperation, I called room service and requested a pot of café Americano. It arrived swiftly, a beautiful sterling silver presentation complete with a pink rose in a crystal vase.

I sip my coffee, pardon, *café*, and touch the soft petals of the rose. The sensation reminds me of running my fingers down Cecilia's arm, soft, sexy. I remember the first moment we met, her eyes twinkling even in sadness, her beauty unobstructed by the black hat and black dress she wore to Esther's funeral service.

Esther. My final love in Palm Beach. I remember her, too, of course, because I spent what seemed like an eternity as her companion, though in reality it was only a little more than a year. Her skin was not like a rose petal, not anymore, at seventy-two years young, as she professed her age to be. Her ex-husband, George, who I met at a social function at her home, guessed her age was closer to eighty-two, but none of us really knew. The funeral director refused to release her age, or the cause of death, to the press, so it was left up to the collective imagination to decide those particular facts. Gossipmongers had a field day with it. I even heard someone guess she was ninety-six years old, of all things.

I cannot bear to imagine a woman of almost a hundred years on my arm. So I won't.

Esther had no children, which I'd known. What I hadn't known is that she had a sole surviving relative, her sister Eunice, who lives in Santa Barbara, California. Eunice declined to be interviewed for the obituary in the *New York Times*, and she didn't make the funeral, either.

Likely because she didn't make it into the will.

What was true about Esther is that she had been lovely in her youth, as she often pointed out to me. Her mansion was dotted with photos of herself: radiant, blonde Esther as a young woman, Esther the debutante in a flowing white gown, Esther the socialite at various charity events, and Esther the matriarch of Palm Beach society wearing what became her signature over-sized white sunglasses, her hair still blonde.

I think of Esther now, smiling at me over a long luncheon at the club, and smile too. We did have some fun together, we really did. I touch the rose petal again, realizing Esther would have insisted on a single white rose for her coffee service. She only liked white flowers.

The bathroom door slides open. My bride is ready for the day. And what a special day it will be.

"Coffee, darling?" I ask.

"Yes, of course," she says, crossing the room. "What do you think of this outfit? I had trouble picking something suitable for our last day."

I bite my tongue and don't tell her that if she hadn't over-packed, she wouldn't have so many choices left. I pour the coffee instead.

"I like the outfit," I say, noting her dark, fitted jeans, white blouse, navy blazer, Gucci loafers. "Classy. Traditional. I'll wear a similar look. I'll just go get ready."

"How is your stomach?" she asks, sitting across from me. She takes a sip of coffee. The giant gemstone on her engagement ring flashes in the sunlight streaming through the window. I splurged on the diamond because I could. Her crossed leg swings back and forth as if she's agitated about something. "Yum."

"It is very good coffee," I agree. "My stomach, well, it will resolve once we're back home and away from this rich food."

"Of course." She smiles. "It's just a shame to be so ill on vacation. If you'd like to stay in this morning, I could go out alone, stroll around. You could rest? Take it easy. I know you've made special plans for tonight, so I want you to be at your best. I mean, feeling good."

"How sweet. I'm fine. No need for rest. I can do that when I'm back home." I stand and walk to the bathroom. "OK, I'll be right out and we can go to breakfast as planned." I'm hungry but dreading the consequences of another French meal.

"Sounds fabulous," she says as I slide the bathroom door closed.

It must be nice for Cecilia. She's so young, and now because she married me, so wealthy. I walk into the closet and changing area that separates the bathroom from the bedroom of the suite, run my hand along her hanging garments, admiring their beauty. Some of the items still have price tags attached to them. I imagine Esther's face: she'd be aghast at such extravagance. I reach up and yank a Neiman Marcus tag from an unworn blouse. I resist the urge to remove all the tags I see on her side of the closet. On a closet shelf she's placed five purses, including a tiny lavender Chanel number with a gold metal strap and a $5,200 price tag attached. I yank the tag off with disgust and toss it into the trash.

I try to calm my temper, at her spending and her tag leaving. I did not approve all these purchases. I take a deep breath and remind myself Cecilia doesn't know any better. She wasn't raised in wealth like this. She's doing her best to learn. I am doing my best to teach her. I expect a certain level of order in my life, and Cecilia knew that going into our relationship. From what I can tell, her life had been chaos up until we met. She had nothing, no one. And I picked her. She had been grateful. She will be again. It's all part of my romantic plans for today, the reason for the trip to Paris.

I pull on a white button-down and a navy blazer. I decide on khaki pants, so we don't match exactly. In a sense, I have created Cecilia in my image. I've refined her, elevated her appearance, her presence.

Of course, it was easy. Cecilia is a natural beauty, and, as she told me, she'd never fallen for someone like me before. I still remember when Cecilia put her hand on my thigh, leaned over close and whispered, "I didn't know Esther. I just read about her and thought she was really cool. So here I am, paying my respects. I created the program for today. I painted this rose on the front of it."

Interesting, I'd thought at the time. I'd never chosen to attend a funeral for someone I didn't know well, but it was a kind gesture.

"I knew her well. She loved white roses. She would appreciate you being here." I placed my hand on top of hers, patting it, and felt the zing of immediate attraction. It had been so long since I'd touched a young woman's hand: smooth, soft, vein-free.

"Good. OK if I come to the celebration of life, too?" she had whispered.

"It's at the club," I whispered, removing my hand from hers. "I don't know if that's appropriate." A woman in the pew in front of us turned and stared at me with dark, penetrating eyes.

I glared back before whispering, "Sure, come to the party. Be my guest."

Esther's celebration of life became our first date. I know Esther would have approved of my choice. In fact, Cecilia reminded me of a young Esther, Esther at thirty perhaps, sexy and flirtatious. I'd asked Cecilia to remove the ridiculous black hat before escorting her to my car for a ride to the club.

"Why don't you like my hat?" she'd asked innocently as I opened the door of my Bentley, one of Esther's first gifts to me, for Cecilia. I watched as she slipped inside before leaning in.

"It's a lovely hat. Anything would look wonderful on you, of course, but did you notice any other women wearing a hat?" I'd asked. "Buckle up." I closed her door.

When I slid into the driver's seat, she'd said, "It's good to stand out. To be unique."

"Not here," I said. "Here, you conform – you join a private club, you look like everyone else."

Cecilia considered my response for a moment as I considered her. All I wanted to do was kiss those lips, hold her body against mine. And I would, but not that evening.

I lick my lips and pull myself back to the present. I check my outfit one more time and decide to change out of the navy blazer, replacing it with a blue cashmere sweater. Much better.

I don't want Cecilia to think I'm learning anything from her. That would be ridiculous. I slide open the door to the closet changing area and step into the bedroom of the suite.

Cecilia's on her mobile phone. She hangs up as I cross the room.

"Who were you talking to?" I ask.

"Confirming our tour reservations for later this afternoon," she says. "You look very handsome. I'm glad you bought yourself that expensive watch yesterday in that intimidating jewelry store. It really pulls your whole outfit together."

"I know," I say. Again, I'm the teacher, you are the pupil. I force a smile. I wonder, briefly, if she's bringing up yesterday's little shopping adventure to pout about the diamond necklace I didn't buy for her. It was too flashy. Surely she's let that go? "Time for brunch. Shall we?"

"I'm starving," she says. She knows I hate it when she says she's starving. Victims of war and famine are starving. She will never lack for anything. She's never known what it's *really* like to struggle. She looks at me and smiles. "I'm kidding. Sorry. But I am hungry."

My stomach rolls. I gasp. I may have grunted. My god.

"What's wrong?" she asks.

"Nothing," I tell her. "Everything is perfect." At least I will pretend it is. What's that saying, "fake it until you make it"? That's always worked for me.

FOUR

Cecilia

The sanctuary of the Church of Bethany-by-the-Sea is overflowing with flower arrangements, mostly white roses, a show of respect befitting a queen. And, I suppose, the late Esther Wilmot was as close to a queen as West Palm Beach has seen, one of the last of her kind. I stand in the doorway, handing out the memorial programs I'd designed and had printed for the occasion. Esther's house manager, Julio, who I got to know in yoga class, often calls on me to handle these sorts of tasks and I jump at the chance. This, of course, will be the last of those projects. I'd selected a heavy card stock in light cream, and had hand-painted each program cover with a single white rose. Esther would have loved it, I'm certain of it.

Creating invitations and signage for Esther's parties has kept me afloat. It's expensive to live in this town, even if I do reside across the tracks in a one-bedroom apartment the leasing agent called precious, which means small. It's one room with a bed, a tiny kitchen and tinier bathroom. And it's hot, without air-conditioning but with plenty of mice scampering in the walls who keep me awake at night. I live alone, except for the mice. Truth be told, I've been alone my whole life. But I'm happy enough. My home is still considered Palm Beach, and that sounds quite fancy, but it's a world away from the Palm Beach of Esther Wilmot.

Disappointingly, my oil paintings and watercolors haven't been flying off the art gallery's walls. In fact, I haven't sold a single painting yet, despite heaps of praise from the gallery owner and my art teacher. It's expected from my teacher, I suppose, as he taught me how to paint as he was supposed to through the community outreach class. But he also has a huge crush on me, which he shouldn't. He's too old. I am happy with him loving my art up close, but I'd prefer he loved me from a respectable distance. He tells me it only takes one collector to start a feeding frenzy. But that hasn't happened yet. It seems the rich of Palm Beach only want to invest in established artists, not someone starting out, like me.

"Young lady, may I have a program?" an old man wagging his cane demands in a rather rude voice. It's that entitlement that kills me around here. They're all like this guy: seventy-plus, filthy rich and mean.

I paste on my fake smile. "Of course, here you go, sir. Enjoy."

"Enjoy? A woman is dead," he says. "What's the matter with you young people?" I watch as he gives me the once-over, no doubt looking for tattoos. He won't find any and I know that will disappoint him, and his preconceived notions of who I am. I'm a chameleon, though, but he doesn't know it. The old man finally moves inside the church.

I look at the program in my hand. Beneath the single white rose I'd painted Esther's full name in gold brushstrokes. Classy. Elegant. Inside, I've written a short story of her life, approved by Julio, because Esther was brilliant at making things up about her life to suit her own purposes, or so I've heard. Until her recent death of heart failure, Esther lived at her oceanfront estate, next door to the estates of the Pulitzers and the Kennedys, on North Ocean Boulevard Drive in West Palm Beach. I wasn't invited inside ever, but I did catch glimpses of the place when dropping off printed invitations or signage, although that was only ever to the servants' quarters, not to the front door of her palatial pink home.

It took me a few days of online research to gather the content for the interior of the brochure. I didn't know before she died that Esther was born in Nebraska, though she'd told many interviewers over the years that she had been born in Paris at the Ritz Hotel. Esther always lived life as if she'd been born in the lap of luxury, surrounded by anything and everything money could buy, doted on by a caring staff who looked after her every need. She hadn't been. She'd simply married well. Continuously.

I adjust the large black hat I've added to my appropriately somber black dress, a sale item from the rack at Target. Esther never visited Target, I'm certain. Quite the opposite. Going by a rumor I'd considered unbelievable but had heard too many times to dismiss, Esther didn't trust any of the local dry cleaners in Palm Beach, so she sent most of her clothing to Manhattan for cleaning.

I cannot imagine being the servant who oversaw boxing the dirty clothes once a week and sending them off to New York. I mean, the excessiveness of it all, the waste. I also happen to know her most special items of clothing, designer ball gowns and the like, were shipped to Paris for cleaning, an unimaginable luxury. My clothes come from secondhand shops. I make great finds in Goodwill down here because when the ultrarich tire of this season's fashions, off they go to charity. That's where I've found some of my favorite outfits. Well, there and an occasional Target run for essentials. And my laundry is done by me, at the coin-operated place down the street. I live in a world none of these people even know exists, and it's right under their noses.

I hand another couple of memorial programs out to an octogenarian couple before stepping inside to scan the crowd. *Nice turnout, Esther.* You must have been loved, or at least appreciated, by most of the who's who in this town. I didn't know Esther had a sole surviving relative, her sister Eunice, who lives in California and didn't make the funeral. From what I've heard, this is because they were estranged, and she didn't make it into the will.

What was true about Esther is that she had been gorgeous in her youth. Julio selected the best photos for the collage I designed for the back cover of the memorial program. I flip one over now and Esther's beaming smile stares up at me from many decades of her life. I flip it back over.

One of the church ladies sidles up next to me, also giving me the once-over like I don't belong. "The service will begin soon, dear, so if you're staying, please find a seat," she says, clearly hoping I'll leave. "You can leave the rest of the programs just there, for any late arrivals."

I scan the crowd. Esther's three ex-husbands are here, up front, and a few rows back is a handsome guy who looks a lot like George Clooney. I head in his direction and slip into the pew beside him.

"Is this seat taken?" I ask, my best flirtation voice activated.

"It is now," he says. "Hello, gorgeous. I'm Paul, Paul Strom."

"I'm Cecilia. Nice to meet you, handsome," I say. "I designed the program for today's service. Did you get one?"

"I did. It's lovely. Esther would be so pleased. How did you know her?" Paul asks.

"I didn't know Esther. I just read about her and thought she was really cool. So here I am, paying my respects. I created the program for today. I painted the rose on the front cover of it," I say. "I'm going to miss working for her. She had so many parties."

"Yes, she did," Paul says.

"How did you know her?" I ask. The organ music begins, and I lean close to continue talking, brushing against his thigh in the process. Our heads touch softly.

"I was her escort, her confidant of sorts, for the final year of her life," he says. "A remarkable woman."

After our brief conversation before the service, we sit side by side in the pew, exchanging glances throughout the pastor's long, boring eulogy.

"Wait, like, you were lovers?" I ask in a whisper as the service continues. I act a bit startled by the idea. I mean, he doesn't look that old, not compared to her three ex-husbands at the front of the church who all look ancient.

"No, no, best friends. I kept her company," he says hastily.

A woman in front of us turns and glares at me. I smile at her, showing my perfect smile, my non-wrinkled face.

"There's a party after this, a celebration of life, at that fancy country club. Do you need a date?" I ask. I've never been to the place, and I always wanted to go. Plus, Paul's cute and he can escort me there since Esther clearly doesn't need him anymore.

Paul smiles. "Sure, come to the party. Be my guest."

My heart swells. Who would have imagined that Esther Wilmot's death would bring me one step closer to my dreams? Well, I did, that's who. You must manifest your own destiny, and mine's starting now.

FIVE

PARIS, 9:50 A.M.

Paul

We settle down at our table in *Le Lobby*, a very fancy way to say
we are in the hotel's lobby, at the only restaurant open for breakfast. It closes in ten minutes so no doubt the waiter is distressed
to see our late arrival. I see him in the corner, judging. I find
myself wanting to grab this guy by the shoulders and shake him.
Remind him he is in the service industry. I am paying a mighty
high rate to dine here, and he should be grateful for that. He
should smile, welcome us in. But instead, he's pouting. Bothered
by our presence.

Too bad. I console myself by remembering I am in charge
here. He will wait on our table.

It's nice in here, of course, with high ceilings, refined
moldings, sparkling crystal chandeliers, and paintings on the
ceiling and walls reflecting the glory of the Beautiful Era.
The French act so superior, but it's all a cover-up. I did my
homework and learned about France once I began escorting
Esther, mostly to impress her during our long conversations
each evening. I'd never been to France, but I needed to be

able to converse with her about such topics. And she loved France, despite the fact I tried to explain the reality of this nation. For example, none of these lovely paintings depict what life was like for the average Parisian from 1870 to the start of World War 1, of course. La Belle Epoque saw the very rich in France unable to deal with the grim reality of most folks' modern life. The schism between the haves and the have-nots was extreme.

Everything began to sparkle on the outside even if life was hard for most as the Eiffel Tower was built, broad boulevards replaced shabby medieval paths, and Paris became the City of Light as the streets were illuminated for the first time by electricity. At the same time, a quarter of the female workforce earned money by hand-laundering – washing, starching, pressing, throwing the full weight of their bodies into guiding their heavy irons. Hard labor. I think of Esther and wonder if she knew of that when she sent her frocks here. Likely not. It's easy for the extremely wealthy to disassociate from anything ugly or physically difficult.

"Can you imagine being here in this room when Gershwin composed 'An American in Paris'?" Cecilia asks, reading the history of the restaurant from the top of the menu. "James Joyce and Picasso and Marcel Proust ate here too."

I meet her eye. "Who is Marcel Proust? Do you know?"

She smiles. "Of course. Doesn't everyone?" She stares at the menu with intensity, but I see her cheeks flushing, revealing her thirty-year-old radiance and ignorance.

"Refresh my memory," I say as the waiter approaches our table.

"Would you like to order?" he asks.

"Yes, please," Cecilia says. "I would like the eggs prestige, scrambled, with caviar please. Oh, and an espresso."

"Eggs Benedict," I say, and he nods and disappears, scurrying to alert the kitchen to our late, rude arrival.

"Eggs Benedict is really rich," Cecilia says. "Maybe you should just have a baguette?"

"I'm fine. The sickness has passed, I'm sure. Back to Marcel," I say, enjoying her discomfort. I did enjoy things much more when she was clueless about a subject, and she admitted it. "Man or woman?"

She squints her beautiful blue eyes at me. "Woman."

"Wrong." I can't help but chuckle. The French seem to be as sexist as I am, truth be told. If Proust had been a woman, we would have never heard of him, I'm afraid.

"This isn't fun," she says. "Or funny."

"You brought him up," I say. "You should know who he is."

"Fine. Who is he?"

"He was a French novelist. He's famous for writing the longest book in history, called *In Search of Lost Time*," I say. "It's the longest novel ever published. Some 4,200 pages with more than 2,000 characters." I don't admit I googled him yesterday at breakfast so I could have this fun discussion.

"I'm impressed," she says, but doesn't seem to be. Instead, she pouts.

"Honey, I'm teasing you with this. I looked him up yesterday morning," I confess, and her face brightens with a smile. That's better. Sometimes it pays to be a bit self-deprecating to boost your spouse's ego. Not often, but sometimes. I'm a giver that way.

She reaches her hand across the table and clasps mine. "Thank you for saying that. I hate feeling dumb," she says.

"You're one of the smartest, most beautiful women I've ever known," I say. I mean that. "That's why we need to have a baby boy. To carry on our great gene pools. He'll have silky blond hair, a big smile, and bright blue eyes, like his mom."

I see her touch her stomach with her other hand, a self-conscious move I doubt she's aware of. "You know I want that, too," she says. "I want everything that you want, Paul. I dream of us having a little girl, a daughter would be so lovely. And a son, of course, an adorable boy, too."

My heart lifts with hope. Maybe this will be our best day in Paris yet. I squeeze her hand and lean over to kiss her cheek.

"I can't believe our whole trip one or the other of us hasn't felt good each night. But I can tell today we're going to feel great," she says.

"I hope so, my love," I agree.

"I can't believe we've been married a whole year," she adds. "It seems like yesterday when you were sneaking me into the club for Mrs. Wilmot's celebration of life."

"That was a great evening, well, for everyone except Mrs. Wilmot," I say.

"Yes, that's true. I was just thinking about her, about Mrs. Wilmot. Esther," Cecilia says.

Me, too, but why were you? "Why? You barely even knew her," I ask.

"I just imagine she would feel at home in a room like this, in a city like Paris," she says.

The city was like a second home to Esther, but she never invited me here with her, which was one of the reasons I decided I had to see it for myself. To find out what she was hiding, or rather, what was so special. And despite the rude people, I do see the charm of the place, of course I do. I feel Cecilia's stare.

"Esther would have loved this room, and would have fit right in here in Paris," I agree. I imagine Esther sitting at the table with us, a bright pink silk suit, high heels, huge white sunglasses, and diamonds, everywhere twinkling diamonds.

"You knew her well," Cecilia says, a twinkle in her eye. Her lingering curiosity, or should I call it suspicion, about our relationship is annoying.

Here's the thing. I never told Cecilia that I was Esther's only companion and lover for the last year of her life. Sure, people came up to me during the celebration of life, offered their condolences, but everyone was sad, and simply remembering a grand lady. I tried to be sure Cecilia didn't know I was somebody special. It was important to me, suddenly, that night, for her to believe I was just another one of Esther's wealthy friends, an escort when she needed one for an event or a party at her home. And I believe it worked.

Nor had I shared with Cecilia that Esther left her entire fortune to me after her death. Esther had a heart attack and passed quickly in her sleep after a six-month struggle with congestive heart failure, the doctor had explained to me as he signed the confidentiality agreement Esther had forced everyone to execute. Including me. I can't tell Cecilia anything, even if I wanted to. But I don't. I like the version of me she saw the night we danced at Esther's celebration of life. Single, rich, attractive man wearing his favorite Brioni suit.

"Like I've told you a million times, darling, Esther was a good friend, a fabulous dinner companion and a great hostess. Some of her parties, well, she was an exuberant force in the social scene, that's for sure," I say. "The night we met, do you remember the full moon?"

"Of course, I do," she says. "We walked outside and danced, just you and me and the moon shining down on us."

Good, we've let Esther go. "And I asked you if I could kiss you," I remind her.

"And I said yes." Cecilia smiles with the memory.

The waiter arrives with our breakfasts and places them in front of us with a flourish. *"Bon appetit."*

"Marcy," I say. Realizing my mistake I add, "Thank you."

"It's not 'marcy,'" Cecilia says. "Think of the word 'mercy.' That could help you sound better, darling."

I take my hand back. I really don't like it when she speaks to me like that. It makes something bitter in my mouth and I swallow, coughing, as I try to clear my throat, and the dark thoughts in my mind. I hope we aren't going to be annoyed by each other today, like we were yesterday.

"I'm sorry, I shouldn't talk to you like that. This is our happy day. I'm so excited for tonight at the Eiffel Tower, too, and maybe we can try to make a baby tonight?" she says. Her voice is soft, loving, promising. She takes a bite of her meal. "Oh my gosh, you have to try this, it's so good." She closes her eyes, savoring the flavors of the eggs and caviar.

"Thanks for the apology, and I'd love to make a baby with you tonight," I say. I love it when she is being agreeable, more like the woman I fell for from the start. "As for tasting your meal, I'm going to stick with mine. It looks plenty rich enough." I notice the side of green beans tucked in next to my Eggs Benedict. Why did they have to do that, stick those there? Triggering, the green beans. Memories compete in my brain. I'm at the round dinner table of our family home, my brother Tommy and I under the awful gaze of my old man.

"You will not leave the table until every last green bean is eaten," my father said. Tommy, the weak one, always, burst into tears.

"We hate green beans," he said.

I simply mustered up all the hate I felt for him, popped another green bean in my mouth and promptly threw up all over the table.

"You're disgusting," he said, leaving the room, calling for my mom to clean up the mess. I'd won that round, though, we both knew it. I'd tried to discipline my own two sons the same way, even though I knew it was wrong. It was my nature. Genetics.

"Sam, Mikey, you will clean your plates before you're excused from this table," I'd said one night at dinner.

My wife, the first Mrs. Strom, was aghast. "Paul, we do not talk to the children in that tone. What is wrong with you?"

Mia always thought she could have an opinion on these things. She'd started laughing at me, ungrateful, and she always took the boys' side. I looked at my two sons, their blue eyes wide and scared.

"It was just a suggestion. My dad always taught us to be grateful for the home-cooked meals we enjoyed," I said. I knew I sounded defensive. My father was a monster, but I was just teaching my sons good manners.

My stomach twists, bringing me back to the present. "Excuse me," I say, fighting back the bile. "I'll be right back." Thankfully I know where the lobby bathroom is, and I make it there on time. While I recover, I reflect on my parents' tragic deaths. They died of carbon monoxide poisoning when my mother, suffering from Alzheimer's, accidentally left her car running in the garage, and the fumes reached the bedroom where they were napping.

They lived next door to us by then, in a small home I bought them next to the grand home we lived in. I discovered their bodies. The silent killer, that's what they call carbon monoxide. A freak accident is what the police called it, even though four hundred people a year die this way. I called it karma.

I realize I need to get back to Cecilia. I don't want her to get bored, or restless. That's the thing when you decide to marry a much younger spouse. You need to be watching them, all the time.

And because I'm always watching her, I like to think I'm one step ahead of her at all times.

SIX

MALIBU, CALIFORNIA, ONE YEAR AGO

Cecilia

I really haven't ever seen a home this majestic, this breathtaking. Sure, Palm Beach has its mansions, but this place in Malibu, a twenty-seven-mile strip of land hugging the Pacific Ocean, close enough to commute to LA, feels a world apart. I'm in awe of the rugged cliffs and the crashing waves, the raw beauty, and the danger. This spot has taken my breath away.

"Pinch me," I say to myself with a smile as I turn away from the stunning view, across our sparkling pool to the ocean beyond, and return to the task at hand: unpacking another box dropped by our regular delivery guy. Fortunately, Paul and I drove across the country to our new home and we didn't bring a lot of stuff. He said we could buy everything we needed here in California, and we have. The interior designer had staged the place, and Paul has made sure everything was exquisite. Linens, crystal, artwork, everything the finest, and all meant to impress.

I found myself, in the space of six months, moving from a tiny apartment on the wrong side of the tracks in Palm Beach, to marrying Paul and moving to this mansion in Malibu. It really has all happened so fast, but it feels so right.

The doorbell rings, and for a moment I'm confused. I think I remembered to close the gate to the driveway, but then again, I'm not used to having a gate protecting me from the world so I often leave it open. I peer through the front door peephole and see a middle-aged woman, maybe like fifty or sixty. I open the door. I haven't met anyone yet. We've only been here two days so far, but I'd love to have a friend.

"Hello! I'm Melissa Reedy. I'm your next-door neighbor, although the way we're all spread out here, you can't even see my home. Welcome to the Point," she says, and wraps her tan, thin arms around me in a big hug. "Tell me you're a tennis player?"

"I'd love to learn," I say, inviting her in. "I mean, we have a tennis court. Can I get you a glass of tea or wine?"

"You know, I'd love a glass of wine, how lovely," Melissa says, following me through the grand living room and dining room, past the spiral stairs, and into the huge kitchen. I still don't know where most things are but I do know where the wine is, and luckily the wine glasses too.

After we settle at the kitchen table, Melissa says, "So tell me about yourself, and your husband. We've been living here more than twenty years. Walter, my husband, is a producer, retired now, and I was a casting director, but also retired. I mostly play tennis and he golfs. We just love getting to know the neighbors. It's such an eclectic bunch out here."

What is my story to tell? I wonder, before I realize I've taken too much time with my answer. "Well, my husband is a producer, of sorts. Just getting started, really. So we moved out here to advance his career. And, well, I love this house. It's so beautiful here. And we're newlyweds."

"How wonderful," Melissa says. Her eyes sparkle at the memory of what that meant for her. "The best year of marriage is the first year. We're on forty years, but I still love the guy."

"Yes, well, I'm an artist, a painter, and I still need to set up my studio. And Paul and I want to have children, at least three, just as soon as possible," I say.

"Oh, lordy, well, I'm a built-in babysitter. How exciting. We better get you playing tennis soon before you get too busy with those little babies," she says. "Cheers!"

We clink glasses together. "Do you want a tour? I can show you the kids' rooms, I mean, the future kids' rooms."

"I'd love that. I've always admired this home. It's stately, if feels like one of those old Main Line homes back east," she says.

I have no idea what she's talking about so I just nod. "My husband, Paul, found this house online, flew here and toured it, bought it, had it completely redecorated, and surprised me."

"How romantic," Melissa says.

It was romantic, and... disarming. What if I hadn't loved the home? I shake my head to dislodge this train of thought. Who wouldn't love an oceanfront home in Malibu? It's just my nerves. I have a big learning curve ahead of me, I've begun to realize. I'm suddenly, almost overnight, the wife of an obscenely wealthy man. And I'm rich, too, I remind myself. Half of Paul's windfall from Esther is mine, essentially. Once we opened that joint bank account, my heart soared. We're so blessed.

For me, it's a huge change. I mean, a blink of an eye ago I was worried about paying rent. It is going to take me a while to figure out this new normal, how to live like this, how to be this rich. But I for one am committed to learning all I can and doing it right.

"This is baby number one's room," I say when we reach the top of the spiral staircase. "With a grand view of the ocean."

"Lucky little kiddo," Melissa says. She throws her arms around me. She's obviously a hugger. "This is all so very excit-ing, Cecilia."

I take a deep breath and try to settle into my good fortune. And I try not to let the voice inside my head tell me it's all just a dream. *You're poor and have nothing, Cecilia*, the voice says.

"No," I say, and then realize I said it aloud. "Sorry, I was miles away. I didn't mean to say no. I meant I am very lucky," I mumble, and Melissa nods, patting my arm.

I am Cecilia Strom now and I have everything I deserve. Almost.

SEVEN

PARIS, 10:30 A.M.

Paul

As I return to our table, I see someone has covered my meal with a silver dome. How nice. Cecilia sits where I left her, plate cleared, busy on her phone. Nobody we know in California would be awake at this hour. It's one thirty in the morning back home.

I wonder who she's texting.

"Oh good, you're back," she says, slipping her phone away. "I was worried. Are you feeling OK?"

"I am now," I say and take my seat. The waiter appears and removes the dome.

"Do you want me to make you a fresh dish, sir?" he asks. I imagine him rolling his eyes at me and my neediness, so I don't look at him.

"No, I'm fine. It's fine, *merci*," I say. I put my hand up to stop Cecilia from criticizing my French and take a bite. "Wonderful. I love Hollandaise sauce—and the egg, perfection right here."

"Glad you like it. Mine was fantastic. So, when you finish,

we should probably take a car to the Tuileries. Or are you up to walking?" she asks.

"I can walk if you can walk," I say. These are the kind of comments that make me feel old. I used to do the same to Esther, I realize. But she was actually old. "Who were you texting with when I got back?"

"Oh, it was Evan. He has insomnia, you know, so he's up all hours of the night," Cecilia says.

Evan works for us, planning our events. He's masterminded intimate dinner parties for eight, up to huge parties for several hundred. We've hosted guests down on the beach, outside around the pool, and, of course, in our home. It just depends on the event's theme, and purpose. My parties always have a purpose, as I've explained to Evan. Networking with the Hollywood crowd being priority number one. In the course of his party-planning duties, it seems Evan has worked himself into a friendship spot with Cecilia, when he should remain at the servant level. I will fix that. "Oh, uh-huh," I say, carefully chewing a bite. "Likely not good when you must be fresh for big events. He should stop texting and sleep."

"He was asking me how our romantic anniversary trip was going," Cecilia says.

"And what did you tell him?"

"I told him that when you're with the love of your life in the City of Light, well, it couldn't be more romantic," she says.

"You didn't tell him about my stomach, thank goodness," I say. "Evan is a bit of a gossip, as you know."

"Didn't mention my migraines, either," she says with a smile. "As far as the world knows, we are having the time of our lives. My Instagram photos and reels are doing great. We look fabulous online. Nothing but bliss. Evan will spread the good news. I told him you might be buying me a necklace today."

"Good," I say, finishing my meal, except for the illogically included green beans. I only like them with mustard, lots of mustard. Dijon or yellow, doesn't matter. I shake my head. Wait, did she bring up that gaudy necklace again? She did. I will ignore it. I wipe my mouth with the thick cotton napkin.

"Hey, did you hire a car service, you know, for the airport run tomorrow?" she asks. "Or should we stop at the concierge desk?"

"You know, I haven't planned a thing after tonight. But we should do that," I say. "Ready to go? We need to make up for lost time today."

"In search of lost time, are we?" she asks. "Proust would be proud."

"Clever," I say as we walk into the hotel reception area. There is a line at the concierge desk.

"Do you want to wait? We can handle this later," she says. "Our flight is at noon, right?"

"Yes, let's handle it later. It will be hard to leave this beautiful city, but alas, all good things must come to an end," I say. "Shall we?"

I point to the doors and Cecilia leads the way outside. "I'm so excited for today."

I love her enthusiasm. She's so beautiful when she's agreeable. I hope the tension coursing between us this week evaporates today.

"I'm excited, too, darling. Let's make it a great day," I say.

"Speaking of that, Paul, I do have a slight modification to propose," she says.

My innate lack of flexibility aside, I have worked hard to plan today down to the minute, and now she's suggesting something else? I don't like it. I feel my neck tighten.

"What might that be, dear?" I ask. The sidewalk is busy, flooded with tourists like us, many with children in tow, too young to appreciate being here. A shame, really, and a waste of money. Like taking a toddler to Disneyland. They won't remember a thing, and you'll end up stressed and hostile. Angry you spent so much on two young boys who have amnesia when asked about the trip only a few years later. But I digress.

"I read about the Palais Galliera and a fabulous *Vogue* Paris exhibit," she says. I can't see her eyes as she's donned dark sunglasses, but I can tell she is thrilled by the notion. "And it's only a ten-minute walk from here. From there, we can go on to the Tuileries."

Usually, I would ask her to stick to the plan. But it is our last day in Paris. We need to make the most of it, I suppose.

"Sure. Let's do it," I say. "You lead the way."

And with that, Cecilia claps her hands and heads southwest down Avenue Kléber, walking at such a clip I have to jog a bit to catch up.

"Cecilia!" I yell because she's so far ahead of me. "Slow down!"

My young bride doesn't even turn around.

EIGHT

PARIS, 11:20 A.M.

Paul

Honestly, I cannot make her slow down and my frustration is growing. Five or six people are between us on the sidewalk. I don't know what she thinks she's doing but it's the opposite of amusing.

"Cecilia!" I yell once more. The couple in front of me turn around and stare in distaste.

"*Mon dieu,*" the man says before turning back around. "Americans."

I give him the stink eye but at this particular moment, I am the "ugly American." OK, I'm not ugly, of course. I'm dressed elegantly for the city, sure, although I do have the middle-age bulge around my waist I've tried to get rid of for years. But my hairline is impressive, and I look good. I glare at him again. OK, Paul, pull yourself together. She's just excited to see the exhibit and so she's being a complete brat and scurrying ahead of you like a runaway runway model. She doesn't care that your stomach hurts when you hurry, but that's because she's young and selfish.

I take a deep breath. Yes, my beautiful second wife is selfish. I suppose all of us are to a certain degree. That's healthy. But too much is, well, problematic, perhaps even narcissistic. I hear that personality trait is quite prevalent these days. Up ahead, Cecilia takes a left onto a street with a sign that says the name is Rue de Belloy.

I seriously don't know where we're going, and I have a huge issue with directions, I'll admit. My mind is spinning me into a panic. I hate being out of control. Cecilia knows this.

I round the corner, almost taking out an elderly French woman carrying a baguette but avoid her just in time. I spot Cecilia trotting ahead and see her turn right onto another street. Is she trying to lose me? After she convinced me, in a very short time frame with all the right answers to my questions, that she was everything I'd ever wanted? Has something changed? No, of course not. I'm just cranky, a little on edge and a little sick if I must admit it. I'm moving slowly. I pick up the pace.

I round the corner where I last saw Cecilia, Place des États-Unis according to the sign. I will remember not to try to repeat that in French in front of my wife. And there she is, finally, waiting for me, leaning against the wall of some fabulous French residence.

"*Bonjour!*" she says. "Glad you caught up. It was so crowded I just figured I'd lead the way. And this is a perfect stopping place halfway to the museum." She points across the street. "We've reached the Place des États-Unis and the Square of Thomas Jefferson!"

"How exciting," I say. I take a moment to wipe sweat, discreetly, from my brow. "Why would the French have a park named after an American?"

"Because he was a Francophile, he loved everything French, and he was minister to France for five years after his wife died," Cecilia says. She smiles. "Impressed?"

"Very," I say. "Although I'm assuming this is a Google search answer, rather than prior knowledge?"

"After my rather poor show at breakfast, I upped my game," she says as we cross the street.

The park is small, and lovely, and does have an American feel to it, I suppose. Like a city park in New York. "Is that Jefferson?" I ask, pointing to a large concrete monument with a bronze figure on top with his arm raised.

"No, that's a tribute to the American soldiers who died for France," she says.

I catch her looking at her phone. Always on the phone, this one. It's like an addiction.

"And those two over there on top of the concrete?" I ask. One of the men looks a bit familiar, but my history is rusty. That's what happens when you bake your brain in the South Florida sunshine for five years, with nothing to dull the daily boredom but tanning and alcohol and the touch of a wrinkled, sun-damaged hand, fingers drenched in diamonds. That's what Cecilia saved me from. Well, to be honest, that's what Esther saved me from by dying, and then Cecilia appeared to make sure I had someone to share all that money with.

"That's George Washington and the Marquis de Lafayette, comrades during the American Revolution and put here to signify the American-French relationship," she says.

I must ask the obvious question as we continue our now reasonably paced stroll through the park. "So, where's Thomas Jefferson's statue?"

"Near the Seine, actually," she quips.

"Seriously? Not here?" I ask. I somehow feel as if this is a slight. "Does he have a good spot where he is? Better than his own square?"

"I think he for sure has a better view. We can go visit him after the museum if you'd like. Although he is across town, over the Seine from the Tuileries," she says. We've stopped at the end of the park. I suppose we have some decisions to make about the rest of the day. She is changing all the plans. I notice a couple of pieces of trash dotting the rather bleak grass of the park. American grass is much better. I look at Cecilia, anger bubbling under the surface of my forced smile.

"I don't know what we have time for today anymore. I mean, we still have lunch at the Crystal Museum, right?" I sound a little like a grumpy child.

"Yes, Paul, that hasn't changed. We're close to that, too," she says, holding up her phone to show me a map that I cannot read. Digital directions drive me insane. Give me a paper tourist map any day. But they don't do that, at least not at The Peninsula, not unless you wait in line for the concierge, but we didn't, so here I am at her mercy.

I look at my petite blonde wife, so small, yet so fast. "How about this? I'll relinquish the day's plans to you, as long as I'm still in charge of the evening," I say. I will control tonight, mark my words.

"Yes, that's a great plan. OK, so, we will see Mr. Jefferson later this afternoon, time permitting, but for now we'll head to the museum. You know, I wonder what the French think of Jefferson these days, actually?"

I take in all the distinguished buildings surrounding this park and realize the French must love Jefferson. This is a nice park, albeit the grass needs work. Fertilizer, perhaps. And he has a statue somewhere, too. "The French think he's great," I say.

"Even with slaves?" she says.

I'm not getting into that discussion with her, not today. Instead, I'll imagine Jefferson strolling on these very grounds with his lovely wife on his arm, just like we are doing today. "Did Jefferson's wife enjoy Paris, do you know?"

"Nope. She died after giving birth to their last daughter. Super sad. The life just drained out of her. She suffered for four months. Ick. I read those kinds of stories and wonder why anyone risks having a baby," she says.

I follow her as she takes a right on Avenue d'Iéna, considering my discussion options. "That was several hundred years ago. Medicine has advanced, honey," I say. "And Jefferson was a great man, don't you agree?"

"It's complicated. He lived here for five years with his daughter and some enslaved people, including Sally Hemings and her brother, who became a chef trained in French cuisine. You of course know what Sally became."

"Interesting, and yes I do," I say, hoping to end the conversation.

"Jefferson first raped Sally here, in Paris, when she was fourteen," she says. Pot-stirring again.

I'm not going to bite. "Enough history for today. Let's focus on our future!"

"What does that mean, exactly?" Cecilia asks, finally stopping at a traffic light.

This forced march is getting on my last nerve. I'm thirsty, too. But this is supposed to be a romantic day, meandering through the city. I take a deep breath.

"I just love strolling the streets of Paris with you," I say, reaching for her left hand, with that huge diamond sparkling in the sunshine. I'm still proud of that ring. Of this wife. This life.

"Oh, me, too," Cecilia says. "I love Paris. And what could be more romantic than celebrating our first anniversary here?"

Suddenly, I'm thinking about the night I proposed. I squeeze Cecilia's hand, hold it high so the ring sparkles. "I was so nervous the night I asked you to marry me."

She looks at me, tilts her head. "I know you were. I can always tell if you're nervous or hiding something. Your eyes give it away. And you lick your bottom lip."

"No, no, you can't, and no, I don't," I say, and find myself dropping her hand and folding my arms across my chest. The light turns and we step onto the crosswalk. I see a charming pastry shop on the corner. Maybe I will stop in there for a bottle of water.

"I can. I knew you were proposing that night, even though you thought it was a surprise. I know a lot of things, Paul," she says. "And sometimes I don't even have to google them."

I walk the rest of the way to the Palais Galliera behind Cecilia, trying to figure out what she's saying, what she really means. I am never wrong, for the record. She couldn't google my proposal, she couldn't know anything. She's teasing me, that's all. I take a deep breath and tell myself to stop overthinking things.

NINE

WEST PALM BEACH, FLORIDA, THIRTEEN MONTHS AGO

Cecilia

I turn into the parking lot of a strip shopping center and pull into a space. I thought I'd been to all of the many swanky West Palm Beach spots, but this one is new to me. I know it's one of Paul's favorite places, but he's never asked me to meet him here until tonight. We've been dating for six months now, and every day brings us closer together. My heart pounds in my chest as I pull open the door to our meeting spot, a bistro called the Blink Monk. I know we aren't staying long; just for a drink. Paul has big plans for tonight and I cannot wait.

I see him sitting at the bar as soon as I step inside the door. The lights are dim, and the place has a boys' clubby feeling, like a bunch of these old guys from West Palm would sit in here and make plans to ruin the world. But not now, not tonight. Tonight is for lovers. Paul's eyes twinkle and he stands up before crossing the space between us and wrapping me in a hug.

"Hello, gorgeous," he whispers. "I have such a special evening planned."

My heart continues to thump. I just know tonight he's going to make my wildest dreams come true.

"Hi, handsome," I say in a whisper. I am wearing the baby-blue dress Paul bought me on our shopping spree together last week. He said it's the color of my eyes. I feel sexy and cared for. I've never felt this way before in my life. Never. "I can't wait to see what you have planned."

He takes my hand and leads me to the bar where a bottle of champagne chills in a silver bucket. A bartender appears behind the counter and expertly pours two champagne flutes.

"Thank you," I say as the bartender hands me a glass. "Cheers."

Paul clinks my glass, and says, "You've never been here before, correct? I wanted to show you my favorite spot before we move on."

"It's lovely," I say, sipping the champagne, bubbles tickling my nose. I could get used to this doting attention, this sparkling life. I think I already have. I lean over and kiss Paul on the lips, a soft promise of more. "How often do you come here? Did you come here with Mrs. Wilmot?"

"No, if you knew Esther you'd feel silly for even asking that question. Esther would never be spotted in a place like this," Paul says shortly.

I feel my lips begin to frown. Sometimes Paul makes me feel stupid. "A place like what?"

Paul puts his hand on top of mine. "Please, don't pout, gorgeous. Esther is quite irrelevant. I mean, I'll always cherish my time with her, and she was a wonderful woman with a rich legacy, literally. Now that some of her fortune has transferred to me without a hitch last week, I'll think of her every time I check my bank account. She's changed my life forever. Both of our lives, as long as we're together."

I feel my smile return. "It's so much money. More than any one person should have, really. I can't imagine how you'll ever spend it all. We should go on another shopping splurge to Worth Avenue. That was the best. The look on your face when I came out of the changing room wearing this dress made me feel so beautiful."

"You are beautiful. You took my breath away," Paul says. "And, we will go shopping again soon. And I can't imagine how I'll spend it all either, but it has been fun getting started. It will take a lifetime, but I'm up to the challenge," he says. "With you by my side."

My heart pings. I just know he's going to propose. He must. I lean in for another kiss. "I'm happy to be by your side." *Happier, still, to be your bride,* I don't say.

"Let's go," Paul says. He stands and I follow.

"Where are we going?" I ask, following him out the door and to his new fancy car. I can't remember what it is, but I remember the quarter-million-dollar price tag. He doesn't answer, just opens the door for me, and I slide inside. He joins me inside the car and we're off.

"I like to spoil you, and surprise you, so you will see," Paul says. "You deserve the finest. Especially after that childhood. Poor orphan girl."

I'm stunned he just said that, tonight of all nights. I fold my arms over my chest in anger and hurt. "Paul! I can't believe you! Don't call me that."

Paul glances my way as he's driving. "Sorry. I didn't mean to upset you."

"I hate being called that. An orphan. I hate that I didn't know my real family growing up. I hate that my adoptive parents were shitty, and sent me back. I hate that I had to go to foster care. So yes, you upset me." I lean back against the soft leather seat and close my eyes. This is not the way I wanted the proposal evening to unfold. Maybe he'll call it off now. I better calm down. I open my eyes, take a deep breath. "I accept your apology."

"Good," Paul says, a smile on his face. "Onward."

But I can't let it go. I need him to never bring this up again. "Promise to never ask about my childhood again," I say. "We all have stuff that is difficult to talk about. You should understand that. You don't like to talk about your relationship with Esther, do you?"

"Stop it," Paul says, jaw tense and eyes flashing. He turns down a small road heading toward the beach and pulls over. We stare at each other, and then I smile. He grins.

"We both have pasts we don't want to talk about. That kind of makes us more perfect for each other. Can't you see that?" I say and touch his leg.

He takes my hand in his and kisses it. "You're right. I promise I won't mention your past again. Let's start this evening over, right here, right now. You're everything I've dreamed of in a partner. You're beautiful, of course, but you're so much more. You're smart, and funny, and when we're apart, I ache to be with you. You complete me, and I hope I do the same for you. We were both searching for our missing piece, and now we've found each other."

"That's the most romantic thing anyone has ever said to me," I say, tears filling my eyes. His words make me believe in love, that I've found something real.

"I have a surprise," Paul says, pulling out his phone.

Darn it. Where is the ring?

I watch as he opens a real estate website. "What do you think of this house, my love?"

I find myself looking at a photograph of a beautiful mansion which the website tells me is in Malibu. "It's in California?" I ask and he nods. "Gosh, it's gorgeous. Why are you showing me this? It costs forty-eight million dollars."

"It's for you," he says. "And me. And for our family-to-be."

I am in shock as he starts the car again and drives toward the beach. He parks and comes around to open my door. He takes my hand, and we walk in the moonlight down a narrow path and out onto the beach. In the sand, the words *Marry Me, Cecilia?* are spelled out in candles. Beside me, Paul drops to his knees. My brain swirls and it feels like everything is in slow motion.

"Marry me?" he says. "Let's start over on the West Coast. I've always wanted to live out there, the place where dreams come true. We'll reinvent ourselves, as they say, together. A fresh start. Forever."

I cover my mouth with my hand, so excited and happy I'm unable to speak. I can only nod as Paul pulls a ring out of his pocket and slides it onto my finger.

"You need to say something soon, gorgeous. Maybe the ring will help. The center diamond is flawless, ten carats with four carats' worth of baguettes. It's stunning, like you, my love."

"Yes!" I say as Paul stands and wraps his arms around me. Fireworks light up the sky as we share a deep kiss. I'm overwhelmed, dazzled and deeply and completely in love. He's the perfect man for me, and it seems I am just what he was looking for, too. Could my life finally be turning around?

The next morning, waking up in bed at Paul's West Palm Beach home with its sleek lines, large windows, high ceilings, and stark, mostly white furnishings, I open my eyes and check my ring finger. It hadn't been a dream. This is real! The huge diamond dances in the morning sunlight.

"I'm so happy," I hear myself say. I sense Paul stir. I didn't mean to wake him, well, maybe I did. "Good morning."

"I'm glad you're happy, gorgeous," Paul says, rolling over to face me in bed. "So I meant to tell you last night, but we got busy with other things." He grins. "The Malibu home is ready, fully redecorated to my standards, with the help of Esther's favorite interior decorator, and Esther's money, of course. It's

West Palm classic with a cool California twist. I can't wait to
carry you across the threshold."

My heart starts thumping in my chest. I would have loved to
have had input on the decor of my first home, but I swallow my
anger and allow a smile to spread across my face. He's just
trying to please me. I should be grateful, and happy. I am so
happy. "I can't wait to see it. Does it really have a pool, and a
tennis court?"

Paul smiles. "It really does. Neither of us has a reason to
stay in West Palm any longer, do we?" he asks, pulling my
naked body closer to his.

"I don't like it here," I say. "I only lingered around because
of you. My lease is month-to-month at my apartment, and I can
leave anytime. I would have bolted after the weekend we met,
truth be told. My paintings aren't selling at the gallery, despite
my best efforts. I just haven't caught on down here. Maybe they
will sell in California. I'm so excited for a fresh start. Most of
the friends I had here have moved to other places. I was feeling
alone and stuck until you came into my life. I can't believe we
found each other at a funeral. My forever love."

"It's fate. Almost like Esther was looking out for us from the
beginning," Paul says.

"She sounds like she was such a lovely person, so loving," I
say, staring again at my huge engagement ring. "Strong and
creative, too, from what you've said."

"Very. And the life of any party, with those vivid outfits,
huge white sunglasses and a gaggle of guests surrounding her,"
Paul says. "But enough about the past. You and me, we are the
future."

"I can't believe I'm going to be Mrs. Paul Strom," I say,
hoisting my left hand in the air, still entranced by the sparkling
diamonds. "This is like a dream come true. I still can't believe
it."

"It's true. It's all true," Paul says. "I have an idea. How about we start our new life now?"

"What do you mean?" I ask.

"How about this? We leave today for California, and get married in Malibu," Paul says. "We could road-trip across the country. My first wife and I always loved a good road trip."

"There you go, bringing up the past. Don't do it," I say. I hate it when he brings up his first wife. I like to imagine him as mine and only mine. "But can we get married here in Palm Beach? Before we leave? I'd just feel so much better if we tied the knot, you know, before we're officially living together? I know there's no waiting period in Florida. One of my friends once eloped here for that reason. We could be married today!" I throw my arms around him. I'm so excited.

"OK, sure, yes, I just need to run a couple of things by my lawyer, but yes, I'd love that. And then we start our new life," Paul says. "I'll call Joseph, Esther's lawyer and ask him how I should handle a quickie prenup. Because of course when this much money is at stake, you can never be too careful, no matter how much we love each other. And I know we are both deeply, madly in love."

What did he just say? I sit up in bed, pulling the sheet up to cover myself. I turn on my side away from him.

"What's wrong?" he asks.

"It's just the idea of a prenup, well, it kinda bothers me. I know it's a practical thing, and people do it all the time, but it sort of feels like you don't really love me. At least not forever," I say, and I feel a tear slide down my cheek. "Don't you trust me? You said you love me."

"Oh sweetheart, of course, I do, silly. I asked you to be my wife," Paul says. "But things can change. I know from experience. I just need to protect what Esther left me, but of course, I will share it all with you. It's just a formality, understand?"

I can't help it. This is upsetting. I can't stop the tears. I wipe them from my cheeks with the sheet.

"Please don't cry," Paul says. "This is a happy time. All good. We'll be together forever. This is just a legal formality. It's nothing. My lawyer is insisting on it. Please, darling, believe me."

"I still don't really get it. This is forever. But fine. If it makes you happy, we can have a prenup."

Paul flashes me a huge smile and adds his signature wink. "You make me happy. We'll have a fabulous life together."

Three days later, after Paul found an online lawyer to draft the prenup because Esther's lawyer was on vacation, we were ready. I had gathered all of the documents we needed, we found a public notary, I signed the prenup and we both signed the marriage license, and then it was official, we were starting over.

As I sit in the car and wait while Paul drops off the marriage license at the county clerk's office, my body pulses with joy and excitement. A new life was waiting for me, I could feel it.

Paul hops back in, a big smile on his face. "No more wasting away in the wrinkle-inducing South Florida swamp. I can't wait to start this next chapter."

"The best chapter," I say. "The only chapter that matters."

"Ready to head west, Mrs. Strom?" Paul asks as we begin our drive, heading toward the interstate.

"Can't wait, husband," I say with a giggle. "That's going to take some getting used to."

"That's why most people have that engagement phase, to sort of settle into the idea," he says with a wink.

"But not us," we both say in unison, one of our cute little phrases.

We feel so smug, so superior, so perfect. Most people date for more than six months before getting married, but not us. Most people talk about their past, share all their worst, hardest but also best memories of childhood and adulthood. But not us.

We are like phoenixes, rising from the ashes. We are what we are in this very moment. Right now. And that makes us both happy. A dream come true.

I laugh and put my hand on his thigh. "I love how spontaneous we're being."

"I know. I agree. We get things done. And speaking of that, I can't wait to start a family with you. I can already picture the little rascals, three of them. Each has a room waiting for him," Paul says.

I smile. "I know all about your dreams, Mr. Strom."

"And we'll make them come true," he says.

"You know it." I turn to look out the window. I cannot believe I'm finally leaving Florida, finally getting the life I deserve. I'm glad to leave everything behind here. I turn back to Paul. He's looking at the console in front of me, but then he meets my eye.

"Where do you want to stop tonight? We could stay in Orlando, it's about three hours from here, or we could try to go a little farther," he says. "We could, um, even start trying for baby number one tonight?"

"I need to get off birth control, give it a couple months. But we can practice," I say with a big grin. "I just want you to be happy."

The perfect man really did exist. And I had found him. At least that's what I told myself that day. And I really did want to believe it.

TEN

PARIS, 11:40 A.M.

Paul

There is so much to love about Cecilia. I think back to the night of our engagement, kissing on the beach, as if we were the only two people who mattered in the world. I had assured myself this time around I would get things just right. My wife would be loyal and happy, my children would have it all, and I would break into the movie industry as a producer and financier. I'm a natural-born salesman with a practiced poker face that I'm proud of. I'm not bragging, it's just a fact. That night, I was certain I'd become somebody in Hollywood and come home in the evenings to a sparkling mansion by the sea where my wife waited eagerly to greet me with dinner in the oven, a cocktail in her hand and a smile on her face. I mean, life just couldn't get any better than that. If only.

I don't know where Cecilia is. She's disappeared again. In front of me is a beautiful palace, with three domed arches, a lot of marble and a lush green yard, if that's what you call grass in front of palaces. Who knows?

I pull out my phone and text Cecilia.

Where are you?

This is ridiculous. I don't see my wife anywhere. I still need water. I am not having fun.

"Hey," Cecilia says and touches my shoulder, sneaking up on me so that I jump.

"Why are you running and hiding from me?" I ask, trying to calm my racing heart.

"I wasn't hiding from you, darling. I was just anxious to get here. This is going to be so fabulous. A chic Beaux-Arts fashion museum that houses three centuries' worth of clothing, accessories and photography. So fun! I got us tickets to the 'Love Brings Love' exhibit. *Très romantique*! Let's go."

Clearly she's lost her mind. She thinks I'm going to enjoy this? Clothing? The building in front of me is huge. I do not want to go to a huge museum of clothes. Who would want to do that? Besides, I could use a little break from Mrs. Strom.

"I'll wait for you out here. On that bench over there, enjoying a bottle of water from that street vendor. I don't want to look at old clothing," I say. I want to say more. She has made me very angry this morning. For a moment, I imagine grabbing her wrists, pulling her with me back into my plans, my schedule, my way. When we first got engaged, that's all she wanted – to do whatever I wanted. Now, though, a year later, well, we seem to have lost the newlywed glow. But I'm not going to use force, not in this crowded park. Besides, I will manipulate her with my words, my displeasure. In my experience, women are so easy to persuade. They just want to please me. When we first married and for months later, Cecilia would respond to my displeasure and quickly course-correct. She was conformable. I wrinkle my face into a pinch, as if I'm smelling something rotten while simultaneously bored.

"This is not my idea of *très romantique*," I say. I fold my arms across my chest. *Please me,* I'm saying. *You know how to please me. You used to please me all the time.*

Cecilia shakes her head. "Paul. Did you hear yourself? Please stop trying to speak French," she says. "Fine. I'll go in by myself. See you in an hour or so."

I'm stunned by her lack of empathy. What about me?

"Can you try to hurry? We have the Rodin, the Tuileries, lunch at two. This is our last day together in Paris," I say. "We should be strolling hand in hand."

She sighs, turns and walks away. I turn to buy water from the street vendor, but then see a bistro across the lush grounds. Perhaps I'll have water and a glass of rosé. Rosé all day, as they say, especially when your romantic trip to Paris isn't *romantique* at all.

Dear Diary,

Even though my parents don't approve, I know I have to make my own decisions. It's my life to live. The only one I've got, and I need to follow my dreams. It's a testament to how much they love me that they're supporting my decision.

"We didn't send you to college just to turn around and move to LA. That was never part of the plan," Mommy said.

"An actor? Nobody just moves out there and becomes an actor. You have to know people," Daddy said.

But I wouldn't let up. I was like, look, just give me a year. If it doesn't work out, I'll move back here, back home near you all. But I need to try, don't you see that? My dreams are too big for this town.

Mommy had looked at me with tears in her eyes but she nodded yes. Daddy does whatever she says so I've got the green light.

I'm leaving at the end of the summer. I'm doing this. Going for my dreams. Mommy said she wants to fly out and help me find a place to live, help me buy a car, get me all settled. I couldn't ask for more support. They really are the best. But they can't give me what I want, not here, not ever.

I want to be a star. I want fame, and money, and I want people to ask for my autograph wherever I go.

I practice different ways to sign my name, figuring out which one looks most famous. I just can't wait to get out there and get my big break. It won't be long now.

ELEVEN
PARIS, 12:10 P.M.

Paul

I watch Cecilia climb the steps of the palace, and sigh. I'd paused for a moment where she'd left me, hoping she'd change her mind and want to stay with me, but I guess not.

Now I'm sitting at the bistro, Les Petites Mains, just across the gardens from the stupid palatial clothing museum and I've made myself at home at an outdoor table. I send a text to let Cecilia know where I am. I ask her to come find me whenever she's finished looking at old clothes like she's at some huge Goodwill, which hopefully is soon.

I am enjoying my third glass of water and have ordered my second rosé. I'm tempted to order from the menu but know I should wait until lunch with Cecilia. *Love is at the heart of Palais Galliera*, the menu reads, *and this restaurant is like a secret garden for lovers.*

I'm fine, I remind myself. It's a perfectly lovely spring day in the most beautiful city in the world. And this bistro is a great spot for me, here, alone. It gives me a moment of reflection, I suppose. A chance to consider the course of our romance, the state of our marriage, so to speak. We are not pregnant with our hoped-for first child, despite repeated attempts. But we are gaining friends and clout in Malibu and Hollywood, slowly, through a combination of my personal charm, Cecilia's looks and our fabulous mansion. I may even have a chance to produce a huge summer blockbuster, which really means give a bunch of cash to finance the movie so your name appears in the credits. I'm close to signing on to the project. Once that happens, the Hollywood film opportunities will come rolling in. We have an awe-inspiring home and more money in the bank than I could have ever dreamed of. The future is full of possibilities, or so it seems.

We must look perfect from the outside. Our Malibu parties have become the sought-after invitation and I know Esther would be pleased. I think of her often these days, not just because of my bank account. But also, truth be told, I think it's because I miss our relationship. No, not the sex, not that. That was a very small part of the arrangement. What I miss is our sophisticated banter, the many cultural opportunities she provided me with. I learned so much from her.

I have not learned anything from Cecilia.

But I have learned something about her. In addition to not being as pliant and pleasing as I had thought, Cecilia has a lot of secrets. Although it turns out that Esther did, too. One in particular that is quite troubling, in fact.

"Monsieur, votre rosé," the waiter says, swooping in on my table like an efficient seagull.

"*Merci*," I say with perfect pronunciation. Cecilia isn't the boss of me and I can speak French when I want to.

The waiter frowns, nods, swoops away.

I pull out my phone and scroll to the email message, the one that changed everything when it landed in my inbox a month ago. The email is from Esther's estate executor, Joseph Grant, the attorney to anyone who is anyone in Palm Beach.

Dear Mr. Strom,

I hope all is well with you and you are enjoying the quite generous estate left to you by my client and friend, the late great Esther Wilmot. I write to inform you of some surprising, yet manageable news that is swirling around the Palm Beach gossip mill. This is nothing for you to be concerned about, but I did want to give you a heads up since you are no longer in town.

It seems that Ms. Wilmot may have had a child I was unaware of. This person has not reached out to our firm but has made some noise in the West Palm community about challenging the estate settlement. There has been no legal maneuvering as of yet and I don't expect there to be. Your estate agreement is ironclad, and while this individual may try to challenge the estate beneficiary plan, ultimately you are Esther's sole heir and her wishes cannot be overturned.

As you remember, shortly after Esther's death, her estranged sister also attempted to make a claim on the estate. Without success. I predict a similar fate for this person's claim should they pursue it as it has even less standing in court. I have had my private investigator digging into the issue. Despite the individual's DNA test that proves the relationship, Esther signed away the rights to the baby upon birth and had no contact with the individual whatsoever from that day forward. The child was given up for adoption, and that is the end of Esther's relationship with the individual.

We believe this claim is without merit and will be dismissed by the judge if it is ever filed in court. I did, however, want to bring this to your attention. It could be, as many things are, just an ugly rumor propagated by a shady attorney. Sometimes these types of nuisance cases do in fact draw a payout from clients who wish the matter to simply go away. I do not advise that in this case, of course.

Should you have any questions, don't hesitate to reach out.

Very sincerely,

Joseph Grant Jr., Esquire

Just when I had begun to believe the fortune really was all mine, someone had crawled out of wherever they had been hiding to try to make a claim for Esther's estate. It was gross, opportunistic and completely unfair to me, who had devoted more than a year to Esther's happiness and comfort. And of course, because it was just a nasty rumor, feeding the gossip crows for a bit, I could let it go. Ignore it and carry on with my fabulous life. Of course, I could. But it was an annoyance.

As soon as I'd read the email, I'd called the law firm. Despite the fact the letter said not to worry, I was nervous. Anyone would be. Joseph was in a meeting and his assistant promised he'd call me as soon as possible. I only needed to know one thing. Who could think of challenging my estate? Who was this rumored person? Was it a man, a woman? Why didn't my lawyer know who the individual was? Turns out, Joseph really didn't know. The rumors were so varied it was almost funny: a young man, a young woman, a long-lost sister, a long-lost brother. Joseph counseled me to put it all out of my mind. Apologized for even bringing it to my attention. But he did. And so it continued to nag a bit, in the back of my mind.

I take a sip of my rosé and check the time. Cecilia has been inside that place for almost forty-five minutes so far. I imagine her inside, contemplating some royal person's wardrobe from the 1800s. What is she trying to learn exactly? What could possibly be appealing about that? I picture her tilting her head, concentrating in that cute way she does. At our parties in Malibu she's so great, leaning in to conversations, making everyone feel welcome and heard. Like she did to me from the moment we first met. Such intense eye contact, such a caring, empathetic demeanor. She speaks to you like you're the only person in the room, the only one who matters.

And then, like a light switch, she turns off the charm and turns away, excusing herself to meet the next guest, to regale a more important person with sparkling conversation. Times like those, at our parties, I'd often wondered where she got her natural entertainment instincts. I mean, of course, I'm a natural at parties myself, but I'm my father's son, although he always worked in sales at boring corporate jobs and I am much more creative. I came by this fake charm biologically. He would say or do anything to be the center of attention, until he lost his looks. By the time he and my mom were living in the tiny home next to my mansion, everyone could see him as the ugly ogre of a man he was.

Cecilia is an entertainer. A mesmerizing, gorgeous woman who makes even the most famous of our guests feel welcome and at ease. Of course, I've learned recently that she inherited the trait from her mother.

When Joseph called me back I asked for the name of the individual trying to take my fortune away from me, a forgotten love child Esther never wanted to know, likely never wanted to have, and for certain did not want to keep.

"We don't know the individual's name. I've heard that it's a woman, possibly named Babcock," Joseph said on the phone. "But don't worry about it. She really has no claim on the estate. Keep enjoying yourself in California. I'll let you know if anything else develops."

I swallowed. Cecilia's maiden name is Babcock. It seemed my new wife was trying to steal the estate when she already had access to everything she wanted and desired through me. I was shocked. Still am, truth be told.

"Mr. Strom? Are you there?" Joseph asked. "Again, it's

nothing to worry about. The judge will dismiss the claim if one is ever filed. I'm certain."

I regained my composure and thanked him for his time. And since then, I haven't been able to look at my wife in the same way. I see Esther's eyes in Cecilia's, which is somehow comforting but also not. And ever since then, I can see what Cecilia wants me to see, but I am trying to figure out what's underneath. Who is she, really?

And now here we are on our one-year anniversary trip. I suppose I wanted to go on this trip to get to the truth, to discover if Cecilia really loves me for me, or whether she found me and married me just to get access to her mother's money.

I want to believe that our love is what I think it is: superior, beautiful, true. Worthy of being in this romantic city, worthy of a Hollywood happy ending. A love connection meant to happen.

She loves me. I love her. The money is ours, sort of, now. She doesn't need to make a claim on it because I share it happily —despite the hastily drawn-up prenup that says I don't have to, I do.

Except, if the rumor is to be believed, she has contacted an attorney, discussed making a petition to the court to be recognized as a rightful heir. And, if she does it, in the process she will challenge my right to the estate. Did she think I wouldn't discover the truth? What could she possibly want that she doesn't already have? Does she want control of the money? No, that's ridiculous. She already has the money through me. Does she want a divorce? Does she want the money and not me? Is she planning to try to steal it all from me?

"Hey there, handsome," my wife says, interrupting my troubled thoughts. She appears like a dream, kisses my cheek, before pulling out a chair and sitting beside me. "How's the rosé?"

"Very nice. Refreshing," I say. "Would you like a glass before we head to our next stop?"

"Sure, why not?" she says.

"How was the clothing museum?" I ask. She likely realizes I don't want to hear much about it.

"Oh, it was fabulous. You really should have come with me. I learned so much."

The waiter swoops in. "Un verre de rosé?"

"Oui, merci," Cecilia says.

Her *merci* isn't that much better than mine, just saying.

"So, the *Vogue* exhibit was fabulous. And the old gowns were one thing, but it was also interesting to learn about the way people lived back then. It's just hard to imagine for me but this museum brought it all to life," Cecilia continues. The sunshine glistens on her wedding ring as she speaks. The diamond band she's added to her right wrist shoots light my way. "The exhibit is called 'Love Brings Love.' Isn't that perfect?"

I tell myself not to ask another question and simply smile. "It's perfect."

The waiter brings Cecilia's rosé and I ask for the check. After almost a week here, I have this one down. "L'addition, s'il vous plaît."

Cecilia drops her head into her hands. Her glee vanishes. So dramatic.

My neck tenses. "Everyone says the French like it when foreigners try to speak their language."

"Well, I'm not everyone and I think I've made my opinion clear," she says and gulps the rosé.

I check my temper and hold my breath. "Excuse me. I need to find the toilet. Give him this when he comes back, *s'il vous plaît.*"

"Ugh," I hear Cecilia say under her breath.

But if she's uttered anything else I'm too far away to hear her. Again, this isn't the Cecilia I know, the one I married. She's changing, literally before my eyes, right at the end of our vacation together. But I will take charge. The rest of the day will go as I planned.

By the time I'm headed back to our table, I've forced my expression into a blasé look of nonchalance, one of my favorites: mouth relaxed, shoulders down. Poker-face Paul. I inhale a deep breath and join my bride at the table.

"Did you pay? Are we all set?" I ask. "It's time to get going on the rest of the day's adventures."

"Oh, yes, let's do this," Cecilia says, standing up. As we begin to stroll through the grounds surrounding the museum, she turns to me. "Paul, when you were married before, did you have more than one affair? I mean, you said you cheated on Mia when she was sick. Was it just a one-night slip-up?"

Sure. Sounds like a great answer. "Correct. I'm not proud of it, but it is what it is. Is there something you need to tell me? Why are you bringing this up?" I feel my shoulders inching up toward my ears, my neck tightening.

"What? Me? Cecilia laughs. "I've never been married before so how could I have had affairs?"

You're married now, though. I look at my wife and she smiles.

TWELVE
ST. LUCKY, FLORIDA

Cecilia, Age Ten

It's not my fault, it's hers. These people, the Sinclairs, said they would be my forever parents. They said I would save them from their heartache. But I wasn't enough, it turns out. Mommy Sinclair decided to get pregnant, with this baby girl, and that was her real dream all along. Not me. And just like that, they wanted to send me back. Without a warning. Without even much of an apology. They told the staff at the foster home that I had behavior problems and they couldn't cope with me anymore.

I didn't have any behavior problems until they replaced me with a baby of their own. Sure, I refused to hold the baby, and I didn't like to watch as they fed and fussed over the baby. So I'd just glare at them. That's all. When the baby was six months old, I accidentally let her roll off the couch. It was an accident. She barely even cried.

That was enough to send me packing. They said they were afraid I'd hurt their precious child.

I wouldn't have. I just wanted that baby to disappear. I

wanted to go back to how it had been for the year I was with them as their daughter. All about me. The focus of their love.

I told the director at the foster home that they lied about me. She says the truth is usually somewhere in the middle, that I'd better watch myself if I had any hope of finding another forever family.

I told her that it seems like forever is a pretty short time. She told me to watch my mouth and sent me to my room.

THIRTEEN

PARIS, 1:15 P.M.

Paul

I stare at Cecilia. She reaches out and takes my hand as we continue our unpleasant stroll. "You'll recall I had an affair because my wife was cheating on me with our neighbor, Buck. That's what started it."

"Really?" she asks. "Your jaw is twitching. And you just licked your bottom lip. I thought you said your wife was sick? I thought that was a reason for your weakness, your one-night stand, as you put it?"

I slide my mouth back and forth. My skills are slipping. I glance at Cecilia, who seems amused by her own question and my discomfort.

"Really. I told you. My wife had the affair," I say, keeping my tone light. I don't have any proof Mia cheated on me, of course, but I strongly suspect she wanted to. And heck, they're together now, so I'm right. "But we aren't talking about the past, remember?"

"Oh, I know, I was just having fun. The museum was full of stories of love, affairs and forbidden romance. Just got me thinking. You just seem like you're too sexy for one lover sometimes," she says. And then she starts laughing.

"What?"

"You should see your face. Ha!" she says. "And no, you are not allowed to have an affair while you're married to me. Understood?"

"Of course. Same applies to you, my dear," I say. I'm beginning to wonder if perhaps Cecilia and I are even more alike than I thought. No; she's just my sweet Cece, although she forbids me from using that nickname because that is what her adoptive parents called her growing up.

"I wouldn't dream of it. Look, we need to make a decision. Are we keeping our lunch reservation at the Crystal Museum, or shall we stroll along the Seine, be spontaneous and then keep to our plans to visit the Tuileries?" She's looking at her phone again. Presumably at the map.

"We should keep our lunch reservation at the museum," I say. "We've already been to the Louvre and the gardens. We did that two days ago."

"I want to walk. I'm not hungry for another heavy meal. Let's wait until this evening for that," Cecilia says. "Look, the river is just over there. Come on!"

She grabs my hand again and pulls me after her. It's not the gentle touch she used to get my attention during our multi-day road trip from Florida to California. Not at all. I yank my hand away.

"But we have reservations. It's been planned for months," I say. My jaw clenches and I rub the back of my neck with my left hand. I feel like she's trying to start a fight, pushing me too hard. But why?

"Cancel them. It's easy. Just find the email confirmation and push cancel," she says, holding up her phone. "I'll wait."

Back in my days at the advertising agency I had assistants to do such things. At Thompson Payne, I was in charge of the show as director of client services. My job was to make the agency sizzle, from the staff to the gleaming office space. I never made my own reservations, and quite frankly, I didn't have to do such menial things during my time with Esther or with the society mavens who I dated before her either. They had servants, staff for these things. I decide when I arrive back in Malibu, I will hire a personal assistant. I deserve it, and I can afford it.

"I need a personal assistant. I don't like handling these things and I won't anymore," I say. "During my advertising agency days, I—"

Cecilia puts her hand up. Her diamond ring sparkles like the edge of a knife blade when the sun hits it just right. "Stop. I don't want to hear about that right now, how magnificent you were, how the clients all loved you. Unless you want to tell me why you left there? I mean, if you loved it so much, why did you move down to Florida?"

"I needed a change of scenery, I told you that," I say. "I was torn up over the divorce, Mia's betrayal. I couldn't work, I couldn't function." I don't like her tone, or her defiance. Why is she prodding me? It really is like prodding a sleeping lion. It's dangerous. Inside I feel a fire ignite. My stomach, already on edge, twists.

"Poor dear Paul. You've been through so much." Cecilia pushes her sunglasses up on her head, squinting in the bright sunshine. "Hand me your phone. I'll cancel the reservation. I'll be your personal assistant, darling." She touches my shoulder and I almost jump.

As I hand her my phone I wonder again if my suspicions have been correct all along. I watch her carefully as she searches my inbox. I want to ask for her phone, search its contents, but that would be rude. I would seem untrusting. All is well. I have the money—the most important piece of my happiness—and Cecilia. I try to calm myself.

"Found it. All you do is click this blue button and your reservation is cancelled," she says. "All set."

I watch her with mounting, seething anger. Still trying to calm myself, I think of my bank account, all that glorious money from Esther still unspent. I think of the romantic meal I'd planned at the Crystal Museum.

"Maybe I just didn't want to cancel it. Maybe that was it," I say.

Cecilia's phone rings and she takes the call. She turns away from me so I cannot hear what she's saying, who she's talking to, but I don't care. I walk a few steps away from her and tune her out. I take a moment to breathe.

Maybe I should ask her directly if she is the person rumored to be challenging my claim to Esther's estate. Whoever it is, they would know already that Esther's sister lost. It just doesn't seem logical.

What is logical, what I dread may be the case, is that she married me for the money. Not in the traditional gold digger sense, but in the "that's my estate" sense. Is Cecilia Esther's secret, illegitimate daughter? I know Cecilia was adopted, and I know her adoptive parents called her Cece, which she hated. She hasn't shown me any photos of the parents, and she doesn't keep in touch. She hasn't told me anything else.

I've never thought Cecilia and Esther looked alike; never thought of myself as having a type. Sure, they both have blonde hair and blue eyes, but their features are quite different, aren't they? My heart squeezes with the realization.

I turn and watch her, back still turned to me, still on the telephone. But she loves me, she does. She's perfect and perfectly in love with me. Everyone else has a boring love. *But not us.* She is the perfect reflection of my success in the world. Plus we have a prenup—albeit hastily drafted—so she should know the only way to have access to Esther's fortune is through me. With me. By staying in our marriage, together. That's it.

Period. She didn't marry me for the money. I know she didn't. I'm in control, regardless of Cecilia's lineage.

I take a deep breath. I watch Cecilia continue to talk on the phone and I make a decision.

Cecilia walks toward me with a sunny smile on her face. "Sorry. I had to take that. The caterer for our fundraiser at the end of the month. Remember, we're helping the state senator who has all the Hollywood connections? The one who looks like he is a movie star?"

"Right, yes, Senator Stein. But it's four in the morning in LA," I say and watch her smile fade. "Who are you talking to?"

She chuckles. "Evan is in Miami for some big art show. He had to talk to me before he left for the day. Busy guy."

"So what exactly was his burning question for you at seven in the morning?" I ask.

Cecilia steps closer and then, quite unexpectedly, wraps her arms around my neck and gives me a kiss. "He needed to confirm the menu and the head count for the event. That's all. It just took a minute. I'm sorry if I upset you."

She's right. I am grumpy. "Well, that kiss was nice," I say, wrapping my arms around her slim waist. "Let's do more of that."

"I agree, we should. We need to stop being so terse with each other," she says. "It's our last day in Paris."

Is terse what we're being? I'm not certain, so I just say, "This day has been anything but what I thought it would be, but I'm sure things will turn around by tonight."

"I'm certain of that, too," Cecilia says. "Now, let's get going."

This time when she pulls on my hand, I go along with her. Really, if I decide to believe she is true and that she loves me, what other choice do I have?

FOURTEEN
ST. LUCKY, FLORIDA

Cecilia, Age Fifteen

It was five years before I was adopted again. Most adoptive parents want infants, or toddlers at the oldest, not teen girls. So I was fortunate, compared to others I knew in the foster home. Some of those girls would probably be stuck there until they aged out. My new forever home smells like mold and cigarettes, and it is farther inland, darker and a little scary. It is a quiet house, where nobody talks much. But by now, I am pretty and popular at school, despite my unusual background. Boys think I'm hot, so the girls think I'm cool. It works for me.

The baby girl from my first family, well, she goes to my school now, too—because we're such a small town, we're all on the same campus. She's in kindergarten. She has all the trappings of a spoiled brat. The expensive clothes, the new shoes, the spending money. Mrs. Sinclair, the woman I used to think of as "Mommy," walks her to the door every day, kissing her little cheek before she walks into her classroom. Mrs. Sinclair looks right through me, never acknowledges me. Like I'm a ghost.

When I see the little girl, I glare at her. Her eyes get big and she runs away. She deserves it.

My new parents cannot seem to remember my full name, so they call me Cece. That's not my name. I hate it. I sort of hate them. But I'm going to stick it out and hope they'll pay for college if I behave myself. Anything is better than that foster home.

I really want to go to college. That brat girl, she's only five years old right now, but I know for sure she will get to go to college. She'll grow up in my house, in my room, with a family who loves her more than anything in the world.

I'll never have that.

FIFTEEN

PARIS, 1:45 P.M.

Paul

Cecilia and I stroll along the bank of the Seine, holding hands, taking in the energy of the city as sunlight bounces off the water below. I know people who walk past us think we're important, celebrities even. I see the double takes, the whispers, the stares. And I love that.

And as we stroll, I think about how fast and special our love is, how we started out so great. Sometimes it felt like Cecilia had materialized on that sad rainy day of Esther's memorial just for me, as if Esther sent her to me. I became her sun, and she told me as much. She would hang on my every word, ask what I wanted to do each day, leave me little love notes everywhere in my home.

She even gave up her whole life just to spend more time together, so we could get to know each other "at the cellular level," as she said. I remember those days with such joy, even though, of course, I was grieving poor Esther's death. Cecilia went out of her way to cheer me up, suggesting bike rides and beach picnics, bringing me little surprises like my favorite bottle of red wine, or a new cologne to try.

For my part, I showed her my best, most charming self. I was instantly drawn to Cecilia. Aside from the fact she was gorgeous, she was artsy. I found that incredibly appealing. Plus, her painting career was portable; she could create anywhere, she told me.

She was, as she still often reminds me, primed to take over from a successful gallery owner in Palm Beach; a career she gave up for me when we fell in love. I think the guy had a crush on her, never sold a single one of her paintings, and was holding out the hope that the promise of owning a gallery might keep her around. But who knows? She picked me, so it doesn't matter.

"I will quit my job for you," Cecilia had said at some point after we'd been dating for three months or so. "I mean, they want me to take over the gallery someday, but I'm not so sure that speaks to me. Bottom line is that I'm an artist, not a business owner."

"You don't need to own a gallery, darling," I said. "You'll be much too busy for that. We're going to have an amazing life. A fun life."

"I hate having to leave you here, all alone," she said. "But I'll be late for work if I don't go now."

"I hate it too," I'd said, pulling her back into bed with me. "As soon as my big business deal goes through, I'll be more than able to provide for us both. It should be any day now."

"And then I'll quit and never look back," she said, giving me a delicious kiss.

Those were the days when my job was waiting for my attorney to call with an update about Esther's money transferring to me, and long workouts to keep in top physical condition for my new, young lover.

"When do you think it will happen, the deal?" she asked, snuggling back into me.

"Any day now, love, and then you and I can do whatever we want, go wherever we'd like," I said.

"Remind me of the business again?" she'd said.

"Remember, I invested in an early-phase startup and pow, it's on fire," I said. I couldn't quite remember what I had told her before, so I kept the details vague. I didn't want her to think my only source of income would be due to Esther's demise. That didn't seem very grand. And I am grand. I deserved the money that was coming my way from the estate, but I wanted Cecilia to think of me as so much more.

"Right. A startup." Cecilia stretched and hopped back out of bed. "And then there's Esther's fortune. She is leaving a lot to you, right?"

"Yes, of course. She was so lovely. I'm sure that will be the case," I said. "But that is just icing on the cake. The IPO of the company I invested in will be the cake. Ha!"

She shook her lovely head. "Corny old-guy joke. You need to work on that. I'm hopping in the shower."

Considering that an invitation, as it always was back then, I joined her. In comparison, on this romantic week-long trip to Paris, we've barely kissed. *My fault with the stomach issues*, I remind myself. I will eat clean the rest of the day.

"Say, Cecilia, where do you plan on taking me for lunch?" I ask as we dodge oncoming tourists. "Do you have somewhere fabulous in mind?"

"I do. We're going to cross to the Left Bank and eat at a special family-owned café. Evan told me about it just now on the phone. He's set it all up and they're waiting for us. He has connections to the foodie world everywhere and he insisted this will be fabulous. It's all arranged," she says.

I try to keep my happiness intact even though she has

decided Evan's restaurant is better than mine. It's not. My choice for our lunch spot was elegant, with crystal chandeliers, fine china, exquisite food. I'm certain this place will not compare.

"How exciting," I say as we cross over the river. I realize we haven't been on this side of the Seine our entire trip. Perhaps a change of scene will be good?

"I'm glad you're happy," she says. "We can go to the Rodin Museum before or after."

"After, please," I say. "Where are we? What is this park? Whose palace is this?"

A group of schoolboys runs past us, and a pang hits my heart. I haven't seen my boys in five years, and likely never will again. That's why we were supposed to be pregnant already, Cecilia and I, with a replacement son followed by two more. It's easier to imagine the future than dwell on the past, I've learned.

"We are in the park of the *invalides*," she says. "And in front of you is a military museum. Napoleon's Tomb is in there under that huge golden dome."

"I'd like to see that. After lunch," I say. I imagine Napoleon planned a huge tomb to compensate for his small size. Men do compensate, well, some must. I am one of the blessed; just ask Cecilia.

"I saw you watching those boys run past us. You miss Mikey and Sam, don't you?" she asks. She stops, reaches out and touches my shoulder. "It must be hard on you."

Cecilia has pushed her sunglasses up on her head. She looks at me with squinted eyes, watching me like you would a snake you came across on a hiking trail, with both interest and apprehension.

"What?" I say. I really cannot believe what she just asked me. I also cannot believe she spoke my sons' names. She never mentions their names. They are the boys, my boys. That's it. She knows how much it hurts me that they were stolen from me. OK, they weren't actually stolen but taken to Mia's parents' palatial home in New York. I was warned in no uncertain terms that if I tried to reach out to them, ever, she'd press charges. Stolen is easier to explain.

Right at this moment, I wonder what Cecilia sees in me. Does she still see me as the sophisticated older man, at the top of Palm Beach and LA society, that she promised to love, honor, and obey for as long as we both shall live? Does she still long for my experienced touch? Am I still the best she's ever had?

Cecilia pulls her sunglasses back down, her challenge over for the time being.

"Never mind. The café is just down Rue de Grenelle. Come," she says and once again takes off walking at the speed of sound in the City of Light.

It's annoying, to put it mildly. And I cannot just brush it aside. I won't.

SIXTEEN

MALIBU, CALIFORNIA, TEN MONTHS AGO

Cecilia

I'm beginning to think I'll never learn this game. But I need to, it's what we all do out here every morning, according to my new friend. We must play tennis. Melissa smiles at me from across the net.

"Don't give up. You're a natural. Maybe some lessons would be a good idea?" she says. She's been patient and helpful, but I can tell I'm boring her. "I need to run to my clinic, but I can send you an instructor's name. He's great, and quite cute. Hope Paul won't mind."

I walk to the net. "Of course not. He knows I only have eyes for him. Thanks for trying to help me, though. Call me later?"

As Melissa hurries off the court, slips into her car and begins to drive away, I hear a familiar song blasting on her radio. "Need You Now" by Lady A prompts a strong vision of the day with my first adoptive parents, the day I was placed in my "forever home." My new mom was singing along as she prepared dinner. All I could feel was love. I needed them and they were there, like a dream come true.

A chill runs down my spine. I tried everything I knew to please them, but I was never good enough, could never be a replacement for the daughter they'd lost as an infant. And then they replaced me...

"Cecilia! Hey! What are you doing?" Paul yells from the window of his car. I've learned it's a Bentley. It's very nice. We had so much fun on our road trip out here that I smile every time I see it. And him.

"Trying to learn tennis. But I can't do it, I'm terrible," I say, hurrying off the court to give him a kiss. He climbs out of the car and swoops me into an embrace.

"You don't need tennis, gorgeous. You have many other talents, especially in bed." He grins.

"You've taught me everything I know," I say and feel my face flush. He has. He's an experienced lover. I've never felt so sexy. I've never felt so truly loved.

"Well, if you aren't busy, I have some time for another lesson before I need to head into LA," he says. "Oh, and I need to make sure we're all set for the party tonight. It's our coming-out party, so to speak. Everyone who is anyone in Hollywood has been invited, and so many have said yes. They'll be here, at our home. We've arrived!"

We hop into his car before heading down the winding driveway to our mansion perched on the edge of the sparkling sea. This view, this life, I can't imagine it ever getting old.

"I think everything is handled for tonight. The event guy, Evan, will be here by 1 p.m. to start setting up. He says he'll make our place even more fabulous," I say. I've had fun working with him—and with an unlimited budget, anything is possible.

Tonight's theme is *The Great Gatsby*. I've ordered an authentic flapper outfit, a bright yellow sequin dress, and the hair and makeup team will make sure I really sparkle.

Paul stops in front of our house. "Did they figure out how to make the champagne fountain work? I've always wanted to have an over-the-top champagne fountain."

"They did," I say. "I hope all those Hollywood people will be impressed. They seem like a scary crowd to try to please."

"But not for us." Paul turns to me with another grin. "I've already caused quite a buzz around town. People are interested in working with rich, gorgeous people like us. It's only a matter of time before Paul Strom Productions is attached to a block-buster movie. The deal terms are coming through next week, according to the attorneys."

"I know it's going to happen. I can see us walking the red carpet at the premiere," I say as we rush inside, almost running up the stairs to our five-room master suite. Paul locks the door behind us. We have a staff of four—full-time, every weekday and on the weekends when needed—but they are discreet and always seem to disappear at times like these.

Afterward, as I sit in bed and stare out at the ocean, a hummingbird pauses and hovers mid-flight, seemingly staring at me through the window. Perhaps it's admiring my American Dream like in *The Great Gatsby*? Or maybe it's a good luck omen. I check the time and realize I need to get ready for the event planner. We each have our own full bathroom, our own showers, bathtubs, vanities, and huge walk-in closets. I start making a move toward my own personal bathroom.

Paul appears as I'm getting out of bed. "I'll see you in a few hours, love."

"I wish you didn't have so many meetings," I say.

"It's what it takes to break into the business, I've told you that," he says. He kisses my forehead. "I'll be home soon, in time to see our home transformed into Gatsby's mansion, West Coast style. Watch every detail. Also, I know I'm probably asking too much, but would you mind picking up my tux from the tailor? I would send a staffer, but we need all hands on deck here."

"Sure, no problem," I say as he hurries out the door. I notice that the hummingbird is still hovering around outside. I type in my phone: *What does it mean when a hummingbird visits you?* I smile. I was right! Hummingbirds are positive omens and bring healing and good luck. *If you see a hummingbird*, the search results say, *it could be a sign that you need to add more joy and sweetness to your life.*

"But I'm fine, hummingbird, I'm so lucky! You should visit someone else," I say as the tiny bird finally disappears. I reach for my sketchbook to make a quick drawing of the bird, inspired by its presence, as well as its ability to disappear in the blink of an eye.

My phone rings. It's Evan, the event planner.

"Are you getting excited for your coming-out party?" he asks. "I'm headed your way. Everything is coming together so perfectly. You're going to be the talk of the town."

I laugh. "As long as the talk is good. And yes, Paul and I hope to make a great impression."

"You can't help but make a great impression," Evan assures me. "And with your house for entertaining, well, they're all going to be wanting the next invitation. Mark my words. I'll see you in twenty minutes."

I climb out of bed and hurry to my dream bathroom. I never would have imagined, as a teenager looking out of my second forever family's kitchen window at the swamp behind our house, that I'd live a life this glamorous.

Dreams do come true—not all of them, but maybe just the ones you need—as long as you work hard to make them happen.

SEVENTEEN
PARIS, 2:00 P.M.

Paul

Café Nobo isn't anything special. If fact, it's more of a casual coffee shop-type place. Nothing sparkles with crystal or light like it would have at the museum where I had our lunch reservation – the reservation that Cecilia rudely cancelled.

There are seven tables in the place, and only one of them is occupied. This definitely isn't special. It's fast food in Paris.

"Paul, stop pouting. This is going to be great," Cecilia says, ushering us to a table since no one is around to greet us.

"I'm not pouting," I say. In fact, I'm currently experiencing an emotion much more dangerous than that one that I accidentally allowed to slide across my face. My patience with this day, with the plans all messed up, well, I've just about had it. And that's not good for anyone, trust me. Just ask some of the people in my past who found out the hard way what happens when you push my patience to the limit. Of course, I'm more mature now. More measured. I don't usually allow myself to get depleted. I know what and who I need. And I usually get what I want. I'm sure you've figured that out by now.

The only good thing about finding myself in this miserable restaurant is I can finally rest from our forced march through Paris. And although this place lacks a view, or really anything of interest or distinction, at least across from me Cecilia is all sunshine again.

"I hope you're hungry because Evan says this is the best-kept secret in Paris," she says.

"Sometimes there is a reason places are kept as an embarrassing secret," I mutter.

"Honestly, stop it," Cecilia says. She pulls out her phone and starts texting. "I'm letting them know we're here."

A petite woman appears from the back of the restaurant with dark hair pulled into a bun, a black apron and a shy French smile.

"Cecilia! *Bonjour!* So happy Evan sent you my way," she says, scurrying to our table. "So nice to meet you. Thank you for coming!" She wraps my wife in a big hug. The two women do the cheek kiss thing and then, finally, someone notices me.

"*Bonjour*. My name is Phoebe. Welcome to my restaurant," she says, extending her hand.

I realize I should stand, so I do, and she kisses me on both cheeks. I try to do the same but I'm not good at that. I'm American. "Hello, Phoebe."

The three of us stand awkwardly for a moment until Phoebe says, "*Alors*, I know you are quite hungry, Paul. Let me go and get your meal ready."

"Evan mentioned that you are a great chef, and that your kitchen is fabulous," Cecilia says.

"Would you like a tour? To me, it's very special but I don't know if you'll agree," Phoebe says.

"Oh, I don't want to be in the way. And, well, Paul, I don't want you to be bored." Cecilia glances at me.

"Oh, I'm fine, honey. I know how you love kitchen tours," I say. It's true. Cecilia can get excited walking through just about any kitchen, any home, any restaurant. "Go ahead. Some partners might be angry, but not us." I toss our loving phrase at her but she barely seems to register it.

"Come along," Phoebe says. "We will make something very special for you two, a traditional French lunch. You can help!"

"OK, yes. I get to see a real French kitchen! And learn real French cooking, how fun!" Cecilia squeals and claps her hands like she's won the lottery. Well, she already did. With me. "We'll be back!"

With a wave, my wife disappears into the back of the restaurant out of sight and once again, on our last day in Paris, I am alone. At a café. Not of my original choosing. And I'm thirsty. A kid with the hint of a mustache and long gangly arms is lurking in the corner of the restaurant. Does he work here? Intend to rob the place? Who knows?

"Pardon?" I call out. "Could I get a drink? *S'il vous plaît?*" I cringe as I try the French, hearing Cecilia's scorn imprinted on my brain.

"*Oui,*" the kid says. "What do you want?"

"A glass of rosé?" I say. Rosé all day, am I right? It keeps the fire tamped down. At least for a while.

"*Oui,*" he says without making eye contact.

"Oh, and water," I say.

"*Oui,*" he repeats, slinking away. I want to make a comment on his slouchy, slinky behavior but I won't.

The young, slouchy, likely tattooed waiter is soon back. "Here," he says when he slides my glass—a tiny glass—of rosé on the table. "Be back with water."

You know, if I didn't know any better, I'd think this kid was American, from Ohio or the middle of anywhere. He doesn't sound French, and while his treatment of me is very French, there's something else going on here. When he comes back, placing the clearly typical small glass of water lacking ice on the table, I meet his eye.

"Are you American?" I ask.

"Half," he grunts.

"Is that your mom, in the kitchen?" I ask.

"I spend summers with her, to help with all the tourists, and then I go back home to the States," he explains.

"Do you know somebody named Evan?" I ask, trying to tie the annoying caterer to the reason I am at this spot, suffering through what will surely be a less-than-elegant lunch. I'm furious with him for intruding on my day.

He shakes his head and turns and walks away. Rude. He must be more French than American. I open my phone, wondering what time it is back in the states, back in Southern California particularly. But I remind myself to stay present, stay in the moment on our special anniversary day, despite the temptation to turn elsewhere. There will be time for that later, but for now, I will once again wait for Cecilia. I stare at the back of the restaurant, at the spot where she disappeared into the kitchen, and will her to return quickly.

Dear Diary,

OK, so the most amazing thing happened today!!! I was excited for this audition for a variety of reasons but mainly because it was being held at a famous guy's office. I mean, a lot of times these casting calls are held at casting directors' offices, or some other cold, soul-crushing, sterile facility.

But today, I got to go to an amazing office building in Santa Monica, with views of the coast as far as the eye can see, and meet one-on-one with the producer. OMG!!

As I sat in the reception area, I checked out the competition. Brunettes as far as I could tell, all of them, so I stood out with my long blonde hair. I also stood out because I'm almost six feet tall. Most of these other girls are tiny. They should be going out for teen roles, not adult roles. I'm ready, more than ready, for a grown-up part. I knew it.

Turns out he agreed!! I walked into his huge office and sat down across from his desk. He smiled at me and told me to go ahead with my lines. So I stood up again and delivered like my future depended on it. And it does. It really does.

He told me to come back tomorrow!!! I got a call back!! OMG, this is the break I've been waiting for this whole time.

This is the one I deserve.

EIGHTEEN

PARIS, 2:40 P.M.

Paul

My wine and water glasses are empty. The unfriendly stick-figure boy-man is nowhere to be seen, and neither, of course, is Cecilia. She has been in the kitchen for almost forty minutes as I continue to sit alone, waiting.

It has given me a chance to settle with my thoughts. To crystallize—even without being at the Crystal Museum restaurant—my plans. I realize I have been in a whirlwind of love and happiness, caught up in an illusion of my own making.

I'll never forget the night that Esther intimated she was leaving her vast estate to me. It was a feeling beyond description, a dream I never thought would come true. I had kissed a lot of frogs during my time in West Palm, but it turned out that my exciting, final Palm Beach paramour would be the answer to my dreams when she died.

And then Cecilia appeared. And we fell in love. And we married. And now this. Her recent behavior has convinced me that she is planning to divorce me soon and have our hasty prenup voided so she can steal Esther's estate, or at least half of it, from me. I am also now more convinced than ever that she is the one behind the rumor of an estate challenge. Cecilia must be Esther's illegitimate, long-forgotten and mistreated daughter.

I have made the decision that I will confront her with my suspicions. I dash off a quick email to Joseph on my phone asking if he's heard anything else about the so-called heir who will challenge the estate. And then I turn my attention to the back of the restaurant as Cecilia, likely that very heir, emerges holding a large platter of food.

"I hope you're hungry, darling," she says. She looks so proud of herself, so smug. She's reminding me a bit of Mia, or at least working girl Mia, who started to rear her ugly head during our Lakeside getaway all those years ago. It was there where Mia told me, in no uncertain terms, that she was going back to work at an ad agency. *I forbid it.* My wife does not work outside the home. Mia was disobeying me. I didn't enjoy the behavior from wife number one, and I certainly don't from wife number two.

"Famished," I say, just because I do not allow Cecilia to use such gross overstatements. I hate exaggeration. Unless it's for a purpose. As it is now to make a point to the gangly creature. "Parched, too." I point to my empty glasses as Phoebe appears with a full bottle of rosé and a pitcher of water.

"So sorry," she says. "Theo was supposed to take care of you."

"Let's eat, shall we?" I say as Cecilia settles in. Phoebe sits down beside her. Apparently, we are now the only patrons of what is supposed to be a popular restaurant, according to Evan. It clearly is not.

"I asked the chef to join us. Here, Paul, this is your plate. Made just for you with love." Cecilia hands me a huge plate of food. I must admit it looks and smells divine. I grab a French fry and pop it into my mouth. Chewing allows me to recover from the unpleasant realization that we are having lunch on our last day in Paris with the mother of an obnoxious stick-figure man-boy and that this whole situation is based on Evan's connections. Evan is on my last nerve.

What a joy. I'd really wanted to speak with my bride alone, but now I can't.

"Please enjoy the traditional French casual meal," Phoebe says, watching me. "There is a *tarte* with tomatoes and basil. The *pommes frites*, and the *salade niçoise* with endive and fresh seared tuna."

My mouth is watering. I can eat first and then I'll talk. I smile and dive in. This was worth the wait.

"It's great, right? I mean, nobody makes fries like the French," Cecilia says in between bites. I notice her cheeks are flushed. They were drinking wine in the kitchen, I'd bet my fortune on it. "I learned so much, Phoebe. Thank you."

"My pleasure," she says. "Paul, you do what in the US, for work?"

I hate this question. I force a smile. "I am a producer in Hollywood," I say.

"*Mon dieu.* How exciting. Evan didn't mention I had a celebrity guest. What movies do you do?"

Phoebe is beginning to grow on me, what with her enthusiasm and her clear enchantment with me now she knows I'm somebody from Hollywood.

"He's just getting started out there, really," Cecilia says, draining the enthusiasm from my new fan's face like pulling the stopper out in a bathtub.

"Oh," Phoebe says.

"That isn't true, darling. We've had several meetings. I'm about to produce a limited series, remember?" I say. "The salad is spectacular, I must say, Phoebe."

My host is back to being engaged. "What is the series about?"

Good question, since I'm making this up. "About a husband and wife, they're perfect together but there is something off. We learn the wife is up to terrible things. It's quite an entertaining script."

Across the table Cecilia smiles, but not with her eyes, while continuing to gobble French fries like they are the last ones available on the planet. Perhaps she's pregnant. I think back to the last time we made love, embarrassingly a couple of months ago now. Just enough time for hormonal changes and morning sickness. That could explain it all. Her terse temperament, her demanding behavior, the way she's tried to take over and ruin our last day. The realization makes me smile. It's just what we need, what we dream of, what we talk about. My son. The boy who will carry on the Strom family name and legacy.

"How are you feeling, darling?" I ask Cecilia.

"Fine. Why?" she asks. "The migraine is gone, if that's what you mean."

"Oh, so sorry you have to suffer a migraine on your holiday vacation," Phoebe says.

"It's Paul who has been most ill, actually," Cecilia says. "Stomach issues. How are you feeling?"

And that's when it hits me. A burning sensation in my mouth and my heart starts racing. What is wrong with me? Across the table, Phoebe and Cecilia's faces blur, and then come back into focus.

"He looks like he is ill suddenly," Phoebe says, her eyes bright with alarm. "I hope you aren't allergic to anything?"

"You know, he doesn't think he has food allergies, but I'm beginning to think he does. To French food. Is that possible?" Cecilia says. "Paul, drink some water, you look horrible."

"What can I do?" Phoebe asks.

"He'll be fine in a little bit. It always passes, poor dear," Cecilia says.

My hand shakes as I place my water glass back on the table. I can't believe this is happening again, here, at this charming, simple restaurant. There weren't even any heavy sauces on this meal.

"Maybe it's a certain spice you use that we don't?" Cecilia asks Phoebe.

Phoebe stares at me with huge brown eyes. "I don't know. I'm sorry."

"It's fine. He'll be OK. Just give him a minute," Cecilia says. "Now, take nice deep breaths, dear. There, you're getting a bit of your color back. Handsome as ever." She pats my hand. It's still shaking. I feel awful. I take another breath.

"Did you know, when I met Paul, I thought he was the most handsome man I'd ever seen, for his age? I know he looks a little sweaty at the moment, but he really has movie star good looks. That's why Hollywood is perfect for him."

"OK, yes," Phoebe says. She still looks concerned.

"I looked him up on the internet after the first night we met. I cyberstalked him, so to speak." She pats my hand again across the table. "There are so many things you can learn about people on the internet, the little details that betray a person if only you know where to look."

Phoebe nods her head. "Good idea. Should have done that with Theo's dad."

"When you love someone there's nothing about them that feels unimportant. You want to notice everything, figure out everything about them," Cecilia continues. "Everything is important when you've found your true love. Every little detail."

Like talking about my boys. My career in advertising. My past. She learned all about me because she loves me.

Why didn't I do the same with her? I take another sip of water. I meet Cecilia's eyes across the table.

"I do know," I finally say. The tremors and burning in my mouth have subsided. All that's left is the gnawing pain in my stomach and a growing dread in my heart. Why didn't I research Cecilia more thoroughly? An initial search revealed nothing. She'd had no social media presence, no business website, although she was listed as "staff" at the gallery where she worked, nothing except an apartment address on the wrong side of town. She'd told me that as an artist, she hated the online world, that she only created in the real world. Why did I take her word for everything she told me about herself, her life? I was too anxious to move on, too eager to date a young, gorgeous woman and make her my wife. I hope I have not been a fool.

Cecilia looks at me and again pats my hand across the table. Like I'm a child. At least my hand has stopped shaking now.

"We are just so lucky, Phoebe. It was love at first sight. I hope you find that too—I do," Cecilia says as if she's talking to a long-lost friend.

"*Oui*, I will try for love at first sight next time if I ever date again. It's so horrible out there. People are not what they seem," Phoebe says. "How are you feeling now, Paul?"

"Better, thank you," I say. "Look, this was quite a meal, but I do need to whisk Cecilia away. It's our last day in Paris. We have so much to do."

And so much more to talk about.

NINETEEN

Paul

As soon as we are outside the restaurant, on the sidewalk, I grab Cecilia's arm.

"What do you mean, you stalked me online?" I ask. I'll admit I still I don't feel good and I'm also angry.

"Everybody does it. You didn't stalk me?" she says. "That's dumb. Ready for the Rodin Museum?"

"Of course, I searched the internet. I couldn't find anything about you, no digital footprint at all. Who lives like that? I mean, you said you had a business doing event invitations, and you were selling art at some gallery, but I couldn't find anything." Was that on purpose? So I couldn't learn her real connection to Esther? No, I surely wouldn't have been able to find that truth, anyway. She appeared in my life like a dream. She's my soulmate. I felt lucky she picked me, and me her. She hooked me and reeled me in. My mind is racing, and I know I'm not thinking clearly. Who am I married to?

"Some people don't like to be found. I'm more private, more

cautious than you are," she says. "But you, you have a very public persona, especially once you began dating Esther."

"We weren't dating. I was her companion. She didn't like to be alone. I'd escort her to galas and to the movies. We'd have long talks together every evening over cocktails. It was innocent companionship," I say. "For the last and final time."

"Right, darling," Cecilia says. "We have a couple of blocks to walk. Do you think you can handle that?"

Another wave of nausea rolls over me. "I can handle anything. Just walk slowly."

"Of course," she says. "Wasn't Phoebe fabulous?"

I don't want to talk about Phoebe or the food that is making me so ill. I want to know what is going on with my wife. "Did you plan to meet me that day at the funeral? Was it all part of a bigger scheme?"

"What are you talking about?" she asks, again walking too fast for me.

"You married me to get your hands on the money," I say carefully.

That gets her to stop in her tracks. "Paul, don't be ridiculous. We both know it was fate that brought us together. I was there handing out the programs I'd designed for the occasion, to honor Esther. By then, I'd read all about her amazing life. And of course, I'd helped behind the scenes with some of her fabulous parties."

"And?" I ask, my hands now on my hips.

"And what? My name is Cecilia Strom now! I grew up, dirt-poor, in a tiny town in central Florida. I was adopted by a family when I was eight years old, and it really felt like home. It felt like they loved me. But then they got pregnant with a baby girl. So, by age ten I was back in the foster care system. I was finally adopted again when I was fifteen years old. The second family didn't even pretend to love me. I think they liked the checks they got for taking me in. The only saving grace was that I got to stay at the same school. The teachers liked me. I was popular, despite all this upheaval in my life." She pauses, tears in her eyes.

Poor girl. Her childhood does sound horrible. I wonder why she never told me this. "I'm sorry," is all I say.

"Thank you. Everybody's got something hard in their past. I don't have any relationship with Esther, never have, except now through you. I never even met the woman. All I was doing at her funeral was paying my respects, passing out the programs I designed in her honor. You know this. I can't understand what's gotten into you, but it sort of feels like you're losing your mind."

Maybe I am. Crap. I don't know what to believe. Another wave of nausea hits and I grab my stomach.

"Sorry. I don't know why I'm doubting you," I say. Although there are a number of reasons.

"Oh, Paul. It's OK. I know you don't feel well. Let's go see *The Thinker*. That will brighten our day. Let me hold your hand, until you feel better," she says. She wraps her arm around me and my heart surges with love. It's nice to feel her body against mine after all we've been through today.

"I like it when you take care of me," I say. I feel the strong pulse of desire pulse between us, as it always used to. "I like taking care of you, too. Maybe we should skip the museum, go back to the hotel for a bit of fun?" I imagine hurrying inside our hotel room, desire burning in both of us. I would swoop Cecilia up in my arms and carry her to the luxurious bed in the suite. She'll sigh and begin to undress as I yank my clothes off. And then we'll make love, like we did when we first met and even during the first few months in Malibu when we still couldn't keep our hands off each other. The thought of an afternoon back in our sumptuous suite at The Peninsula makes me smile. And after, while we linger in bed, we can talk about how wonderful tonight will be.

I really cannot wait.

"I've always wanted to see *The Thinker*," she says. She places both hands on my chest and I lean in to kiss her. My head swirls with lust. "Let's go see it. It's a four-minute walk. Please. And then we can go back to the hotel."

It feels so nice to have her hands on my chest. She leans her head into me, her ear on my heart. People pass us on the sidewalk, glance at us in envy. This type of love is so rare to see these days, you know? "Do you hear it racing?" I murmur.

"What?" she asks.

"My heart. It's racing. It's what you do to me," I say.

"It is," she agrees. She looks up into my eyes. How can I say no to that gorgeous face?

"Let's go see *The Thinker*," I say. How long can that take? Patience, that's my new virtue.

No, it's not.

TWENTY

SOMEWHERE IN GEORGIA, ONE YEAR AGO

Cecilia

I never knew driving across the country could be so fun. I've already seen more of the United States than I ever have before. In fact, it's the first time I've left the state of Florida, and when we crossed over into Georgia, I was grinning from ear to ear.

I glance over at Paul, and he senses me watching him. He turns his head and smiles. "Hey, gorgeous. Do you need to stop for anything? I'm thinking outside of Atlanta we could find a nice hotel for the night. Maybe Buckhead?"

I shrug my shoulders. "I've never been to Atlanta, so you pick. Whatever you like I'll love. This is so fun! I've never had someone take care of me like this before. Ever. Thank you."

"Stick with me, kid. I'm going to spoil you rotten. And our kids." Paul grins.

"I'm all for that," I say.

Paul turns up the music, his Spotify playlist. "Come Away with Me" by Norah Jones starts playing. I'm learning all of Paul's favorite songs on the drive. He says he picked them just for me, just for this trip. I sing along to the music. A Frank Sinatra song begins and I smile.

"I'm glad you're enjoying the music. I was afraid you'd find my choices too old-fashioned," he says. "'As Time Goes By' by Frank Sinatra is a classic, of course. So is 'Mack the Knife.'"

"I love them all," I say. And I do. I've never had anyone make me a playlist. Sure, my high school boyfriend loved me, and he was great. He had that picture-perfect family that I dreamed of being a part of. I knew his parents didn't approve of me, but for a while I won. As soon as he went off to college, though, and I didn't, everything changed. I hear he's happily married to his college sweetheart now with a couple of kids. He stayed in the same small town, lives two blocks from his parents.

I never wanted that.

Maybe because I knew I couldn't have it...

Paul

Paris is such an interesting city. There are layers and layers of history here, right on top of each other. In America, we sanitize our cities, bulldoze the old and raise the new. We scrape away hints of history and keep marching forward. I'm definitely more American in my actions.

In Paris, the old—the beautiful and the squalid—are here now and always. I suppose that offers a certain charm, too.

I glance at Cecilia. She's in the corner of the sculpture garden at the Rodin Museum, pretending to appreciate a sculpture, while I am thinking in front of *The Thinker*. Of course, you're familiar with Rodin's most famous sculpture. The massive bronze statue of a handsome nude man, sitting on a rock, leaning over, right elbow on left thigh, holding the weight of his chin on the back of his right hand.

What exactly is *The Thinker* thinking about? Clearly, he's thinking with his whole body, clenched fist, flexed arms, and the like. Apparently, according to my museum brochure, Auguste

Rodin chose to depict *The Thinker* as a strong, athletic figure to convey that the act of thinking is a powerful exercise.

He's right, of course. I, for one, can get totally lost in my own head. For example, I can create an entire world where my lovely wife is in love with me and not my money. Cecilia seems to be delaying things, and I'm beginning to wonder if she actually wants to go back to the hotel and make love as we planned? I watch as she texts frantically in the corner of the garden next to a sculpted hedge. I had thought by bringing her here to Paris, she would focus on us, not the ever-growing list of friends and acquaintances she has in her orbit daily. It appears I was wrong about that, too. I'm tempted to pull out my phone and text with someone. Someone who wants to spend time with me instead of staring at a sculpture. But I do not.

Instead, I read more of my brochure. Interestingly, *The Thinker* was originally planned to be one part of a set of bronze doors for a museum in Paris. This figure also represented Dante reflecting on *The Divine Comedy*, his epic poem about heaven, hell and the fate of all humankind—the spiritual journey of man through life. Sin and consequences. It's a manly journey Dante takes us on, as I recall from college. Evil is to be punished and good rewarded. Us humans are subject to temptation and commit sins, of course, because we have free will. The good go to heaven, and, well, the bad go to hell to suffer relentlessly. My stomach twists and I feel another wave of nausea.

"You've been over here a long time," Cecilia says, sneaking up on me from behind. I swear she was just in the other corner. "Having a think with *The Thinker*, are we?"

"Clever. Actually, I was thinking about *The Divine Comedy*," I say. "A particularly grim view of what waits for us on the other side. 'Abandon all hope, ye who enter here,' and all that. Incidentally, *The Gates of Hell* are out here somewhere, by the way."

"Well, that's some happy stuff right there," Cecilia says. "Can we head out?"

"Sure," I answer. "Did you read *The Divine Comedy* in college?"

"No." She leads the way out of the sculpture garden. "You know I went to work after high school. I didn't have the money for college."

"Right," I say. "A shame."

"We are going back to the hotel now, aren't we?" Cecilia asks. "That's what you want to do."

It's what I wanted to do when I envisioned wild sex. Now, I have other ideas.

"I'd like to see Napoleon's Tomb but I'm flexible, really, until dinner. That I really don't want to miss, and we won't," I say. It takes careful planning to snag a reservation at Madame Brasserie at the Eiffel Tower. She will not disrupt that experience. "Who were you texting with in the garden, by the way? And why?"

"Just a couple of friends, asking about our trip," she says. "Didn't know I needed your permission to talk to my friends."

I feel like Cecilia has suddenly become an impertinent teen, not my wonderful, loving wife.

"I like my friends," Cecilia continues, "but I love you. Let's go back to the hotel. We've had a long day out in the sun. I could use a rest. I'm sure you could, too."

She loves me was all I heard in that statement. Everything else was blah, blah, blah. "So what do you want to do?"

"You aren't listening. I hate it when you do that," Cecilia says.

Hmm. I thought I was. I rearrange my face into what I hope is a look of concern and care. "I'll do whatever you would like to do."

"Ugh. Follow me," she says and stomps down the street. At

this point I'm not sure where she's taking me so I trail along behind.

You know, at home, in Malibu, I am king of the castle. My queen does not act like this, not there. I wonder who is influencing this behavior? One of her friends? Evan, the caterer, the hired help who suddenly seems to have undue sway on my wife's opinions and even the restaurant she frequents for lunch in Paris? She couldn't possibly be considering leaving me, at least that's what I've told myself since the estate challenge rumor. My heart beats rapidly with all the possibilities here. She and I are committed to creating a family, the type she longed for as a kid. And I need my second-chance boys, because I don't know if my first sons will keep my last name. I need a Strom heir. I need to get to the truth here.

I stride to catch up to her. It appears we aren't heading back to the hotel just yet.

"Why are you being so rude to me?" I ask. "Are you trying to tell me something?"

She looks away. She's hiding something. After a moment, she turns and looks at me. "Why are you so jealous when I talk to my friends? Is it because you don't have any?"

"I have plenty of friends," I say. But she's right. I don't have friends per se. I focus on my wife and, time permitting, my paramour, Susan. I imagine her in bed, her long blonde hair fanned out on the pillow, waiting for me to visit her in the bungalow I bought for her in Brentwood. I couldn't believe my luck when she walked in for an audition at my offices. She was stunning, just my type. And she wasn't bad at delivering her lines. I really could have seen her getting the part, but the movie didn't get the rest of the funding it needed, so it's a dead project. I'll help her find something else, perhaps. I'm excited to see her as soon as I get back to LA. But that's not important now.

"You have a lot of acquaintances, true, but that's because you're working them to get into the movie business. Who is your best friend?" she asks. I look up and notice we've reached the splendid entrance to what looks like another palace. The building is a marvel. But I need to focus on my wife.

"You are, darling. Who needs friends when we have each other?" I wonder why Cecilia is asking me all these questions. She hasn't shown any interest in my friends since we met. I go to play golf with guys, and she does whatever it is she does with her Malibu friends: usually, working out, hiking, paddleboarding, tennis. She has a very easy, active life, courtesy of yours truly.

"Aww, how sweet," she says. "Oh, and welcome to Napoleon's Tomb, inside that beautiful gold dome. Impressive, right? Little man, big tomb."

"Thank you for escorting me here," I say. "I'm a fan of Napoleon."

"I thought you would be," she says.

Maybe this will take her mind off asking me so many questions. So far today she's prodded me about my first wife, brought up my sons, wondered about my advertising agency days, and now she's asking about my friends, or lack thereof. Troubling. She is not normally so inquisitive. As we make our way inside the dome where Napoleon is buried, I see the huge coffin fit for a Roman emperor, surrounded by large statues representing his victories. It occurs to me that the entire situation is a little overdone, but then Napoleon was a legend; you can't take that away from him. I'd like to think I could be remembered in this way, well, you know, in an American Hollywood royalty sort of way? A star on the Walk of Fame, perhaps?

As we're stepping outside and back into the grounds surrounding the Hôtel des Invalides, I notice Cecilia on her phone again. Hopefully just for directions back to the hotel, but likely more. I've figured out, even without a sense of direction, that we should head to the river.

"We should head toward the river, correct?" I say to my distracted companion.

"Yes, good," she says. "Oh, I have some news. I've been offered a job. Isn't that fabulous?"

I felt like the air had been knocked out of me. "No, my wife will not be working. Darling, you just keep enjoying the life of luxurious leisure I've provided," I say. "And you have your paintings and me. Who needs anything more?" She doesn't. I forbid it. How could she spring this on me, here, now, on the last day of vacation?

"Ha ha, that's funny," she says but there's a flash of steel in her eyes. "I need more. Evan wants me to join as a partner in his events company. He wants me to illustrate his invitations and printed materials, and redesign his website and e-newsletter. It's right up my alley. I've already said yes. I know you don't know him that well, but he's super talented and blowing up on social media. His events are so social media perfect and, well, I'm just so excited about this. I'll be his new creative director."

Evan has gone from a person I mostly ignore, somebody who whisks food and decor in and out of our home during parties, to a tour guide who suggests restaurants in Paris—and now to my wife's potential employer? No way. I'm the one who hired him when we first arrived in Malibu. I'll be the one to fire him now.

We are crossing the bridge, leaving the Left Bank, but I am not focused on the beauty of Paris, not anymore. All I'm thinking about are my narrowing options and my simmering rage.

Cecilia

I don't know what I've done to upset her, but Melissa Reedy, my first friend in Malibu and my next-door neighbor, isn't returning my calls. She hasn't come over for wine or tried to help me learn to play tennis. I see glimpses of her, and we've driven past each other in town. I think she's avoiding me. She simply disappeared from my life.

"Cecilia, where are you?" Paul is bellowing for me from the first floor. That's the only problem with a 10,000-square-foot home, it's hard to find your spouse sometimes. I hurry to the top of the steps.

"Hi, what's up?" I ask. It's Saturday, and Paul is dressed for golf.

"This dry cleaning just got delivered, and my things cannot remain on these hangers until Monday when the staff get here. Unacceptable," he says. He holds up a cluster of shirts on wire hangers, covered in thin plastic.

"What exactly are you asking?" I sigh. Lately, there have been more of these over-the-top demands.

It's weird.

"I need you to take these to my closet and put them on proper hangers. That's all," he says.

"Sure," I say. "Just leave them there. I'll get around to it."

"Thanks, and I'll see you after golf. Oh, and have you been tracking your cycle with that app I showed you?" he asks.

"Yes," I say. But that's a lie. It creeps me out giving an app that kind of information. What if the government gets hold of it and tries to take control of your reproductive rights?

"Good. I have been, too. Tonight's a very fertile night," he says.

I hate it when he talks like this. Like I'm some sort of baby machine he just needs to impregnate on the right evening. It's taking all the fun out of sex.

"Don't talk like that," I say and fold my arms across my chest. "It's not romantic or fun."

Paul tilts his head. "Neither is not getting you pregnant already."

"We haven't been married long," I say. "There really isn't a rush. We're just settling in, hosting parties. That takes a lot of work. I wouldn't want to do that pregnant."

Paul smiles. "You are a natural. Better than me with the party guests. Of course, they're all a means to an end. Remember that. They aren't our friends, they're our targets. We're climbing the social ladder together, darling. And networking leads to big opportunities in Hollywood. We're catching fire, well, I am as a producer, but you're the wind beneath my wings. For some couples this would all be too much of a challenge. But not us!"

I smile at our catchphrase and realize he might be right. I am good at this, but unlike Paul, I also genuinely like getting to know people. And I'd like to make some new friends, although none of these people seem like they want to get to know me properly. But, still, I work the crowd. I know how long to chat with each guest, and just what to compliment him or her on. I study the guest lists ahead of time, make notes, like it's my job. And, I suppose, it is. I like to people watch, and I'm quickly learning about how the rich and powerful can be easily flattered and imitated.

"Maybe I should be a producer with you?" I say. "We could be a great team."

"No, Hollywood is a man's world. Always has been. You just leave the business world to me. Anyway, I've really got to run. Can you come get these shirts? Just so I don't have to worry about it."

"Have fun playing golf," I say. And instead of trotting down the stairs as he's expecting, I turn and walk toward our bedroom.

I call Evan, my only other real friend in Malibu. We talk every day, sometimes more than once a day. This week, we've been planning a beach party for sixty people on the private beach below our home. But even without an event to plan, we talk daily.

"Hey, don't worry. I figured out how to light the pathway down to the beach so nobody will trip and sue us. Or you," Evan says almost as soon as I get through to him.

"Great," I say without enthusiasm.

"What's wrong?" he asks.

"It's Paul. I'm not sure what it is, but he's changing," I say. "He used to be so loving, so attentive, and now it's more like I'm his least favorite member of the staff."

"No," Evan reassures me. "He adores you. I see him watching you."

Watching who I'm talking to. That's the other thing I've noticed lately. If I speak with a man, a handsome actor or producer or even one of the gardeners, he'll make a point of giving me the look. The look that says enough with that person.

"He is always watching me," I say to Evan. "It's fine. I'm just lonely. Melissa still isn't returning my calls or texts."

"That's strange. Well, how about I come over and we do a walk-through? We can take some wine down to the beach with us. Sound good?"

"Sure, yes. And Evan, don't tell anybody what I said. I sound like a spoiled brat. I know I have a privileged life here," I say.

Privileged doesn't mean perfect, I'm discovering.

TWENTY-THREE
PARIS, 5:00 P.M.

Paul

We reach the other side of the river in silence.

"We need to talk about this so-called job offer from Evan," I say to break our standoff. I am the oldest and wisest here. "You have no need to work. I have taken care of everything for you."

"I'm bored. I know I don't need to work, but I want to work, " Cecilia says and she's off again, power walking, I assume toward our hotel. I rush to catch up.

I realize this moment in time calls for compassion, an attempt to listen to her logic, or at least to appear to be doing so, and to feel some sort of emotion about this other than rage. I must channel my energy into seeming reasonable. I am not good at these sorts of emotions. I do not like to talk about feelings. I like an emotional distance from everyone, but, as I'm finding, perhaps especially from my wife...

"How could you be bored?" I ask, resuming the conversation. "Your days and nights are full. You're working out daily at the gym, and painting again, which is nice. You've even sold a couple right off the wall of our living room during a party. We lead a life others would kill for, darling." I'm smiling, tilting my head with sympathetic understanding, like when you're addressing a toddler who just scribbled on your library wall with a black Sharpie. They're embarrassed, they don't understand what they did wrong. So you treat them with compassion, not anger. That's what I've learned to try to do. It's not easy, though, feigning care.

Cecilia's face gathers into a storm. She pushes her sunglasses on top of her head, blue eyes narrowed, chin pointed up at me in anger. "My days are filled with working out and my nights are spent entertaining mostly boring old people. Painting is the only thing keeping me sane but it's not enough. I can't do it any longer," she says. "I am starting my new job when we return from Paris. I need to use my creativity. Evan has a huge event coming up and I'm designing all of the invitations, creating the look for the whole thing. You should be happy for me."

"What about me? You and I spend every evening together, and most weekends. Isn't that enough?" I ask my tempestuous one. "What about our baby? I mean, it has to happen soon or we'll go to a fertility doctor."

"No, we won't," she says. "Those doctors are creepy. I had a friend go to one guy once and he touched her inappropriately. So gross. I don't trust them, I trust mother nature."

"You won't think like this once you have a baby on the way. Once you're pregnant, life will be full. And anyway, I've scheduled an appointment for us—upon our return from Paris, in fact. With a specialist, a woman, so you don't have to worry about anything untoward happening."

"I don't think I'll go, even to a woman doctor. What will be, will be," Cecilia says. "Anyway, aren't you going to congratulate me on my new position? Creative director has quite a grand ring to it."

"I can't congratulate you on this new 'job' because I forbid it." My hands are clenched in fists by my sides. My stomach twists with its usual pain but I barely feel it. In front of me, Cecilia begins to shake all over.

And then she starts to laugh, at me, on the street in Paris in front of countless strangers. And she doesn't stop. It isn't a happy laugh.

"You want me barefoot, pregnant and at home, is that it?" she asks between bursts of sinister chuckles. "You do know I can be a mom and have a job? It's like, what people do. Women can handle boardrooms and babies. It is the twenty-first century."

"Don't put it that way. I love our time together. I value it. We're living a dream few but the point-one percent could ever hope to achieve. Don't try to ruin that, darling." I need to get her off this street before we attract more attention.

"You're really something, you know that?" she says.

I will choose to believe that it is a compliment. "Thank you."

"I need to make a call," she says, suddenly sobering up. "You can find your way back, can't you? Thomas Jefferson Square is just up there, and then take a right on Kléber." And with those sparse directions, she heads off in the opposite direction.

"We have dinner at nine thirty sharp," I call after her. She doesn't turn around. Susan would turn around. Well, actually, Susan would never leave my side in the first place. I miss Susan.

This is interesting. I watch Cecilia hurry away on the side-walk, darting through the crowd, until she disappears. I know I need to calm her down, defuse this tension between us, and I will. My wife shouldn't be running away from me in Paris, she should be running toward me with a loving smile on her face. I am good at this, I remind myself. I'm typically calm and in control, hiding the fire deep inside. But the last month has been tough, what with the rumored challenge of the estate, and with Cecilia's recent attitude. I feel as if the power is shifting between us. It is apparent, now, that my wife is not pleased with me. But I'm not worried. I know that most of the time Cecilia is empathetic and sweet. That's why she was perfect for me. She'll come back around. And of course, I also have a plan.

I briefly consider making a call, too. It would be nice to speak with someone kind and loving, someone still enamored with me. Susan would answer my call right away, any hour of the day or night. But I resist the urge.

It appears there will be more than enough time for that later given these recent developments.

TWENTY-FOUR

WEST PALM BEACH, FLORIDA, SEVENTEEN
MONTHS AGO

Cecilia

I'm sitting on Paul's balcony, watching the sun rise. I'm not usually an early riser but I've found lately that I have too much energy. I think it's Paul's fault. I'm too in love to sleep. I never saw this coming.

It's true what I told Paul when we were first falling for each other. I had always dreamed of an older, more sophisticated man who could provide for me and teach me the meaning of true love. Someone who could show me the world, but also show me all the places I have never been, all the experiences I'd missed by not being able to afford to go to college, by not having a family who cared about me.

After the Sinclairs adopted me to replace their dead daughter because they were told my mom couldn't conceive again, I had a glorious year—well, until Mom got pregnant. At the Sinclairs', birthdays were celebrated, Thanksgiving and Christmas were over-the-top with presents and love. Every celebration was for me, about me, until the baby arrived. After the Sinclairs sent me back to the foster home when their precious replacement baby girl was six months old, I'd never had another birthday party again. I was *return to sender*, and I felt so alone— have done ever since, despite my second adoption. The Babcocks, my second family, were only in it for the money. We didn't even acknowledge Christmas in that house; every day was the same. I've never heard from them since I aged out, but the feeling is mutual.

All I ever wanted was a home filled with people who loved me. I never had that.

Until now, with Paul. I feel as if I'm his sun, the center of his universe. We spend virtually every minute together and he's asked me to move in with him. I agreed, even though I've only known him for three weeks. It just feels right.

"Hey, gorgeous." Paul joins me on the balcony and hands me a steaming hot cup of coffee. "Just a drop of almond milk."

"Perfect." I take a sip as he sits down beside me.

"Why are you up so early?" he asks.

"I think I'm too happy to sleep." I grin. "Are you happy?"

"Happier than I've ever been in my life," he says. "So, I have a question for you. I'm looking toward the future."

"Me too," I say, and my heart thumps in my chest. "With you, I hope."

"I hope so, too. You should know that I'd like the next stage of life to involve marriage and children. I need to know if that sounds like what you want as well. I'd love at least two boys."

I smile. In a perfect world, I'd want that, too. We'll see.

"Sure, and a girl, too, why not?" I say. I turn to look at the sunrise. "Kids are expensive, I hear."

"Don't you worry about that, my dear, I'm loaded," Paul says with a grin. "Most people have to worry about expenses, but not us."

"Not us! Esther sure was good to you," I say. "Must be nice."

"It wasn't without sacrifice, gorgeous. All that time I could have been with someone like you."

"But then you'd still be poor." I laugh.

"Well, not poor, but not like this. So, back to my questions. Family. Check. Travel?"

"Oh, yes, I'd love to travel. I've always wanted to go to Paris, and London, and Rome, and well, everywhere," I say. "I've never left Florida."

"So yes, check," he says.

"Do you have some kind of checklist you run through when you're starting to date someone?" I ask him. I see his face flush. He does. "That's funny."

"It's prudent. I know what I want."

I put my coffee down, stand and grab his hands, pulling him after me back to the bedroom. "I know what I want, too."

Paul

For some reason, as I wander alone on the streets of Paris, hopefully heading in the right direction, my thoughts drift to Esther. I miss her wit, her over-the-top style. I miss the way she would touch my arm and say, "You're too good to me, Paul. It's hard to believe you're real."

I'd reach out, touch her wrinkled hand, carefully avoiding the large, bejeweled rings that would leave bruises on her thin skin if squeezed too tightly, and say, "You're the one who is too good to be true."

Every evening, if we didn't have a charity event, we'd be seated on her outdoor terrace, the sunset turning the ocean a pleasing bright orange, waiting for our drinks to be served on a silver platter by one of her many staff members. Some evenings, we'd dine al fresco, enjoying all that her oceanfront, one-acre chunk of paradise could provide. Other nights, we'd take a swim in the pool under the glow of a full moon. I must admit, it wasn't half bad. If she had been fifty years younger, we would have had so much fun.

Where am I?

I take off my sunglasses and begin to slow my stride. I realize I've reached the avenue called Kléber and turn right, as instructed. Did Cecilia tell me that to confuse me? I stop, causing a French man behind me to yell something at me as he passes by. *Too bad, I don't understand a word you're yelling, nor do I care.* I smile. He flips me off.

Oh no! In front of me I spot the Arc de Triomphe. I have gone too far. I turn around and head back down the street, finally recognizing the hotel's grand exterior. And just in time, as another wave of nausea washes over me. The doormen invite me through and I'm inside, finally back where I belong.

I note the lack of a line in front of the concierge desk and make my way over.

"Sir, may I help you?" the friendly woman asks. She's wearing reader glasses around her neck on glittering threads; her nails are painted bright red. She is the personification of efficiency, and she gives me a warm smile. I like friendly women, French or American. I detest unfriendly ones.

"Yes, thank you. I need transport to the airport tomorrow. For this flight," I hand her my phone with the airplane details.

"*Oui*, yes, of course. A van or a sedan?" she asks.

"The smallest vehicle you have will suffice," I say.

"How has your stay been with us, sir?"

"Oh, great, just wonderful. Everything I imagined and so much more," I say. I'm thinking again, stewing. I need to go to my room. "Thank you for your assistance."

"Of course. Your car will be here at 11 a.m. tomorrow," she says. "Enjoy your last night in Paris."

I smile, assuring her that I will. Despite the current issues with Cecilia. I ride the elevator up to our suite. The room has been cleaned and everything is as it should be. I welcome the chance to have the room to myself and decide I should shower and change for dinner. I assume my wife will be back soon. As I finish dressing—I've put on a dark navy suit and white button-down for the occasion—the door opens. It's Cecilia. Relief washes over me.

"Darling, let's not fight anymore," I say, pulling her into my arms. "It's our last night in Paris. And, as for the job, can I just get used to the idea for a bit? It was all so sudden, such a surprise. And, more importantly, with your many talents, there are a host of jobs you should consider if you're serious about having a career. I mean, like I said, soon you will be having our baby and your days of boredom will be over." There. All fixed. I'm apologizing without apologizing because I hate apologizing.

Cecilia smiles and gives me a quick kiss on the cheek. "You're right. I did surprise you. I know you hate surprises."

That's very true. And now it's time to change the subject.

"It's almost time for dinner. Why don't you go hop in the shower? I'm sure you have something special you plan to wear this evening," I say.

"I do. You know that dress you love, the strawberry red one with the low back? That's what I was thinking about."

I feel myself coming alive, desire coursing through my veins. I do love that dress. That dress has instigated many of our lovemaking sessions. Perhaps it will be our lucky charm again tonight.

"Perfect, darling," I say as she slips into the dressing area and pulls the door closed. I take the time to examine my reflection in the full-length mirror hanging on the wall. I see that my stomach, once pudgy with the midlife, middle-of-the-country lifestyle, is flat. I do look the part of a successful, handsome movie producer. I just need to find the right project. It was tough, at first, getting the word out. But once I'd met the right people, started throwing a little money into independent films and the like, I gained some traction. I even have my own IMDb listing. I'm credible, and somewhat connected. I'm becoming somebody of note in the insular, hard-to-break-into entertainment industry.

And to find the right project, I must meet a lot of people, including, it seems, young screenwriters and young actors, mostly women so far—and mostly all very attractive. All of them are looking for their big break in La La Land. My money and I can help those I choose. That's how I met my Susan. The proverbial casting couch is alive and well, it seems, even if you're just a producer with a vague idea of what he wants. I knew I wanted her, though, the minute I saw her. I close my eyes, wonder if I have time to give her a call.

It's nine thirty in the morning in LA. I imagine Susan, long blonde hair—yes, I have a type—sitting at her kitchen table, laptop open, latte half finished, writing away. I bought the place for her in Brentwood, and she still says she can't believe it. It's cozy and warm, a bungalow made for two. I plan to surprise her with the gift I bought at the jewelry store here in Paris as soon as I can sneak away.

No, I did not buy Susan the gaudy necklace Cecilia was eyeing. That would be wrong.

I'm about to pull out my phone when I hear the water in the shower turn off. I missed my chance, but it's OK. I will be home tomorrow evening. The thought gives me immense joy, it really does.

It takes a few more minutes before Cecilia slides the doors open and appears, red dress clinging to her slim, beautiful body, the very picture of elegance. And in the delicate space between her two breasts hangs the gaudy, overpriced diamond necklace that I refused to buy her yesterday. I'm certain it's one and the same.

Cecilia proceeds to do a little spin across the room, sending her dress swirling around her, and the huge diamond around her neck also spins like a glittering top until she's by my side.

"What do you think? Am I 'last night in Paris' suitable?" she asks. She wraps her arms around my neck and leans back, making sure I can't help but notice that huge necklace glinting like a dagger between us.

For once, I'm speechless. I'm trying to figure out just what to say to express how angry I am at this latest betrayal of my trust, my rules, my plans.

Dear Diary,

It's hard to face all the rejections you get in this town. I mean, at least I'm not totally alone, but still, I don't have much to show for my time here yet.

Hollywood is filled with beautiful people like me who are trying to make it as stars. I just don't know how to get a break, but I do trust that with hard work it is going to happen. I've just started acting classes with a famous Hollywood casting agent. She promises to tell us if we've got it or not, and what to do to enhance what we've got.

I paid a fortune for the opportunity. A little voice in the back of my head is saying, you spent waaayyy too much and what if she tells you that you DON'T have it. Then what???

Calm down. You have it. You have everything you need except loads of money and fame. That's why you're here. To get what you've been missing all along. To become glamorous, and famous, and rich.

I'm going out tonight. I'm sick of sitting around just waiting. So I'm off to a bar, a social media hotspot. I need to get my numbers up, I know that. I look in the mirror. I look good in my very tiny dress with high heels and very blown-out hair.

I look the part. I just need someone to give me a break.

TWENTY-SIX

PARIS, 6:35 P.M.

Paul

Cecilia smiles at me. I haven't said a word. She tickles me under the chin. "I know you like this dress."

"I do, but I don't like secrets," I say. Whatever has come over Cecilia, whoever has gotten in her head, well, it has gone too far. That necklace is worth $350,000 dollars, three times what I spent on my new watch. I don't even know how she paid for it. I'm still literally speechless.

Cecilia spins across the room and back into the closet. She reappears with her shoes, strappy silver sandals, dangling from her left hand.

"I hope you don't mind," she says. "I just had to have it."

"I do mind. I mind a lot," I say as we lock eyes.

She sits down on the chair by the window and begins putting on her sandals. "I invited a friend to join us for cocktails, before we head over to the restaurant," she says. "Just one drink."

She isn't looking at me; her sandals clearly demand her full attention. But I do, too.

"Who is this friend? Now, suddenly, you have a friend in Paris?" I hear myself. My voice is too loud but I'm too angry to control it.

"Calm down. Christopher is a friend from Malibu. He saw my social media posts and realized we were here at the same time," she says. "One drink. You will really like him. He's like a younger version of you. He's up on the rooftop terrace right now, waiting."

I am once again speechless. She has invited her friend, Christopher, to have drinks with us on our last night in Paris. I look at my bride and don't like what I see. Again.

She stands up, sandals fully buckled. "Stop giving me the silent treatment, Paul. Your gift is talking. I know it's killing you to stay quiet. Come on, say something."

I wish, right now, my initial internet search into Cecilia's past had led to more ammunition, more information, more to throw her off-balance like she has me. But alas, it has not. There is only one topic I'm certain of. She is Esther's daughter. But that conversation will not result in any movement. She'll deny it.

I should have known better than to marry a nobody. It's far better to marry up, I've decided. What do I really know about Cecilia? She tells me she has no siblings, and that she's estranged from her adoptive parents. She was in South Florida working as a gallery assistant and freelanced as an invitation designer for Esther, although I never met her until Esther's funeral service. Now that she is showing me her true self, not mirroring what I wanted to see in her, who is she? And when did she meet this Christopher guy? Where in Malibu? I've never even heard of this so-called friend.

She's a liar and a gold digger. And she will not take half of Esther's estate. Nor will she take all of it from me.

Cecilia sniffs her wrist. "Oh, shoot, forgot perfume." She sashays past me, back into the changing area, and re-emerges smelling like someone else. This is not her scent. She smells like a tropical rainforest. I don't like it.

"What's with the new perfume?" I ask.

"When in Paris, you must buy perfume. All the guidebooks say that," she says. "You like it?"

"No, and that's not what they say." I stare at Cecilia, and she winks at me.

"Lighten up, Paul. You're going to give yourself a heart attack. Isn't that how your dad died?"

No, not exactly, Cecilia. And you really don't want to know the truth, not right now. "My parents died of carbon monoxide poisoning. It was a tragedy."

"Right. Sorry. OK, ready to go up and meet Christopher?" She holds the door open for me. I notice she has a new purse hanging from her shoulder, a silver sparkling number. When did she have time to do all this shopping? We were only apart for forty-five minutes this afternoon.

"New purse?" I ask.

"Yes, don't you love love love it?" she chirps with glee like a bird.

"When did you have time to do all this shopping? I mean, we were at the jewelry store yesterday when I bought my watch, but you didn't get the necklace then."

"You wouldn't buy it for me, so I dropped a pin to help me find the store again and circled back," she says with a smile. "I really do love it. I'll always remember Paris because of it. The purse and perfume were at the same charming boutique, next to the jeweler."

"How convenient," I mutter as we walk to the elevator. "But how did you pay for it all?"

"We're rich, silly, I just put it on my card. I mean, I deserve to treat myself on our wedding anniversary. It's something special to remember our trip," she says. The doors slide open. No one else is inside. I push the button marked terrace.

"I didn't get a notification," I say. "American Express always notifies me when you make an expenditure."

"That's creepy." She shudders. The elevator doors slide open once more, and we step out onto a beautiful garden terrace. The Eiffel Tower beckons darkly in the distance, and elaborate plants and trellises wrap around the railings of the place like elaborate nooses. I wonder if you sat up here too long, would the vines make you into some sort of living topiary, too? I imagine Cecilia, vine-encrusted, held in place. I like it.

Paul

Cecilia is the opposite of tied down. She springs from the elevator like she's launched from a cannon and squeals with delight. *Mon dieu.*

"Christopher! Oh my gosh, it's really you, in Paris!" She beelines to the café table where a man wearing a dark suit, like mine, and a big smile, not like mine, stands and gives a wave. Next to him sits a young woman with short dark hair, large sunglasses, and full pouty lips. At least he has a date.

"It's me," he says to Cecilia as the two of them hug and do the ridiculous kiss on each cheek trick. Oh good, he gives her a third kiss, for good luck, I suppose. *Well, good luck yourself, jerk. She's mine.*

I remind myself not to be jealous. I am rich, successful, handsome. She loves me, not him. But if that is the case, why on earth are we meeting this man, here at our hotel, on the last night of our Parisian adventures? The entire point of my little trip to Paris was to isolate my new bride, although I have already done a fairly good job of that, plopping her in Malibu at a mansion by the sea and only allowing her to circulate at parties hosted at our home. She does not join me for the Hollywood events, of course. But still, some people have managed to get close to her, like this guy, apparently. It's frustrating. She was meant to be all mine on this trip. It was supposed to be a chance for me to evaluate where we stand, what is true and what is not.

"Paul, meet Christopher. I met him when I joined the gym, like six months ago," she says. "It feels like we've been friends forever. Why are you here again?"

"Just a one-night stopover on the way to see family in the south of France," Christopher says. "And this is Sabrina, by the way, an old friend from Paris."

"*Enchanté*," Sabrina says, although she looks completely bored with the situation at hand. Why are we even sitting with these people?

Christopher and I settle into seats across the table from each other with a nod. There will be no cheek kissing. What does this guy know about me, about my wife, our life?

I remember a similar circumstance I found myself in with Mia's father. He did not take to me from the beginning, even though by the time his daughter had told him of our love, it was too late for him to do anything about it. So, while he thought we were playing a bit of cat and mouse when Mia told him we were dating, by the time we were engaged Donald Pilmer Jr. realized he was the mouse indeed. He was not accustomed to that position.

One day, he called me at my office at the ad agency, one of the few times he had initiated any communication with me. Mia's parents infrequently visited us in Ohio, preferring to summon us to their palatial New York apartment, or their home in the Hamptons.

I'd welcomed his call with a friendly hello and made a suggestion to build a bond between us. "I'm not sure why you don't like me, but I wish you and I could build a relationship. It could benefit both of us, you see. I help you keep your relationship with Mia and your grandchildren, and you get a son you never had. Let's take a trip together, to Scotland or somewhere. How about it? You might just change your mind about me."

I can still imagine his smug, entitled frown, his distinguished gray hair adding gravity to his words as he paced his library. "We will not be friends, young man, and you are certainly not my son. You are my daughter's husband. That's it. Nothing more."

I'd smiled at his dismissal. I knew I had him where I wanted him. I lowered my voice to match his tone and said, "Well, your loss. But like you, I'm king of my castle and if you ever want to see your grandkids, you better make sure the king is happy. Talk soon."

After that call, I made sure their invitations to visit were few and far between, absence making the heart grow fonder as they say. Mia's mom, Phyllis, learned to love me—she had to, to see her grandkids—and seemed to get over our hasty marriage. Donald never did. But it didn't matter because the stock dividends rolled in every quarter, and every Christmas, they sent all of us, the boys included, a huge check, wrapped inside a thick linen envelope. Had I known about those gifts sooner, I would have agreed to more children with Mia. Oh well. One day soon Donald Pilmer Jr. will get what's coming to him. He's a corrupt investment banker from New York. You know the type. His days are numbered, his luck will run out. The thought makes me smile.

Until I look across the table. Times have changed. And now I'm the one with the cash, not my wife. This is the opposite of my first wife Mia. Being the one holding the cash makes things easier. Mia was a spoiled rich girl who thought she was the one in control. Cecilia is not.

But Cecilia is playing games with me, I'm afraid.

I'm not good with games, not unless I'm the cat.

"Cecilia has told me so much about you, Paul," Christopher says as a waiter places a bottle of champagne in a silver bucket next to our table.

"That's funny. She's told me nothing about you," I say. Our eyes have locked on each other's. He has weird green specks in his brown eyes. Mine are blue. Superior.

"We met a little while back, at the gym, when you guys first moved to the West Coast," he says.

"That's hardly a lifelong friendship, my dear," I say to Cecilia rather than to Christopher.

"Christopher is my oldest friend since I became Mrs. Paul Strom," she says to me. To the waiter pouring her champagne she says, "*Merci!*"

"Cecilia was working out at Malibu Fitness on the treadmill next to me and we started talking," Christopher says. He raises his glass. "Cheers."

"I wonder why I've never met you, then, since you two are so close? She's never even mentioned your existence," I say. "Cheers." I'm rewarded by Cecilia's flushed cheeks. Christopher averts his eyes while Sabrina stares at me. I stare back.

After we've all clinked glasses and taken our first sips, I decide my course of action. We, of course, have an elaborate home gym with all the workout equipment and machines money can buy. But Cecilia insists on going to this other gym. Now I know why. I can remain angry and jealous, or I can try to figure out why they are such great friends, what his angle is, and more importantly, what Cecilia's motive is in asking him here tonight. I take a deep breath and try the friendlier route.

"What do you do, Christopher?" I ask.

Sabrina smiles for the first time all evening. "Whatever he'd like whenever he'd like to do it."

He laughs. "True. I'm one of those lucky bastards born with a silver spoon, as they say."

When he laughs he looks like a horse. Big teeth, mouth too wide. Ears pointy. I'm not threatened anymore. He isn't charming. He's a horseface. He doesn't work, just works out, and flirts with other people's wives. "Are you married?"

"Not currently," he says. "Thought about it a couple times but just was never quite right. I have time, though. I'm young."

I know what he's saying without saying it, as do you. He's young. I'm old.

"I doubt Christopher will ever settle down," Sabrina says and winks at him. "He's my favorite playboy."

Cecilia places a hand on my thigh. But instead of exciting me as it usually does, it's bothersome, like a large mosquito about to bite me. I push her hand back onto her own lap.

"Anyway, Paul, Christopher and I struck up a convo because he was new to Malibu, too," she says. "And since then, we've been working out together almost every day. It's the best." She flips her hair over her shoulder and, once again, reveals the dagger necklace.

"It was so funny, really, like it was meant to be, because we both hate working out, truth be told," Christopher says.

"And who does? But really, it's a must if you want to look the way Cecilia looks, for the long haul, as they say." He is younger than me, but I know I look just fine. I carry on. "So are you in the industry, Christopher? I've met a lot of Hollywood movers and shakers, but haven't come across your name," I say. I am proud of how many industry connections I've made in just one short year. Of course, Cecilia has helped immensely, hosting parties and working the crowd so well. We are the epitome of a power couple.

"Oh, I'm not a Hollywood guy," Christopher says. "I'm more of a world citizen, a traveler. A collector of people. I'm proud to have friends everywhere, far and wide, near and far."

Sabrina laughs. "He's what you'd call a playboy, actually."

Cecilia shakes her head almost imperceptibly. "He's not. He's my workout buddy, right, Christopher?"

"Sabrina, stop it. I have many women as friends. Cecilia is one of them," Christopher says playfully.

Beside me Cecilia takes in a big breath. Sabrina tilts her head.

"How interesting, the friends part," Sabrina says, leaning forward for the first time all night. She smiles at me, and then at Cecilia.

I want to smack her. She's implying there's more between Christopher and my wife. There better not be. That would be very stupid of Cecilia.

Inside the fire is burning bright.

TWENTY-EIGHT

MALIBU, CALIFORNIA, SIX MONTHS AGO

Cecilia

I'm putting the finishing touches to my home artist studio when Paul appears in the doorway, hands on hips. He must have quit golf early or skipped the nineteenth hole. Unlike him. But that's fine, I'm almost finished here.

"What's going on?" he asks.

I remember when he used to come home from golf or LA and hurry into my arms, or hold his out to me, so excited to be reunited. Now he stands in the doorway with a frown on his face. I don't want to hug him when he's like this. Sourpuss.

"The staff and I spent all day turning this bedroom into my artist's studio," I say. "Isn't it lovely? I can paint by the window, this table is great for sketching, and all my paints look so beautiful on display, don't you agree?"

"This is the nursery, Cece, not an artist's studio," he says.

"Don't call me that." My body tenses now, mirroring his.

"Where is the crib? The rocking chair? The changing table?" he asks.

"In the other bedroom. I mean, there are two other rooms that can become nurseries. This one has the best light for painting," I say. "See, I've already started a new canvas." I point to the abstract seascape that is taking shape. I love it, with all its various shades of blue and green, the swirls, the calm chaos. Somebody at our next party will love it, too, and soon my art will be hanging in homes throughout LA.

Paul shakes his head. "This will be the nursery."

I glance at my watch. It's almost five thirty. "Look, I have to run. I'll be back in an hour or so. I'm taking a Pilates class at the gym."

"You didn't make me breakfast this morning," he says, still standing in the doorway, blocking my exit. I wish I hadn't gotten into the habit of making breakfast for him. That was early on, when we first arrived in Malibu. When I was completely head over heels in love. But now, things have changed.

The tension between us is intense, and this has been happening more frequently. I don't understand why everything I do is wrong these days, nothing I do is good enough. I can't please him.

"You know, I just forgot. I was excited about setting up the studio," I say. "Excuse me."

Paul steps aside but I feel his eyes on my back as I head down the hall. "We have a state-of-the-art home gym that you should be using. It has everything you could possibly need."

Except other people, I think to myself but I don't say. I'm beginning to realize that if Paul had his way, I'd never leave this house for any reason.

"It's a lovely gym, and you're right, it does have a lot of equipment, but I'm learning Pilates so I need an instructor," I say. "I don't know how to work a reformer on my own. I'll be back in an hour or so."

I hurry down the stairs, through the house and to the garage without looking back. I hop in my white BMW, and as soon as I pull through the gate at the end of the driveway, my shoulders drop in relief.

I pull into the parking lot of Malibu Fitness just in time for class and I'm walking up the steps to the second floor when I spot Christopher.

"Hey you," I say. "Are you doing Pilates with me?"

"Wouldn't miss it. Say, I just realized the oddest coincidence." Christopher pulls me to the side of the walkway, a concerned look on his face. "I know your husband's brother, Tommy. From Santa Barbara. We went to college together."

"I didn't know Paul had a brother," I say, stunned. He told me he was an only child. Why would he lie about that?

"Apparently they haven't talked for years. But Tommy is afraid of him, Cecilia. He wanted me to tell you to be careful," Christopher says. "And this is confidential, OK? Tommy doesn't want Paul to know where he lives, or anything about his family. But he did want me to warn you since I'd made the connection between you guys and him. And I told him I would see you here."

"Warn me about what?" I ask, a chill running down my spine.

Christopher shrugs. "It's not really my place to get involved, and I hate gossip, but Tommy says you're married to a monster."

I look at Christopher and can't help but smile. "Ridiculous. Paul's a loving husband, and has never been anything but kind to me." I'm trying to convince myself as much as I'm trying to convince Christopher. "They likely had some sort of falling-out, and now he's spreading bad rumors. Tell him thanks, but I don't believe him. But I'd love to have him and his family down for dinner sometime."

Christopher pushes his hand through his thick dark hair, shakes his head. "OK, well, that's not going to happen. He's afraid of Paul. But if you're happy, that's cool. Remember, don't tell Paul where Tommy is, or that I know him."

"Sure, of course, your secret is safe with me," I say. I am good at keeping secrets, it's one of my strengths. I swallow and take a deep breath, unnerved by Christopher's warning, despite the fact I acted otherwise.

Paul

Cecilia looks at me with a smile. It's all I can do not to wipe it off her face.

"Well, this has been lovely. I'm so glad you could meet us for a drink," she says. "I guess we should get going, right, darling? Paul's been a little off all this week. His stomach doesn't tolerate French food, unfortunately. Leaves him a bit grumpy, but I keep trying to cheer him up. So, let's head out. We have a very special evening planned."

Not so fast. "So, Christopher, you do know Cecilia is my wife, not some global plaything?" I don't think I'm smiling. I don't like horseface Christopher. I don't want to ever see him again. And I will forbid my wife from doing so as well.

"Of course, Paul. Cecilia and I are friends, nothing more," Christopher says and shifts in his seat.

Cecilia touches my arm and I bristle. I must be riled up, more than I realize. "Paul, we should go," she whispers.

"Why, darling, it was your idea to spend our last evening in Paris with a man you see, now I realize, almost daily at home.

I'm surprised you haven't come by the house or been invited to one of our parties. You must not be that special. So why exactly are you here now, Christopher?" I reach over and pull Cecilia into me. It's meant to be a loving gesture, but it may have been a little rough.

"Paul, come on. Let's go," she says, placing her hand on my shoulder, pushing away from me, as if my touch is unbearable. When I look over at her I notice her shoulders are up to her ears, her eyes wide and unblinking. Is she frightened of something?

"Yes, darling. One minute. Why are you here, Christopher?" I ask again.

"Don't be rude. He is here to see me before he goes on holiday," Sabrina says.

"My family vacations in the south of France. I'm heading there in the morning to join them. Just wanted to spend one night in Paris on the way, catch up with my friend, Sabrina," Christopher says. "Not that it's any of your business."

I put my arm around Cecilia again and pull her over to me. She puts her hand on my shoulder and pushes away. Fine. I release Cecilia and she almost tumbles out of her chair.

"I forgot something in the room. Can I have the key? I'll meet you in the lobby," she says. "See you back home, Christopher. Nice to meet you, Sabrina." This time there are no cheek kisses, just a brief wave and she's gone.

"I'm going to powder my nose. I'll meet you in the lobby," Sabrina says, kissing Christopher's cheek and nodding a solemn goodbye in my direction. I have the feeling she isn't a fan of mine, but the feeling is mutual.

The waiter appears and drops the bill. I don't make any sort of move to pick it up. Christopher chuckles a bit and pulls out a credit card.

"You're an asshole," Christopher says. He looks so pleased

with himself, so smug. I want to punch him right now. I know I can't. Not in front of all of the people on the terrace.

"You don't know anything about me," I say.

"I know more than you think," Christopher says. He hands his credit card to the waiter, who slips it into the reader, efficiently giving him a receipt. A record of our special time together.

"Do not go to the gym with my wife anymore. Do you understand?"

"Um, I think that's her choice, not yours," he says.

"Well, you're wrong. And Christopher, if you don't stay away, you'll be sorry." I stand up and lean forward over the table.

He's been busying himself with his phone instead of looking at me. He continues his mistake. "You don't scare me. In fact, I guess you should watch yourself. I mean, a young wife, an old guy like you. Well, I wouldn't let your guard down either, if I were you. I guess I understand why you feel so threatened by me." He finally looks at me instead of his phone, finally sees me. His eyes widen. "Or... well, fine. OK, maybe you've got a point."

I take a deep breath and step away from the table. I cannot cause a scene here, for many reasons, but most importantly because I have plans for the rest of the evening and this punk will not ruin them.

"Certainly was interesting meeting you," I say calmly. "And I hope I never see you again."

Christopher's face has gone white. None of the pomposity is left in him. He's popped like a balloon. I guess he didn't really understand what Cecilia was getting him into tonight, did he? Poor horseface.

"You're right, I don't need to work out at the same time as Cecilia. It's good to change things up."

And before I know it, he's scampered away like a terrified little mouse. His departure will give me a little time to explore this rooftop area. Somewhere up here, high above the streets of Paris, perhaps Cecilia and I will enjoy a nightcap. Alone. I walk to the back of the terrace, away from Christopher and the whole situation. I always win.

Dear Diary,

My acting coach is AMAZING!! She thinks I've got it, like as in I'm going to be a star. This is what I needed to keep going.

A famous casting director believes in me. I am signing up for her next series of classes. She says this will make all the difference. Sure, it's expensive, but I'm worth it. I wrote to Mom and Dad and asked them for a little bump in my allowance. It's a loan, really, until I book my first job.

The casting director says I have star power. OMG! Like leading lady vibes. She also says that because Mercury is in retrograde I have time to work on my craft. She says not to go out on any auditions until the planets are in a more favorable line-up.

That's fine with me. I want everything to work together in the best possible way for my dreams to come true. She says the universe wants that for me, too.

I'm going to manifest a huge role in a blockbuster movie. She said I would.

I will do this. I will be famous. I just have to wait for my moment. I'm filled with love for everything and everyone. My parents seem to be worried about my expenses, but I told them not to worry. I'm biohacking my budget, I'm getting grounded, getting energy from source, and I'm going to shine.

Mom said she didn't understand what I was saying.

I need to go to yoga. That's all for now.

THIRTY

Paul

When the elevator doors open and I step into the lobby, I spot Cecilia speaking to the concierge. She's added a colorful scarf to her ensemble, tied around her purse strap, and she appears, to anyone looking her way—and who wouldn't?—to be a happy, beautiful American enjoying her last evening in Paris.

I hurry over and quietly walk up behind her. She doesn't know I'm here.

"I'm so glad, *merci* for the plans," she says to the concierge. "*Bonne nuit!*" As I wonder what plans she's making, she turns and screams, her purse tumbling to the marble floor of the lobby. "Paul! Why did you sneak up on me like that?"

I hold up my hands, shocked by her outburst, as are the other hotel guests. I see the fear in her eyes. I have no idea why she's so jumpy, but I attribute it to our non-happy meet-up with Christopher and the rather tense way it all ended. I need to calm her down. Get our last, best evening back on track. She needs a drink, clearly. I watch as she bends down and picks up her sparkly purse. She's lucky the clasp held or that would have been quite embarrassing, I imagine.

"Cecilia—" I begin, but she holds her hand out to stop me.

"Pardon me, *monsieur*," she says to the concierge, who's looking rather concerned. "My husband surprised me, that's all."

"Oui, madame. Passe une bonne soirée," the concierge says.

I have no idea what he just told my wife, so I simply shrug.

"Thank you again." Cecilia nods at him.

"Shall we go?" I ask, indicating the front doors. We begin walking across the lobby, but she stops halfway across the ornate space.

"Were you spying on me? What were you doing?" she asks.

"Calm down." I take a step toward her, hoping to pull her into my arms. I'd like that to be the last thing people see of us as a couple in this lobby this evening. A loving embrace would do us both so much good. Except, as I step closer to her for that embrace, Susan's lovely face pops into my mind.

Cecilia steps back, avoiding my tender gesture, and folds her arms across her chest. The dagger diamond glistens menacingly at me.

"Obviously I was just coming to find you after saying good evening to your friend Christopher," I say. "Maybe we should go get a cocktail. Relax a bit."

"Yes, a cocktail sounds lovely. Do you have a place in mind?" she asks. She's unfolded her arms and seems almost amenable to a kiss.

"Anywhere without Christopher is fine with me," I say, and then kick myself. I shouldn't have brought him up. He's handled, like Monday morning's recycling. You feel good about it when you put the waste out on your driveway, then the trash truck comes, and it's gone. Someone else's sorting headache.

"I wish you hadn't been so nasty to Christopher." She folds her arms again, eyes flashing in anger.

"I wasn't the one who started it. He implied I was old, not worthy of you," I say. Now I'm the one with fire in my eyes. "Besides, I still don't understand why we had that little meeting."

Cecilia bites her bottom lip, tilts her head. She blinks, breaking eye contact. "I thought it would be fun. I mean, you're gone nearly all day every day doing the Hollywood hustle, no real time to socialize other than at our parties, so I thought you'd like to meet a friend of mine who happened to be in town. Guess I was wrong."

I take a step toward her.

"I thought you and Christopher would like each other, that's all," she says. She must know she's lying. I don't like knowing she's with anyone but me, women or men. I'm strange that way, I suppose. Every time Cecilia tries to bring a new friend into her orbit, I typically find a way to sabotage the relationship, usually before it can take hold. If I had known anything about Christopher, I would have ended that relationship immediately. I have experience. Take, for example, our neighbors Walter and Melissa Reedy. A lovely older couple. A retired producer and casting director turned tennis player. Tanned and tucked and overly friendly.

Melissa Reedy began appearing at our kitchen table, having coffee with Cecilia, teaching her how to play tennis, making plans for beach walks and shopping trips. I'd had to intervene.

When Melissa opened the door to her grand estate, smaller than ours but still grand, I'd apologized for bothering her.

"Not at all, Paul, do come in," she'd said, and I had. "What can I do for you?"

"Thank you so much," I'd said, metaphorical hat in hand. "It's uncomfortable for me to be here, but I felt I had to warn you about Cecilia."

"What do you mean?" Melissa asked, eyes wide, a small vein in her neck throbbing with interest. "Your wife is lovely."

"She seems that way, especially at first. But she's not well," I explained. "She turns on people, I've found. She's already turned on you, but you don't know it. She's spreading rumors about you and your husband, that your husband is having an affair. That he's not attracted to you anymore, and you're the last to know. She tells people it's sad to watch because you're so clueless."

"What? That's ridiculous, and she knows it." Melissa said, face flushed. "I'll talk to her."

"It won't help, and will likely make it worse. She'll just deny it but I've heard it from a few people now. I'm so sorry, Melissa. She's done this to friends before, and I have no idea why. It's the reason she hasn't kept any friends that I know of. It's sad, and I'm sorry to have to tell you about this. I just thought you should know. You should steer clear of her."

"What's causing this? What did I ever do to her besides being her friend?" Melissa asked.

"It's not you. It's her, I'm afraid," I said, pointing to my head. "The problem is when she drinks too much, she gets mean. It's happening more often lately. She can be quite nasty."

"Oh, my word. She drinks too much? I've never seen any indication of that," she said. "She's been perfectly pleasant. Fun to be around. I've loved getting to know her."

"She saves the worst of it for me, I'm afraid. But I love her. I can't leave her. So if you do hear fighting, harsh words, you'll know the cause," I said. "This bruise is from two nights ago. She has quite a punch." I push up my sleeve to display a round bruise on my left forearm. One little bang with the hammer and voila, proof of violence.

"She hit you?" Melissa's face has gone white. "I never imagined. I'm sorry."

"I felt as if I had to warn you, before she turned on you, too. She's spread other rumors about you and your husband as well, I'm afraid—it's not just the cheating rumor."

"He's absolutely not cheating on me." Melissa folds her arms across her chest. "What else is she saying?"

"They're too awful to repeat, but back in Florida, well, she accused her best friend of shoplifting, if you can believe it. Pure fabrication. She accused another friend of having an affair. She likes to use that one, as you now know."

"I'm shocked and, if I'm honest, I don't know what to do," Melissa gasped. "I have really enjoyed getting to know Cecilia. She just seems so great and... well, I just enjoy her company. So much."

"Of course I can't tell you or her who to be friends with, but you seem like such a good person," I said. "I don't want you to have to find out the hard way what she is really like. I'm only telling you what she's been saying because I care about you. I love my wife, but I know how she is. I'm very sorry, but I had to tell you the truth."

Melissa swallowed and nodded. "Well, if you ever need anything, please just reach out. We'll be here. I'm so sorry."

"Thank you so much for your concern. I love her, despite everything, but I don't want others to have to suffer," I said. "It's awful, what happened in West Palm. She took the lies too far, tried to ruin too many marriages. She said too many mean things about her friends behind their backs. She was ostracized eventually. It's why we had to move out here. A fresh start for her, and for me."

"I never would have imagined such a thing," Melissa said. And then she gave me a hug. "You just let me know if you need anything. And I'll cancel that beach walk today. That would be best, right?"

I agreed, and that was it. She was out of our lives. My process works well, typically. I took pleasure in Cecilia's confusion over losing her friend, the fact Melissa would cross to the other side of the street to avoid Cecilia on walks. Cecilia didn't understand what had happened, poor girl, but how could she?

By this point, I had also noticed Cecilia buddying up with some of the help. I haven't yet figured out how to keep her from befriending the staff, but I have done my best to correct that behavior. I didn't know about Christopher. He's handled now. Although I wonder if there are others who I don't know about...

Evan has bothered me on this trip. He's overstepped, over-reached, and I'm over him. There are plenty of professional event planners in LA.

I think about the café owner Phoebe and her son Theo. They were surprise additions to our trip, but innocuous. And we'll never see them again. Did I mention how much I hate surprises?

I'm assuming there will be no more surprises the rest of the evening. I'm in charge now.

Cecilia has applied lipstick and her lips now match the bright red of her dress. She's waiting for me to escalate over Christopher, or let it go.

"You really do look beautiful tonight, darling," I say, pushing thoughts of Susan's full lips out of my mind. I need to focus on Cecilia. "Let's start the evening now. Start it over." I lean in and give her a kiss, knowing I'm ruining the perfectly applied lipstick, knowing it is now on my lips, too.

I release her from our embrace, and she smiles. "The color is good on you."

"The color of blood, am I right?" I lick my lips—it tastes remarkably good—before using my handkerchief to clean my face. This is something I'm accustomed to with Susan, as she's fond of a dark red lipstick, and I must check myself after being with her. Her lipstick does not taste like Cecilia's does.

"It's the color of love, silly," Cecilia says. "How is your stomach feeling, by the way?"

I haven't focused on it for a while, but as soon as she mentions it, a wave of nausea sweeps over me. I check my new watch and see it's after seven thirty. Plenty of time until our dinner reservation. Our special final event.

"I'm fine. Nothing a stiff drink won't fix," I say. I offer her my arm and she slips hers through it. We're back together as a team, thank goodness. At least for now.

Paul

As we step outside the hotel, I notice the tourist throngs may have increased since we were last out just a few hours ago. A group of thirty or so octogenarians are pushing past us, earphones in, oblivious, following a small woman with a large red flag. Where did all these old people come from? Why are they walking down our rather quiet, elegant street at this time of night? Do cruise ships land here somehow? Or perhaps they were just bussed in?

Someone hits my shoulder from behind. I turn, aggravated, and see it's just a clueless old man trying to keep up with the flag lady. He really shouldn't. It's not dignified.

"Excuse you!" I yell at his back.

He stops, turns around. "What did you say to me?"

I can't tell where he's from, but he has an accent, and a mean face.

"You ran into me," I say. "You should apologize when you do that."

"You should not block the sidewalk, you arrogant American," he says.

"That was fun. Picking on old men now, are we?" Cecilia says. She's laughing again. At me.

"He ran into me," I say. "Anyway, let's stroll toward the river and try to avoid these caravans of dementia-ridden, sidewalk-hogging seniors." I glance at the shoulder of my jacket, making sure the rude old guy didn't leave any schmutz on my sleeve. I seem to be as perfect as before the encounter.

"Lead the way, *mon cher*," she says.

I do so love it when she's compliant.

As we weave through the throngs clogging the sidewalk, I think about our time in Shakespeare and Company, the famous bookstore on the banks of the Seine, opposite Notre Dame. It was the third day of our trip, if I'm getting my days correct, and seeing the iconic store sent shivers down my spine. I do love to read, time permitting. My favorites are mystery and suspense, figuring out whodunnit, or who is about to do it. Murder and mayhem are so appealing in the fictional world, am I right?

As we'd stepped inside the famed literary bookstore, I'd noticed all the signs prohibiting photographs, but I couldn't understand why. I mean, it is a bookstore, not a museum, and even museums allow photos these days. We worked our way through the rooms, filled with books, and nooks and crannies. The founder, an American, wanted people to explore the bookstore as you would a book, building each room like a chapter. He called it Shakespeare and Company in honor of a bookseller he admired who founded the original store by the same name all the way back in 1919 in this very spot. That store had been a gathering spot for Hemingway, Joyce, Fitzgerald, Eliot and more. This one was just a knockoff, really. But nice, except for the photo thing.

We were about midway through the book, so to speak, when Cecilia disappeared around a corner. I had been reading about how young writers and artists were invited to sleep inside the store on small beds that doubled as benches during the day. I made a mental note not to sit down on any of the upholstered furniture dotted about inside. Then I realized Cecilia wasn't with me.

I hate losing sight of my wife. My heart began to race, and I hurried around the corner after her. She wasn't there. I pushed through to the next room, detecting an unpleasant, unwashed body odor wafting from a young woman standing in my way in the next doorway.

"Pardon," I said.

She ignored me and continued to read whatever hippie book she'd pulled from the shelf.

"Excuse me," I said.

Same response.

"Move," I said, and lightly pushed her to the side.

"Hey, chill," she said as I finally made my way past her.

"Get some sort of awareness about you. You were blocking everyone," I said. She had a nose ring, I hate those, and I assumed also a body covered in tattoos.

"And you're the type of American who gives us all a bad name," she said, beady brown eyes flashing at me.

While I would have liked to have said more to the young smelly creature, my wife was missing so I moved on. She was the one giving us a bad name here. Her smell, her lack of awareness, her sloppiness. I reminded myself I needed to talk to Cecilia about all of this, how our children would not become like these types of creatures. No, they would be classy, and articulate, and powerful. Very powerful.

I entered another room, thankful to leave the hippie where she was, and saw my wife. She was sitting on a velvet sofa, likely one the Tumbleweeds, as they were called by the store back in the day, no doubt slept and drooled on during an overnight stay.

"There you are. You lost me. And you shouldn't sit on that," I said.

"Oh, don't be silly. It's a small store. I knew you'd find me. Are you enjoying yourself? Did you find anything to buy?" She was holding something by Hemingway. And she looked beautiful in a fitted skirt and white blouse. Classy, elegant, literary. In that moment, she reminded me of a very young version of Esther, probably for obvious reasons. In fact, Esther had a photo on the wall of herself in this very store when she was Cecilia's age. The resemblance was uncanny, once you knew what you were looking at.

I decided to take a photo. "Smile, honey."

She dropped her book and lunged at me. "Paul, no photos! It says so everywhere! Why do you always act like the rules don't apply to you? It's so annoying."

I'd stepped back, aghast. Never had my wife spoken to me with such vehemence. It was hard to disguise my rage at that moment, and I'm certain she saw it before I was able to compose myself. I straightened my collar, turned and walked away.

It was gratifying to have her chase after me, which she did, albeit with a delayed response which found me standing alone on the sidewalk beside Shakespeare and Company, pondering my options, wondering why on our romantic vacation to Paris we were not spending most of our time trying to get pregnant, and instead were fighting inside a bookstore on the Left Bank.

Unacceptable.

"Paul, oh my gosh, I'm so sorry I snapped at you," Cecilia said as she rushed to my side. "It's this headache. It's making me into a monster. I really am sorry." When I didn't answer, she added, "Please, don't stay mad at me. We're on vacation. Maybe tonight I'll feel better. I'll really try to feel better."

I looked down into her angelic face and noticed worry etched in tiny lines at the sides of her mouth.

"Forgive me. It won't happen again," she said.

"Of course, darling. I'm sorry you are feeling unwell," I said. She'd clapped her hands and wrapped her arms around me.

And I kissed her. Because I believed her, believed it was an anomaly, not something that would become the new norm.

I release Cecilia's hand now, because the crowd has thinned and because my anger is back. A woman in front of me lights a cigarette, and the smoke wafts toward me, reminding me of my father, the dictator. He had a fondness for yanking his belt out of his pants loops and slashing my brother Tommy and I with it for the smallest infractions. He was the villain of my childhood, and the only male role model I had. As such, I strive to be the opposite of him in as many ways as possible by tamping down the anger that's inside me, the fire-filled rage he instilled in me from an early age. Most people would consider me an easygoing, friendly person, sometimes the life of the party. I work hard to appear to be that.

But the truth is, I am my father's son at heart, and once my fire has been lit, it is almost impossible to put out. If I could see myself in a mirror right now, I know I would see my father's dark, angry eyes staring back at me.

Dear Diary,

It's tough out here on your own. It is. Sure, I'm going after my dreams and I'm committed to making them come true, even though the odds are against me. Mom and Dad have stopped trying to get me to come back home. They know I'm stubborn, and if and when I ever do go back there, well, it would feel like a failure.

I know they love me dearly. I've always been their favorite daughter. I will take a photo of the sun coming through the slats in the shades, hitting the ficus tree and making such beau-

tiful colors. I love my tiny home, love having a place of my own. They are so proud of all I've accomplished.

Even though it's tough out here, something amazing has happened! I've found my forever guy. He bought me this place, that's how much he's into me. I really think I have found Mr. Right. Only problem is I have to share him. But not for long. He promised, and besides, it's me. Look at me! I always win in the love department.

THIRTY-TWO
PARIS, 7:47 P.M.

Paul

I know I'm being too moody on this special day, our wedding anniversary. Instead of focusing on the past, I should be in the here and now, enjoying the softly shifting colors of the sky, the preparation for the upcoming sunset.

The woman smoking the cigarette wears a tight green dress and high heels. How she navigates these sidewalks packed with tourists is amazing to me. In fact, I'm so mesmerized by her, and so lost in the memories her cigarette ignited inside me, I've neglected my wife.

I stop on the sidewalk, bidding a mental *adieu* to the woman in green.

Where's Cecilia? She shouldn't be hard to spot, with her bright red dress, her glowing blonde hair, the diamond necklace large, too large, around her neck.

As I stand on the sidewalk, I am like a salmon trying to swim upstream. People are pushing past me on both sides. I watch their faces. I am a student of people, of their emotions, because I only feel one. I have learned how to initiate the appropriate reaction for specific circumstances—tears or at the very least a droopy mouth for sadness. Smile and twinkling eyes for joy. Worry is a creased forehead and pursed lips.

I have my worried face on right now. I check my watch, 7:47 p.m., and pull my dress shirt down over it, noticing my monogram. I am proud of it: Paul Randolph Strom. *PRS: almost a person. Just missing a couple of things.* I begin backtracking my steps. I'm rather skilled at tailing someone in a car; I've done it before, often actually. It's sort of like in the movies. You wear a black shirt, make sure it's a dark, moonless night if you can. Most of the time, people don't notice their surroundings. They don't notice when the same car follows them for miles. Same for following someone on foot, or, say, sneaking into someone's home. It's easy if you're quiet, methodical. Take my father, for example. It was the middle of the day. He should have seen me sitting in the corner of their cramped living room, waiting for my mom to come home. She'd disappointed me for the last time. My dad didn't see me. He walked right past me on his way to the bedroom, but he didn't notice me. It wouldn't have changed anything, but he should have seen me coming.

But finding my wife somewhere on the sidewalk behind me is proving to be more of a challenge. Did she try to lose me?

I stop again and pull out my phone. Three missed calls from Cecilia.

I call her back, heart racing. Has something happened to my beloved?

"Paul, thank god," she says, picking up the call. "I've been trying to get your attention. I twisted my ankle, stepped in a crack, fell. I don't know how you didn't see me."

I was busy in my head, is the answer, but not satisfactory. I pull my face into "worry" again.

"Oh dear. Where are you? I am so sorry." I begin hurrying back the way I came.

"A lovely man stopped to help me," she says.

I wish she hadn't added that little nugget of information.

"Where are you?" I ask.

"I've been carried over to the little café on the corner. I'm waving to you now," she says.

I spot her sitting at a café table across the street. As I wait for the light to change, I check my watch. We have plenty of time to make our dinner reservation at nine thirty tonight at the Eiffel Tower. I remind myself to relax. I wanted to have a drink, and a snack, so this is perfect. I do hope my wife doesn't need a doctor. That would put a wrench into our—my—plans.

Finally, the light changes and I hurry to Cecilia's table. Fortunately, for both of us, she's seated alone.

"Darling, I'm so sorry I didn't see you fall." I kiss her cheek and and pull out a chair. "Does it hurt a lot?"

"It's mainly just my pride," she says. "And I scraped my palm, skinned my knee. The lovely waiter here gave me a Band-Aid." She pulls up her dress and shows me.

"Ouch. And your ankle?" I ask. "Can you walk?"

"We'll see," she says. "I ordered us both a martini. I thought we could use it. So cheers, and dig in. The foie gras is lovely. Really, everything I ordered looks great."

I notice for the first time there is a considerable spread on the table. I am famished.

"Have you had any?" I ask. I take a large scoop of pâté and place it on my plate, grab a chunk of bread and spread it on with gusto. I take a bite. It's heaven.

"I am saving myself for our fabulous meal at the Eiffel Tower," she says, sipping her martini. It's almost empty, I note. I take a sip of mine. It's strong, a perfect complement for the goose liver pâté.

"And where is the hero, the one who helped you?" I ask, taking another big bite of heaven.

"Oh, he had a dinner reservation to get to. I told him I'd be fine. And I will be. Just need to take a little break," she says.

"Ah, *monsieur* has finally arrived," a man says, approaching our table. He is using that tone I despise. "So nice of you to help your lady."

I take a sip of my martini. Once again, I am fighting fire.

Paul

I look up to see the man accusing me of being a bad protector, and realize it's Theo, Phoebe's son from the café. What is going on?

"Why are you here?" I ask.

"Man, the real question is, why weren't you?" Theo says. His stringy hair flops over his eyes like cobwebs.

"I didn't know she'd fallen, obviously. If you'll excuse us," I say and use my hand to wave him away. "We have a dinner reservation to get to and we've already seen you more than we should have to in one lifetime."

"Paul, honestly," Cecilia says. "Apologies, Theo. He can be a little... ugly."

Stabbing pains assault my stomach and I bend forward with an *oof*. Did my wife call me ugly? I grab her thigh and squeeze.

"Ouch," she says, pulling her leg away from me. I must have grabbed a bit too hard.

I feel Theo staring at me. He needs to leave. His eyes narrow and he says, "Where are you dining tonight?"

Not that it's any of his business. "Madame Brasserie. In the Eiffel Tower," I say. I hope the pronunciation was suitable. But I don't really care.

"Ah, the tourists' favorite place. Of course." He snorts.

"Glad you approve," I say. He's on my last nerve.

"Thank you for everything, Theo. I'm fine. Tell your mom I am OK, I don't want her to worry about anything, and thank you again for being there," Cecilia says.

Theo stares at me through his cobwebs, then smiles at Cecilia. "Bonne chance avec le connard. Appelle-moi plus tard, cherie."

Finally, he takes the hint. I help myself to another spectacular bite of pâté, before saying, "What did he just say to you?"

"I really have no idea. Why don't you just sit, relax, we have plenty of time to finish our drinks," she says. "You're really quite uptight tonight."

Why does Cecilia insist on telling me what to do? She knows I don't like it. Thank goodness I've learned to control my fire. I need to take a walk, to think. "I'll be right back. Do try to stay put, won't you, darling?"

"Of course, darling," Cecilia says.

"Excuse me." I stand and walk inside the busy café. As I make my way to the stairs, to what I know will be a less than acceptable *salle de bain*. I try to calm down. I am in control tonight. I am. This anger firing up inside me is counterproductive. I can feel my blood pressure rising, my chest constricting. The café's bathroom is as dark and disgusting as I thought it would be. As I mind my business, I take deep breaths and remind myself to concentrate on tonight, on Cecilia. I will keep my plans on track for the rest of the evening. It is what should be done, what needs to happen. All day she's been leading me around or disappearing when I least expect it.

She says she tripped. But did she really? I've never known her to be clumsy, and she's a master at dashing about in high heels. The woman in green smoking a cigarette didn't trip. The sidewalks are well kept.

Perhaps I'm overthinking things?

My heart calms a bit when I see that Cecilia is where I left her at our table outside. She hasn't disappeared. No, if anything she looks more peaceful than she has all day. She's smiling, enjoying her second martini.

That's fine. I like her tipsy. She's more talkative.

Perhaps she'll be able to explain, when drunk, how a spider named Theo came to her rescue this evening. I for one can't wait to hear the explanation.

Paul

Cecilia looks my way as I emerge from the restaurant and weave a path through the crowded outdoor section of the café. She has her phone in her hand, as always, but does not seem to be texting or talking to anyone. Her eyes are on me, only me. The way it should be.

The way it was. My palms sweat and I wipe them on my pants as I reach our table.

"How is your second martini?" I ask as I take my seat. "And how is your ankle?"

"The pain in my ankle is inversely related to the number of martinis consumed, it seems." Cecilia's eyes twinkle.

I take a sip of my martini. It soothes my rage for the moment. "I do hope we can still make our dinner tonight?" I say after a while.

"Of course. We can take a taxi if my ankle won't cooperate," she says, her left hand stroking the dagger diamond, taunting me.

"How much was that diamond necklace again?" I ask. "I'll need to add it to our insurance policy."

"We have an umbrella policy, don't we?" she says.

Whatever. I stare at the tip of Cecilia's nose and my mind flashes back to Mia who had a very similar nose, a similarly pleasing face. We were good together for so long, we really were. A decade of bliss, as far as I'm concerned. Plenty of money, a huge house, enviable offspring. Sure, I had a little dalliance on the side, as most men do. I'd met Gretchen innocently enough, purchasing lingerie for my wife from the store where she worked. Well, that became a cover, so I could meet Gretchen. We had so much fun together until she turned on me, too. Although, somehow, I'd like to believe the trouble with everything in my world in Columbus began when Caroline Fisher started working at Thompson Payne Advertising. Caroline was a younger version of Mia, working at the same job Mia had when we'd fallen in love. How could I resist? How could any man?

I close my eyes and open them to find Cecilia staring at me.

"Paul, is something wrong?" she asks.

"I want to know how much that necklace was, and I want to know how you had the money to pay for it," I say. My tone may be a bit harsh, and I remind myself to put patience on my face. "Please. I know it wasn't on the credit card we share."

Cecilia smiles, her red-lip, white-teeth shark smile. "Correct. You didn't get that little notification, did you? You do know, in the state of California, half of everything you own is mine. You are wealthy beyond your wildest dreams. Relax. We can afford it. My half of Esther's estate can afford anything I desire. Seymour helped me set up my own account, my own credit. It's important for women these days."

Seymour. Our banker. My banker. I slip my hand into the pocket of my pants and find the pack of matches I'd grabbed from the bar inside. Right now, I imagine pulling them out, lighting them all and throwing them at my wife. The fire. I take a deep breath and flash a smile. My wife is smiling so I mirror her. Although I'm not quite sure why we're smiling.

"Yes, you're right. We are blessed. I have a sizeable fortune, which I'm happy to share, of course. I just didn't know you'd go off and buy hundreds of thousands of dollars' worth of things without me." I am being calm, not defensive. Stating the facts. I take another sip of my martini. I glance at the remaining foie gras turning old on the table. Why hasn't a waiter been by to remove this? My stomach burns but I return my gaze to my beloved. "Besides, we are married and we have so much to look forward to. And there's the prenup that sort of finalizes things, darling."

"Oh, don't be silly," she says. I watch as she downs the remainder of her martini in one chug. "You and I both know that quickie prenup isn't worth the paper it's written on. You do know that, right? You were in such a rush to get married you couldn't wait for Esther's counsel to return from vacation, as I recall. So I guess you get what you pay for." Cecilia laughs.

She's laughing at me again. She reaches out and places her hand on mine, pats it like I'm a child.

"The prenup is airtight. One of the finest attorneys in West Palm drafted it, as you'll recall," I say, which is a lie because Joseph was out of town and I found the guy online. Who knows whether it is airtight. California has a lot of protections in place for these things, it turns out. The liberals have made it hard to screw your spouse. "Although I don't suppose that matters because we aren't divorcing, darling, we are trying to bring a child into the world." I watch my bride closely. I pull my hand out from under hers. Once again, my left hand closes around the matchbook in my pocket.

"I'm just making the point that what's mine is mine, Paul. That's all," Cecilia says and waves her hand in the air. If I did that, she'd scold me. But I guess there are different standards here now. She attracts the waiter's attention. He smiles and nods. If I waved him over like that, he would have scowled. Double standards is what it is. She's a young, attractive woman, a damsel in some sort of distress in a hot red dress. Me? I'm her older, unsmiling date. This money talk is not what I want us to be discussing on our last evening. I find myself wishing I was in Brentwood, with Susan, right at this moment. I can't believe how this night is going. No, I need to keep Susan separate in my mind. She is youth and happiness, compliance and sweetness. This version of Cecilia is the opposite. We lock eyes.

I need to remind Cecilia that she has nothing, despite her cavalier spending. All she has in the world is what I give her, or, in the case of the necklace, what she buys for herself. I wonder how long this secret credit card has been around, and what else it has purchased. I make a note to talk to, scold actually, our banker when I'm back in the States. He never should have allowed this to happen. I will get him fired. I imagine his big head, his small hands, and stuffy office heavy with dark wood and crown molding. Private banker to the stars, he calls himself.

He has officially crossed the line with me. And who has a name like Seymour Lynch anyway?

"How long have you been meeting with Seymour behind my back?" I ask. I realize I sound aggressive, so I reach over and place my hand, tenderly, on her thigh. A gentle gesture of love and support. *Trust me*, it says, *and please tell me the truth.*

Cecilia looks up. Thinking, I suppose. Remembering or making something up, who is to say?

"Oh, well, we ran into each other in Santa Monica, I think, at Ivy on the Shore or Shutters, one of the two," she says.

"And he told you he had a secret credit card for you? How convenient," I say. My stomach twists but I don't let the pain show.

"No, he said to come see him if I needed anything," Cecilia says. "So I did. He set up an account for me." She shifts in her seat. "I'm going to go to the toilet. Could you please handle the check? I'll be right back."

She stands quickly, seems to wriggle her foot around, decides it's solid and is on her way into the restaurant without so much as a limp. I should be glad, I suppose, that she isn't injured.

Should I also be glad that I know she's had our prenup evaluated? Should I be glad to know she knows how to access my money whenever she wants to, without me being any the wiser? Somehow none of these revelations have made me less angry. Quite the opposite.

I will get my hands on that credit card and destroy it now that I know of her secret plans. She will not get her hands on another cent of Esther's money, not without my permission. And my permission will be subject to strict guidelines.

I earned my money by cozying up to that old hag for so long. To be fair, Esther was the best of the bunch of dried-up hags I had to squire around town, but still. After what happened with Mia, I will not let another woman double-cross me, not ever again. Just the thought of Mia's betrayal makes me want to find her, ruin her. But I must focus on the present.

Tonight, I will give Cecilia the rules. The new rules of our relationship. And she will play by those rules, or else.

THIRTY-FIVE
PARIS, 8:45 P.M.

Paul

It seems to take forever for Cecilia to return to the table. In all that time, the waiter has yet to appear with our check. I am, in a word, frustrated. In another word, furious. I remember that evening, five years ago, when Mia and I were driving to dinner, the first night of what was to be our romantic weekend at the lake.

I had suggested calling the babysitter, Claudia, to check in on the boys. Mia refused, telling me she knew they were at dinner, at a movie theater. But the hairs on my neck had stood up. I knew, without a doubt, she was lying to me. But I didn't yet know why. Still, the very thought of sweet, trusting, loyal Mia, mother of my two sons, lying to me was incompatible with everything I'd known about her. I should have listened to my instincts, but instead, for some time that evening, I told myself I was imagining things. That Mia was who she'd always been. I was wrong. She changed on our romantic weekend away. She double-crossed me. With her parents help and money, she stole the boys from me in the middle of the night. When I returned home from the lake, our house was empty. Our love story suddenly over.

But love is such a complicated thing for us humans. We overcomplicate it all with thoughts. We analyze, we fret. It's easier to understand if you think of us all as animals. Base. With simple needs and desires. That's what we are, all of us. Consider this: Cecilia loves me almost as much as Susan does. Susan, of course, benefits from the carefree me, away from the obligations and social climbing pressures I feel when I'm at home in Malibu. Cecilia, well, she gets a slightly more rigid version of me. Paul the Hollywood producer, Paul the social connector, Paul the husband awaiting his new wife's pregnancy. Pushing for his new wife to become pregnant.

Why isn't Cecilia pregnant yet? I should demand an answer, and I will, tonight.

I bet Susan would get pregnant right away. Now that I think of it, Susan is the person I've been fighting the urge to call since we arrived in Paris. She's called me, and texted, three or four times since we've been here so I know she misses me. It's our three-month anniversary coming up and we'll celebrate properly when I'm back home. I will not call her during my romantic Parisian holiday, and I've deleted her texts and voice messages without listening to them. It wouldn't be appropriate. I do have rules. I don't want you to think less of me because of Susan's existence. I've always had the ability to compartmentalize my life, my loves. My relationship with Susan doesn't harm anyone; it brings more joy to the world as a whole. That's my philosophy, and has been, with all my lovers.

Don't get me wrong, I love Cecilia. She's beautiful, and charming, and learning to be sophisticated. She's Malibu and Hollywood. Susan is simple and fun. She's Brentwood and coffee shops. They don't have anything to do with each other, and they will never meet. That is the way my world works. Neat. Orderly. Defined. I am in control.

Despite my rules, however, Susan has called me, and I know she's angry I'm on this trip with Cecilia instead of with her. And maybe she has a point, given the way things have been going, the tension between Cecilia and I this entire time in Paris, and honestly, for months. But I made it clear to Susan going in. I told her I love my wife and would likely never leave her, although between you and me, there are no real absolutes in life, are there?

The last time Susan and I made love was a couple of days before the Paris trip. She'd cried when I tried to leave to go home, begging me to spend the night.

"I need you to stay over, please, one night," she'd said, tears rolling down her beautiful cheeks.

"You know the rules, sweetie. I must go home," I'd said, sitting up and beginning to get dressed. It was tempting to stay, of course it was. The attraction coursed between us even after a robust lovemaking session.

"Can't you tell her you have work? Hollywood producers travel a lot, I know they do," she said, sniffling.

I walked to the tiny bathroom and pulled a couple tissues from the box on her sink and handed them to her. "Not now, not yet. I need to get more established. I have a couple of projects on the go, and when they do go into production, you will come with me on location. And of course, you'll have a role in the film." I kissed the top of her head.

"Promise?" she said.

And I did promise. Words are so easy to agree to sometimes, aren't they? As I left her tiny bungalow, I made sure to look around. It's habit, from living in such a small community back in Ohio, and then West Palm. People try to catch you doing something so they can have something on you, even if you're not up to anything. Like our former neighbors, the Boones. Doris always snooped on me, told Mia too much. Too bad for Doris I was always one step ahead of her. When their home exploded, they lost everything. No one could prove it was me, of course, but Doris knows. In West LA, nobody really knows me, not yet at least. But they will. I pull out my phone and send a quick text to Susan.

I'll be home tomorrow night. Cannot wait to see you.

Yes, I'm breaking my own rule, but I am the only one who is allowed to do so.

Except now I need to focus on my wife. I'm starting to think Cecilia must have fallen into the toilet because she's still not here, neither is the snooty café waiter.

"Le chèque," the waiter says, materializing as if he read my mind and shoving the credit card machine in my face.

I slip it in, glad they don't expect tipping here because he would get nothing.

"Can you clear the table? The foie gras has turned to something indescribable," I say as I yank the card back.

He looks down his nose at me and walks away. *Whatever.* I stand and decide to go in search of Cecilia. We need to start walking to the Iron Lady before we miss our reservation.

I can assure you we will not miss this reservation.

Dear Diary,

I have this weird feeling that somebody is watching me, but that's ridiculous. I don't know anyone here, well, except for my lover. I just wish he would sleep over. I need to figure out how to convince him. I've tried most of the tricks in my book, but to be honest, I don't have that many left.

I check the time. Oh, he should be arriving any minute. More later!!!

He left again. After we made love. I couldn't help but start crying, begging him to stay. It didn't work. I decided to go for a walk, to blow off some steam, and I almost got run over!! I wasn't in the crosswalk, but still. LA drivers are crazy!! I didn't see the driver, but it was a white car and it came out of nowhere.

All in all, tonight just wasn't the best night ever. Not at all. My lover is going on a trip in a couple of days. I'm debating about telling him a few things before he goes, things he should know. We'll see. Tonight, I'm too shaken to do anything but pour myself a glass of wine.

OK three glasses later, I can't get the white car out of my mind. One second later and I would have been hit. Close calls like that give you perspective, or make you drink too much. I wish I could talk to HIM, but I can't.

I'm drunk. I'm going to sleep.

THIRTY-SIX

PARIS, 8:50 P.M.

Paul

Cecilia is flirting with a man at the bar. I've already paid the bill, so why is she still in there? Talking to a not-handsome man with a wrinkled blue shirt and baggy, saggy eyes. At least, that's what she appears to be doing from my perspective outside. I march inside the café, and she turns, feeling my presence, no doubt.

"Paul, come meet Randy," she says as if we're hosting another one of our cocktail parties in Malibu, not standing in a seedy, annoyingly packed café in Paris. This man, Randy, looks like a French bulldog. Bulgy, saggy eyes and all.

I note my wife stands comfortably in her high heels, no visible sign of any injuries from the supposed fall, and say, "Randy. So nice to meet you. Cecilia, we must go or we'll be late. I'm serious."

"Apologies for my husband. He's a little high-strung tonight, and, well, he lacks a certain ability to read other people's emotions. Paul, can't you see Randy is upset? He just lost his wife, and I reminded him of her."

What am I to say to all of this? *That's a fabulous pick-up line, Randy, but we need to go.* And did my wife throw me under the bus for my lack of emotional intelligence in front of a stranger who's grieving the loss of a woman who looks like Cecilia? Yes, she did. I will address that later. My wife is being kind to a stranger. I can see it in her face. She's being nice. I should try to be as well. I force my face into the look of concern, brow crinkled.

"I'm sorry about your wife," I say.

"Thank you," he says.

Cecilia smiles. I'm behaving with emotional intelligence. But I can't do it for long.

"She was a wonderful woman. Full of life and beauty, like you," Randy says, his French accent clearly pulling Cecilia under his spell.

He really needs to stop talking.

"Oh, thank you, I'm so sorry again," Cecilia says. She reaches over and hugs the stranger.

My fire can't be contained.

"Look, buddy, my actual living and breathing wife and I have a dinner reservation at the Eiffel Tower and if we don't start walking now, we will miss it. Got to live life while you can, am I right?" I say.

"Paul, stop it," Cecilia says. "Au revoir, bonne nuit."

Randy grabs Cecilia's hand and kisses it. "Merci, madame."

Oh, for god's sake. I slide my arm around my wife and escort her out of the restaurant. This melodrama must end.

"You were so rude to the poor man," Cecilia says once we're on the sidewalk finally heading to dinner.

"No, I wasn't. How did she die, anyway?" I ask. I don't care that I was rude. I like to consider it being firm. But I do wonder how she died, because, well, there are all kinds of deaths. Sudden. Slow. Long. Short. Natural. Diseased. Murdered. "What if that guy was a murderer?"

"Oh, honestly, Paul. She died by suicide," Cecilia says, her eyes wide. "So sad. Tragic. He found her."

Still could have been murder, I think, but don't say. Sometimes the police mess up these sorts of things, or they're outsmarted. In my experience it's not too hard to get the better of them.

"Well, that is sad. I wonder how she did it?" I say, although I would like to change the subject to something more romantic.

"Look, Paul, the tower! It's sparkling with lights," Cecilia says and points to our destination aglow in the distance.

"It's beautiful," I say. "Like you, darling." I reach for her hand.

"Thank you. This dress seems to suit me, from the looks I'm getting," she says. "I need to wear it more often."

"Red is gorgeous on blondes," I say. It's true. Lois, Mia, Gretchen, Susan, Cecilia, and even Caroline Fisher looked great in red. But I digress. "So, how did she do it?"

"Will you let it go after I tell you?" she asks.

"Of course, darling," I say.

"She hung herself, from a beam on their bedroom ceiling," she says. "Gives me the chills. It's so desperate. So sad."

"It could have still been Randy. You know what they say, it's always the husband," I say.

We're waiting to cross the street among a crowd of overweight tourists, but our wonderful romantic dinner spot beckons. None of these people can afford dinner at the Eiffel Tower, I know that.

I feel Cecilia staring at me. I turn, stare back.

"What?" I ask.

"Why is it always the husband?" she asks.

I shrug. "I don't know, it just is. It's what they say. I didn't make it up."

The light changes and we step out across the street, bobbing and weaving through the throngs. We reach the other side and enter a large park with fountains and more huge buildings. I'm not sure where we are but the view of the tower is spectacular.

"Oh, you know, we're close to the Passy Cemetery," Cecilia says. "It's where famous artists and musicians are buried, like Edouard Manet and Claude Debussy. They're buried in really extravagant graves, I read. Want to go see it?"

"A cemetery? No thanks," I say, and wonder why my young wife is so focused on death all of a sudden. I guess that guy in the bar really got to her.

"You're not afraid of cemeteries, are you?" Cecilia leans against me. If not for the topic I'd think she was being loving, like she used to be before our trip here.

"Of course not," I say. I speed up my pace and she keeps up easily. We still need to cross over the river.

"Fine, I'll go see it on my next trip here," she says. "You know, sometimes it should be the wife," she adds.

"What?" I ask.

Cecilia shrugs. "Nothing. I'm joking around. I said sometimes a wife just needs to go with the flow, like I am now. See, isn't this pleasant for you?"

No. It's expected.

Paul

All of this talk of death and murder is troubling on what is supposed to be our special night. We cross the river, holding hands, but each lost in thought. I'm not sure what my young wife is pondering, but I cannot help but think of the way she's been challenging me over everything. It's beginning to remind me more and more of Mia toward the end of our marriage. That neighborhood busybody Doris Boone whispered nonsense about me. All lies. Doris had been friends with my brother Tommy growing up, so had been a thorn in my side for decades. She was a problem, yes, but I excel at solving problems. I make a note on my phone with my free hand reminding myself to check in on my Tommy. I glance over at Cecilia.

"Why are you on your phone?" she asks. "Somebody so important you had to text during our last night in Paris?"

"Nope," I say. "Just work. And you'll note I've only been on my phone once, compared to your constant addiction to yours."

"Yes, you're far superior to me," she says. I don't think she means it.

"We're almost there, darling," I say, smiling at her. Cecilia's eyes are bright, and her smile is lovely. She is beautiful, my wife. It's just a shame, really, that she isn't pregnant with my child yet. That would have helped us, kept us focused on the future together. It's what kept Mia and I on track, at least initially. I'd race home from work, skipping client happy hours and the like, to help with the children. It was a busy, exhausting time, of course. Sam was a newborn and Mikey a little over two years old, both in diapers. Mia was exhausted but I would come home to her rescue: the provider, the caretaker, the champion. Did Mia ever thank me? No. But I was fine with that because she was raising my heirs.

I did put my foot down at the thought of a third baby. Her dream of a daughter. That was a big no. We'd taken on enough.

But with Cecilia, I dreamed of three because we're extremely rich and can afford nannies. One for each child. We wouldn't have to struggle with diapers or other messy things that infants and toddlers produce. We'd outsource that part, of course. We would cuddle the children after their baths were over, snuggle with them, breathe in their clean baby smells and then hand them back off to the nanny for the overnight chaos. Yes, Cecilia and I would have an elegant child-rearing experience, unlike my last one.

We're so lucky, so rich, so spoiled. No need to work, no need to struggle at all. We're blessed. I wish good old Rebecca, the evil HR woman from Thompson Payne, could see me now. Walking to the Eiffel Tower for a romantic meal with my gorgeous wife. *Ha.* Living well is the best revenge.

I'll never forget the moment she called me into her office and instructed me to sit down like I was a kid and she was the principal telling me what to do, scolding me when I hadn't done anything wrong. She was ugly, Rebecca, unsuited for work at an advertising agency where image is everything. I almost said that to her, but I didn't. That would have been rude.

"A coworker has filed a harassment claim against you, Mr. Strom. We take these things very seriously," she said. Behind her desk was an Amazon rainforest worth of plants. The whole office smelled like mold. "This is a formal warning. You are to have no unnecessary contact at work with Ms. Caroline Fisher."

I'd felt so betrayed. How could she turn on me like that when we both felt the connection, the attraction? She was my type. And clearly, I was hers. Sure, once she found out I was married, she started pulling away. But this? There had to be a mistake.

Rude Rebecca continued, "She was given the option to take it a step further, but she is giving you a chance here, Mr. Strom."

I'd denied any inappropriate behavior, of course. There is no one who loves and cherishes women like I do, as you know by now.

"One more inappropriate contact with Caroline and your career here is over," Rude Rebecca threatened. "If I could, I would fire you now."

I had never been threatened by a woman before that encounter with the evil plant woman. She was disgusting, and out to get me. I decided then that I really didn't like being threatened by women, not at all.

"Where do we go now?" Cecilia asks, tugging on my arm. "Do you have specific instructions for how we get to the restaurant? It's so crowded. I hope we can find the right entrance."

"Don't worry, darling," I say and pull out the email I printed. "I have it all planned out. We need to go to Pilier Est. Over there."

I wrap my arm around Cecilia's waist to keep her close to me as we plunge into the overwhelmingly huge crowd. This is my now, not some idiot plant lady with a vendetta. Not some young account coordinator either. Sure, I'd messed up. After two months of no contact, ducking into offices when she appeared in the same hallway, for example, I still couldn't get my mind off Caroline. And one evening, in the elevator, it was just the two of us. I might have said "you look amazing," or "god, I've missed you. Drinks tonight?" But that's it.

She turned and stared at me like I was a monster. "You're sick. You really are sick," she'd said and hurried out of the elevator. I'd known then I was in trouble.

That's why the future is so much brighter than the past. We can rewrite our future, ignore all this nonsense, noise. For all anyone in my life knows now, I am a successful Hollywood producer with a gorgeous wife and a huge mansion ready to be filled with offspring.

And that's enough for now, and forever. And it's all thanks to Esther's death. Death does in fact provide new life, for some lucky people like me. And whoever it is that is trying to contest the will, well, they'll find out just how far I'll go to protect what's mine. I'll never share a dollar of my inheritance. I won't.

Dear Diary,

I'm bored and sad.

Here's the thing. I think when I moved out here I thought it would be easy. Like, I'd audition but then they'd see my talent immediately, and voila I'd be discovered. I'd have all the best clothes, because I'd have a stylist. And a hair and makeup team. And a huge bank account.

I've been here six months and it's still just a faraway dream. I really don't want to give up. I want to be an actor so bad. It has to happen. I can't go back home a failure, I can't.

Today, I'm going to go to Venice Beach, go to all the hotspots and see if I can accidentally meet someone famous.

Someone at a coffee shop or on the beach. I need to put myself out there. I need to make myself feel better while my lover is away. I miss him, and his attention.

Wish me well. I'm wearing my most skimpy outfit, so I know at the very least I'll turn heads.

Paul

I slow down, enjoy my last moment of peace before she notices I answered her phone. I look up at the amazing Iron Lady above me. We will be dining on the first floor, which is 187 feet up, and by far the largest floor at almost 15,000 square feet. Our restaurant, Madame Brasserie, is the finest on that floor. After dinner, despite her protest that she is afraid of heights, I will whisk Cecilia up in the lift to the second floor, 377 feet up, and just under 5,000 square feet. We will not walk up to the second floor, as the 1,665 steps would be difficult for her in those heels. On the second level, there's another fancy restaurant, Jules Verne, and the access to the lift for the third floor, 906 feet in the air, and only 800 square feet. Intimate, secluded, perhaps romantic if our dinner goes well.

"Paul, I still cannot believe you talked to Evan," Cecilia hisses, staring at her phone.

"He called. I picked up. You were already going through security. No big deal. Look, over there is where we collect our lift tickets," I say, pointing excitedly. "This is amusing, all these steps, like we're trying to go on a ride at an amusement park for dinner."

"I don't really see you as an amusement park guy," she says. She's applying her blood-red lipstick again. "Please don't answer my phone again, OK? I'm serious."

"Sure, dear, whatever you wish," I say. If I'd had access to her phone when Christopher called, as I saw he did after our little rooftop cocktail party, that would have been fun. Unfortunately, I don't know the security code for her phone, and she doesn't know mine. We trust each other completely, of course, that's why. Also, I wouldn't want her intercepting my private texts with Susan, or others. It's a win/win, this layer of privacy from each other. "In return, could you please stop talking to random men during our last night in Paris? Can you do that?"

Cecilia shrugs with a twinkle in her eye. "Of course."

A small booth is lit up with the restaurant's name. Once again, I present my email confirmation and the smiling woman hands us two lift tickets.

"These will get you up to the first floor of the tower. If you'd like to go to the top, after dinner, you will need to purchase another ticket," she says.

Amusement parks are such a racket. I do hate them, as Cecilia guessed. "Sure, yes please, *oui*," I say and slide her my credit card. "We're going straight to the top after dinner. Sound good?"

Cecilia shrugs. "You know I don't like heights," she says.

"Yes, I just found that out, but it's our last night, it's the Eiffel Tower. I want this to be the best night ever. I'll take care of you, promise," I say. I do mean that. I look above me and imagine us all the way up there.

Cecilia exhales. Her face is tense. She looks angry. Oh, right, the silly phone thing with Evan. "He texted me what you said to him. That's not OK, Paul."

"Here are your tickets," happy lady in the booth exclaims.

"Mercy bow couped," I say. I smile at Cecilia.

Cecilia rolls her eyes, covers her ears with her hands. "Ugh. Honestly." She stomps off toward the lifts, giving me a moment to recalculate. Evan is taken care of, and likely I scared Christopher and he's never going to come around again. I do plan to make a little trip to Santa Barbara sometime soon. I'll bring Susan with me. We'll have a romantic getaway and I'll only leave the resort to do a little reconnaissance, and a little spying on my brother Tommy and his perfect family. Susan will be content to lounge poolside in my absence. It won't take long. I don't want a relationship with him, not at all. I just want to know about him, just in case I need any leverage. I need to keep him quiet. He knows too much about me, about the past. About how our parents really died, especially.

He knows to keep quiet, he's been doing it for years. That's why he's hiding in Santa Barbara. Besides, he doesn't have any proof of what he thinks is my involvement in our parents' tragic deaths by carbon monoxide, or in the Boones' home exploding because of a gas leak. No proof at all. All he could do would be to cast suspicion in my direction. Which wouldn't be good for my Hollywood reputation, although they do attract some of the worst people on the planet in that industry. I mean, genuine monsters. I'm tame, harmless compared to some of those guys. Although I realize that's not saying much.

Cecilia has found the line for one of the two elevators the public can take. A third elevator is exclusively for the Jules Verne restaurant on the second floor. I couldn't get a reservation there, but this will be fine. I check my watch. We will arrive exactly on time for our 9:30 p.m. seating, perhaps even a couple of minutes early. My heart beats with excitement. My plan is working perfectly this evening, finally, and Cecilia is going along with things just fine.

Except she's frowning and texting.

"Darling, can you put your phone away? Please? We'll be home tomorrow afternoon. You can catch up then," I say.

"You were rude to Evan on the phone, and to Christopher at cocktails," she says. "You treated Theo horribly, and that poor man Randy who lost his wife, well, you were terrible to him, too. I don't know what has come over you, Paul. You are not the same man I married. You've changed, or maybe this was who you were all along? Are you feeling sick?"

Come to think of it, my stomach has been fairly calm this evening. I felt terrible after lunch, likely Phoebe's bad cooking, and it hurt briefly at the café where we stopped before coming here, but now I feel happy, excited, good.

"I feel great, darling, and I am the same man you married, the same one who whisked you away to Malibu and made all your dreams come true." I take her soft hand in mine, turn it to make her diamond engagement ring and wedding band sparkle. I really outdid myself with the ring. But then my eyes travel to her chest: the necklace. I feel a flame ignite somewhere deep in my stomach, and now I do feel a little sick again.

Cecilia's right hand twists the diamond necklace. Is she doing that on purpose?

"I'll try to be more kind," I say. "Less grumpy. It's just that I love you so much I don't want to share you."

Or share any more of my money with you without my explicit permission, I don't say.

"Kindness would be appreciated," she says. "I just felt a bit of a chilly breeze." She pulls her hand from mine, unties her scarf from her purse strap, and wraps it around her shoulders. The look is at once chic and sophisticated, and better yet, hides the dagger diamond.

"You'll be warm at dinner," I say. The elevator operator waves us inside, and before I know it, we're closing in on the first floor of the tower. I'm so excited I can barely contain myself. But I do. I arrange my expression into one of mild curiosity. Mouth closed, but corners of lips turned up. Eyes wide and bright.

I tilt my head and look over at Cecilia. Her eyes are dark, and she looks terrified.

"I don't know if I can do this," Cecilia says as the elevator doors open. Her face has gone pale.

"Do what, darling? It's just dinner," I say.

But of course, it's much more.

THIRTY-NINE
PARIS, 9:55 P.M.

Paul

We step out of the elevator and I wrap my arms around Cecilia. She still looks scared.

"Take a deep breath. Everything is fine," I say. I'm using my soothing voice. "I didn't know you were so afraid of heights."

"Let's go to the restaurant," she says. "I need to sit down."

"Perfect, it's just over this way." As we walk, the lights begin to dance, like we're inside a giant strobe light. Incredible. I look at Cecilia and she seems to be enjoying the light show, too. At least she's not on her phone, and she's not backing out of our special dinner. So there's that.

And I will do my part throughout dinner. I will reignite our spark, so to speak. I will launch operation "Make Cecilia Love Me Completely Again" tonight. I think back to how quickly we fell in love. From a funeral encounter to the bedroom in less than two days. It was record-setting, envy-inducing sex those first few months. Like nothing else in the world mattered except the two of us and making love. We were almost always naked, and we loved it.

How different this romantic getaway for our wedding anniversary has been to what I'd imagined it could be. We have everything we could have ever dreamed of. She's told me as much. And if she dreamed of something else, well, I would have bought it for her. Except that necklace. It's horrible. And, of course, there's also the fact that someone claiming to be Esther's child is sniffing around my money.

Cecilia Babcock Strom. Well, no actually, it's Cecilia Wilmot Babcock Strom, isn't it? Of course it is.

"Welcome to Madame Brasserie!" a host in a tux says with enthusiasm as we reach the door. "Do we have a reservation this evening?"

"Oui," I say, and again hand over the email printout.

"Ah, a window table with the best view in all of Paris. Good choice. Please do follow me," he says.

"Oh my god, the floor is glass." Cecilia stops in her tracks.

This is going to be fun. "Don't look down. Come on," I say. I'll have the upper hand this evening, of that I'm certain. She can barely walk across the room.

By the time we reach our table, small, but elegant, and as promised, tucked right beside the window, Cecilia looks like a ghost. A ghost with bright red lips.

"Why didn't I think of this when you told me about tonight's plans?" she says as I help her into her chair. "Obviously there's too much on my mind to worry about the fact we're eating up so high."

"You'll get used to it, dear," I say. "It seems to me you're a woman who can do just about anything she sets her mind to."

"Well, that's sweet of you. I suppose I am a bit driven, have been, you know, it's a by-product of how I grew up," she says.

"And that's why you sat next to me at Esther's funeral, isn't it?" I ask.

Across the table Cecilia's eyes flash with recognition, with the challenge. The color is back in her face.

"I sat next to you at Esther's funeral because you were cute," she says, smoothing her hair with her left hand. She takes a sip of water.

"And because I was Esther's companion, and you knew that, didn't you?"

A waiter appears at our table. He's an older gentleman, thin with white hair, and he has an efficient air about him. He isn't warm, but that's OK. Neither are we.

"Welcome to our very special restaurant. Something to drink to start the evening? Perhaps champagne? Are we celebrating something important?"

I smile and lock eyes with Cecilia.

"It's our last night in Paris. And we're celebrating our one-year anniversary," I say. "It'll be our best night ever, I hope."

Cecilia rolls her eyes.

"Perfect. Champagne then?" the waiter asks.

"I'll have a glass of Chardonnay," Cecilia says. Her tone is off. It's troubling. I thought she would act more contrite now that she knows that I know her little secret. Or at least one of them.

"Double vodka on the rocks. Light on the rocks," I say.

He nods and he's gone. As I wait for Cecilia to speak, I think back to the seduction of my new young wife. It was fast, furious, and now, I'm realizing, completely her plan. I fell into her trap, so to speak, but I enjoyed every moment of it. I really did. I will be so sad to have to divorce her, to end things. But it seems I must, one way or another.

"I told you before, I didn't know Esther. I worked with her house manager and designed the funeral program. When I saw you, well, I just had to flirt with you," she says.

"And you really had no idea who I was to Esther?" I ask. I take a sip of my water. I keep my expression neutral, calm.

Cecilia takes a deep breath. "Like I told you, I'd read all about Esther Wilmot to create the program, and she seemed to be a remarkable woman. I thought I'd stay for the service and pay my respects. I never met her, unfortunately."

"Nice of you, to pay respects to a stranger."

"An employee of sorts. Remember, I did a lot of invitations for her parties through Julio. I liked her style, and she must have liked mine. And I'm a nice person, Paul," she says with a smile that does not reach her eyes.

Yes, I thought she was a nice person. A kind person. A compliant, beautiful person. Was I wrong?

"And what about me? What really made you choose to sit by me at the funeral?" I ask.

Cecilia smiles, and this time it appears to be genuine. "I thought you were cute. I was glad you were cute."

"Cute? Well, I'm not a puppy, darling," I say with a wink. "How about sophisticated, sexy, George Clooney-like, perhaps?"

Cecilia laughs. "Yes, of course, I thought you were all those things. It made things so much easier. But, you know, you can't always judge a book by its cover."

On that much we agree, my dear. I smile.

FORTY

MALIBU, CALIFORNIA, THREE MONTHS AGO

Cecilia

I try Paul's phone again, and still no answer. He tells me he has an assistant at his swanky offices in Santa Monica, but no one ever answers the phone there either.

This is becoming a regular occurrence, and it's not fair. I've spent all day creating a special meal to commemorate the one-year anniversary of our first date. I didn't even ask Evan to help. I wanted it to be a surprise, maybe a way to remind Paul of everything we once had, everything that is slipping away now.

I pull open the oven and poke at the perfectly cooked tenderloin. I marinated it all day, and I've cooked it precisely the way Paul likes it. I close the oven with a too-heavy push on the door.

I take a deep breath and a sip of wine. I wish I had a girl-friend to confide in. I tried again to reach out to Melissa, but she's ghosted me and I have no idea why. I don't know what I did wrong. I wish I had someone to talk to about my seemingly perfect, miserable life. I wish Paul hadn't changed into an unrecognizable bully.

And I really wish he would pick up his phone. This time he does.

"Is everything alright, darling?" Paul says. "You've called four times. No voicemail. Excessive, unless it's an emergency."

"It is an emergency. Dinner is ready. Where are you?" I say. I walk into the dining room where I've set a gorgeous table for two, complete with white roses in crystal vases and slim white taper candles held in elegant crystal candleholders. There's a gift for Paul on his plate, wrapped in gold with a white bow. It's a new watch. A Rolex. He loves watches, and this one is a collector's item. It took me two months to find such a perfect gift. I touch the package with my fingertip.

I'm wearing a new dress, also white, silk, that hugs my body and shows off my figure. Evan said it was "my best look yet" when I FaceTimed him earlier today.

"I'm not going to be home tonight. I have a work conflict," he says. "Raincheck?"

I turn and walk back through the house to the kitchen, then out the doors to the glistening pool area, where the ocean sparkles below the cliff. This all looks like a dream. People would kill to be me, here, right now. I know this. The sun is dipping into the ocean. It's magic hour on the coast, but I'm all alone.

"Are you there? I need to run," Paul says.

Run where? To whom? Why? What could possibly be more important than this? He's hiding something, I know it.

"You've known about our date night for two weeks," I say. The infinity pool seems to blend with the sky and the ocean, everything turning a light pink in the setting sun.

"Yes, well, it can't be helped. It's an important screening and I need to be there," he says. "This is part of the plan. Our plan."

"No, it isn't. It's your plan, not our plan." I turn away from the perfect beauty, heading back to the kitchen. I take another sip of wine and turn off the oven.

"I have to go. I'll see you in the morning, or, well, likely later in the afternoon," he says. "Maybe go paint the sunset or something? Make me one of your little paintings, will you? Oh, and if you don't mind, will you remind the staff to drive the laundry over to the place I like in Santa Monica? You know, good dry cleaners are impossible to find. Thanks, darling. Good night."

I hold the phone in my hand as tears roll down my cheeks. I walk back into the dining room, pick up the present. I'll give it to Evan. He'll appreciate it. I'm such a fool. I thought Paul was the answer, that he would be security and protection, that he would be home and happiness. What a perfect gilded illusion I've created for myself.

And I decide something else that night, too. I will spy on my husband. I will follow him and I will find out what is going on. I will not be treated like this, discarded, lonely. Talked to like I'm his assistant instead of his wife.

If it's an important screening, shouldn't I be there by his side, instead of here, alone and waiting? Yes, I should be. But I'm not. I will find out who is, though. That's a promise I make to myself. He didn't come home until late that night. And the next morning, when he pulls away, headed to work, or so he says, I am following.

We don't drive to Santa Monica, though. He stops in Brentwood on a tree-lined street. And I watch as he hugs his lover. I catch a glimpse of her face and she seems familiar, but from where? One of our parties perhaps? Before I can get another look Paul steps inside her bungalow and they close the door.

FORTY-ONE
PARIS, 10:10 P.M.

Paul

So clever, my wife. So rage-inducing as well. She's the one who isn't true. She's the one who has been out for the money, my money, since we met. I must face it. It's the truth.

I should have seen her coming the moment I learned about her existence. I'll never forget the afternoon. Esther, wearing a canary-yellow caftan, had burst into the sunroom shaking a white envelope. "This is outrageous! She's gone too far. I want you to call my attorney."

"I'm happy to call Joseph, dear, but what is that?" I asked. Joseph and I had become friends since Esther and I began dating. I'd made sure of it.

Esther pulled a plain-looking piece of paper from the envelope. She held it in her shaking hands. "Listen to this." Then she began reading it out. "To the friends and neighbors of Esther Wilmot, it has come to my attention that the way my mother is being perceived and her actions don't currently meet up, and while she would like to hide behind a perfect reputation and public perception, I would like to inform you that everything is not what it seems."

Oh my. I hopped up from the comfortable reading chair where I had been enjoying watching golf on TV and hurried to her side.

"What can I do to help?" I asked. This was the first I'd heard about Esther having a child.

"I had a child. It was the result of a one-night fling, with my yoga instructor of all things," she said. "I was in between husbands. It was such a mistake, and the baby was immediately put up for adoption. I never wanted children. I don't have any children as far as I'm concerned. End of story."

I felt just as strongly about the matter. Esther had been the perfect final swansong for my exile. Single. Childless. Past husbands wealthy and remarried. All I had to do was bide my time, and with her heart issues, well, I knew she wouldn't last long. Everything was as it should be, and, of course, if necessary, I could help the heart failure process along in myriad ways. I had plenty of experience, after all.

"She's trying to ruin my reputation," she cried. "She must be silenced. Sent away again. She was not supposed to be able to know about me, to find me. Ever."

"You are loved here, dear, no one will believe anything horrible about you. Can I read the letter?" I asked. I pulled her into a hug and read the crazy threat over her shoulder. Of course, the creature wanted money from Esther. Didn't we all? But this letter was the opposite of savvy. It had typos and poor grammar. That disqualified the writer from serious consideration from the start.

I began reading it aloud. "My mother gave me up for adoption right after I was born. She probably thought she was doing the right thing by giving birth to me, but then she just abandoned me, so is that the right thing? I have never met her, not once in my whole life, although I have reached out so many times. I didn't want to send this letter but I don't know how else to talk to her and she can't die before we meet. I hear she has congestive heart failure, so I'm running out of time."

How does this person know about Esther's medical condition, the thing she wanted kept a secret? I mean, only myself and her trusted house manager Julio know of her condition. We alone take her to doctor's appointments and refill her medication. And how dare she send this to all of Esther's social circle? My rage ignited on behalf of Esther, an unusual occurrence.

"Did you have a private, closed adoption? Someone has broken privacy rules here," I commented, still embracing Esther.

"I know. I'm going to sue that agency. And this woman for libel or slander. I don't want to meet her, and I won't," Esther said. "What will my friends think of me?"

I silently read the last paragraph of the letter.

I'm scared my mother will pass away before I have the chance to meet her. I've tried everything I can think of, minus this letter, and I don't know what else to do. I cannot live with the regret of never getting to know my mother. I need some type of closure. So I'm asking for your help. Knock on her door and personally tell her I need to meet her. Just one person has the potential to reunite a mother and her daughter, and I think that's worth a shot, don't you? Thank you for any help you can provide and for reading this letter. I've never even received a birthday card from my own mother.

Sincerely, Lila Wilmot.

You can reach me at the email address below.

I released Esther from our embrace, gently took the awful letter from her hand and tucked it back into the envelope.

"I'll call Joseph. We'll handle this. Please do not worry about it. It's not good for you to have your blood pressure up."

"I never should have had that baby. I knew it was a mistake, to keep the pregnancy," Esther said, her face drawn and pale. "I never wanted children. Never. And as far as I'm concerned, I don't have any. Period."

"You need to sit down," I said and helped her onto the couch. "Don't think of this again. It will be handled."

"Thank you. What would I do without you?"

"You'll never need to find out. Go rest," I said. I kissed her on the top of the head, headed out of the room and immediately phoned Joseph. He was equally outraged and promised to send a firm letter to the woman via her email address.

And as far as we knew, it worked. Of course, not one neighbor knocked on Esther's door. Everyone pretended they hadn't even read it. But you know neighbors. They likely savored every word, talked about it during bridge, at the club, on the golf course. But never to Esther's face.

I do think that letter, and the stress it caused, precipitated her decline, among other things. Poor Esther.

And now, I look across the table at my beautiful wife.

"Did you really just want a birthday card from Esther? Is that all? Just a chance to talk to her, Lila?"

FORTY-TWO

PARIS, 10:15 P.M.

Paul

Cecilia's eyes sparkle in the candlelight. If anyone was watching us, they'd see a couple completely in love, enjoying the last night of their Parisian holiday.

"Was it really about getting a birthday card, darling?" I ask again.

Finally, Cecilia smiles. "What are you talking about?" she asks.

"I just wondered if a birthday card or a chat with Esther would have been enough for you, as you suggested in that awful letter?" My heart thuds in my chest. This is, of course, some moment of truth between us. Neither of us will play our full hand of cards, that much is clear. But for now, I will press on. That letter to dear Esther was unconscionable, even though her neigbours never actually mentioned it to her. The threat of such a letter being widely disseminated was enough for that poor old girl and her fragile heart.

"Of course not," she says. "Nothing is ever that simple. You know that."

And now I know I am right. She really is Esther's unwanted daughter. My pulse quickens with a mixture of rage and disappointment. How could I have been so blinded by her beauty that I failed to see the truth. But perhaps there is another explanation. Maybe it was love at first sight for both of us, despite the rather awkward and alarming revelation we now must deal with. Maybe the fact that she is Esther's daughter is just a small bump in the road of our bliss, a footnote to our story?

"But darling, you should have told me the truth much sooner," I say. My stomach turns over leaving a sour taste in my mouth.

Cecilia simply shrugs, takes a sip of her wine.

Of course, I also do not want to speak of these things, of her duplicity, not over our elegant dinner. But I can't help but be curious about us. I swallow, soften my approach. "There was—is —real chemistry between us, you have to admit that," I say. "It was instant attraction. I know you felt it, too."

"Yes, I felt it," she says. She's speaking quietly. I lean forward to hear her words. "It was wonderful. A bonus, actually. Should we look at the menu? I'm starving."

As Cecilia lifts the menu our waiter appears at the table. "What can I get for you?"

I take a deep breath and look at my bride, as if for the first time. "Are you ready to order?"

"Yes. I'll have the soupe à l'oignon gratinée, salade de chèvre chaud and the filets de lieu jaune au beurre tomate," she says. Yes, she's showing off again. No, I will not attempt to say any of that.

"I'll have the same." I hand the distinguished-looking waiter my menu, and he's gone with a nod. It seems efficiency is the name of the game here at Madame Brasserie. Impressive.

"Do you know what you ordered?" Cecilia asks, and looks amused. "Did you understand any of it?"

Snarky. It doesn't matter anymore. "Sometimes we don't

know what we're really getting into, do we? I heard salad, and soup, and some sort of filet. Sounds delicious."

"Good job. You're practically fluent," she says. I am not appreciating the sarcasm. Her face softens, her expression grows tender. "I'm sorry I wasn't completely honest with you. I mean, given the circumstances, it was too awkward, don't you agree? We met and we fell in love instantly. You felt it, and I did, too."

"That's true," I say, wanting to believe her, believe in us. I do. I am never wrong, about people or situations. I refuse to believe I have been wrong about Cecilia. I am the one in charge of our relationship. I look across the table and see worry, and love, reflected back at me.

"To answer your question more completely, we were meant to be together, Paul." Cecilia covers my hand with hers and I allow her gentle touch. It feels nice, romantic. Right. But is it all just a show? No, of course not. Cecilia is young, a woman, she isn't capable of the things I am, but she doesn't know that. My internal flame cools a bit. She loves me. I knew it. If I so choose, I'll be the one to break her heart, not the other way around. That is how my story rolls. *If I decide I don't believe you, it will be too bad, Cecilia. Lila. Whoever you are.*

I smile and take her hand in mine. "I completely agree. We're like a romance novel, a love at first sight story. I'm your knight in shining armor, so to speak," I say.

She takes a small sip of her wine. I notice neither of us has had much of our drink. I suppose we are both keeping our brains sharp, for some reason.

"It was a whirlwind relationship, that's for sure," Cecilia says. "I thought you were so handsome, so special. You were quite the romantic, at first. Remember how you brought me flowers every day for the first couple of months? You left sweet love notes for me when we had to be apart, which wasn't very often."

"And you gave up your gallery job, gave up everything, it seemed, to be with me, night and day," I said. "Was that really true?"

"What?" she asked.

"Did you really have a job at the art gallery?" I ask.

"Of course I did."

I don't know if I believe her, I want to believe her, but she's hidden so much. I bite my lip and wait for her to explain.

"I loved that job, but I loved you more. You swept me off my feet. I couldn't imagine being anywhere but with you. It didn't matter who I was before we met, I became a new person in your arms. It was like a movie, like *Pretty Woman*. Remember when you took me on that shopping spree on Worth Avenue? It was a dream."

I had just been notified by Joseph that I was, in fact, Esther's sole heir as named in the will. It was a cause for celebration, and shopping. A lot of shopping. "I remember. We spent almost a hundred thousand dollars in just a few hours."

"That was so fun. I still love everything we bought that day," she says. "Even though it seems like a lifetime ago. You were so handsome, so romantic. So good in bed."

"Thank you, my darling. The same can be said about you. Until the migraines, of course."

"And your stomach issues," she says, playing with the diamond necklace. "How are you feeling tonight?"

"So far, so good, but I haven't eaten yet," I say. "If you'll excuse me." I decide I need a break from our fun little love discussion. I need to stretch, have a look around, and think. I make my way across the restaurant and back out the door to the first-floor platform. Even at this hour, the place is crowded with tourists. Tall glass walls have been erected on every edge of the platform, I suppose to prevent accidental falls and to keep jumpers at bay, although human ingenuity always outsmarts simple barriers like these. I have read that the second platform is more special, more romantic, and that's why I also bought tickets for that lift.

We'll go up there after dinner. She'll be accustomed to heights by then, I'm sure of it. Or at least she'll pretend to be to appease me, now that she knows that I know who she really is. It's up to me to decide if it matters or not. If I believe her, or not. I knew this night would be an important test of our love, and it has proven to be true. You see, I'm always right.

Paul

I step back inside the restaurant and ask the helpful host where I can find the toilet. Across the glittering room I see Cecilia. She's on her phone, of course.

I decide I don't need to use the toilet after all. I hurry back to our table only to discover our soup has been served. I hope it hasn't been here long. Cecilia sees me coming and puts her phone away.

"Sorry, there was a line," I say, sitting down. "Hope the soup isn't cold."

"It just arrived. I told the waiter it was OK to leave them, that you would be back soon, and here you are." She smiles. I don't think it's genuine, though. "Bon appetit!"

Apparently, we ordered French onion soup. It's different than the normal presentation, though. The cheese – usually sprinkled – is in little balls on top, straddling the vat of onion soup like tightrope walkers.

"Just push those balls into the soup bowl," Cecilia says helpfully and demonstrates. "Voila!"

Why not? I push the cheese balls into the soup, squish them around for good measure before asking the obvious question.

"Darling, did you just marry me for my money?"

Cecilia smiles, her cheeks flushing a little. With embarrassment? "Of course not, silly. You weren't rich yet when we met. Remember?"

"But you knew I would be rich, didn't you? Because of Esther," I say. I take a spoonful of soup and enjoy the warm, salty onion taste. A little more bitter than what I'm used to, but I mix in some more cheese and take another bite.

"How was I to know what Esther would do with her money? Nobody did," Cecilia says. "I would have been the last to know."

I'd known, but I'm not admitting to that. She'd as much as told me I would be inheriting her estate during one of our final nights together. It was a pinch me moment. The opposite of a moment like this one. Poor little orphan Cecilia wouldn't ever see a dime, not from Esther. She must have hoped she would, though.

"Well, it was very kind of Esther indeed," I say, taking another big spoonful of soup.

"It should have been mine," Cecilia says. "I'm her daughter. Her only heir," Her eyes sparkle with amusement, and something darker. I've never seen that look on her face. "How long have you known or suspected my real identity, darling? I mean, it doesn't really change anything now, does it?"

Um, well, yes, it does. And I don't owe you any answers, darling. I take a breath, try to calm my fire. "That letter you sent to the neighbors. It really upset dear Esther. That was in very poor taste, with typos and everything. Besides, she wanted nothing to do with you, from the moment you were conceived, actually. Why didn't you just go after your father, the sperm donor?" I spoon more soup into my mouth. I need time to think.

I know I'm being mean, but she is getting ahead of me here, and this is my night.

"My father is irrelevant. I'm sure it was a one-night stand. I don't care about him. She didn't care about him. He's not even listed on my birth certificate. I cared about her." She shakes her head and chuckles. "And really? You're going to focus on my grammar right now?"

She's laughing at me again. I cannot believe this.

"It's easier than wrapping my head around the fact you've been lying to me since we met," I say. She is doing everything possible to stoke my fire. The soup isn't settling right in my stomach. A sharp stabbing sensation makes me bend forward.

"I'm not the only one with secrets, Paul, we both know that," Cecilia says. "And I didn't lie to you. I didn't know Esther, which is exactly what I told you when we sat next to each other at the funeral service. I never met the woman, despite how hard I tried. It's sad, really, that it had to come to this."

Had to come to what? I wonder. I don't know what her version of the rest of the evening is, let alone the rest of our lives together, but at this moment, just now, we are at a crossroads, that is for sure. We can either continue to dwell on my now dead paramour, my wife's biological mother, or we can move on and enjoy the rest of our final dinner together in Paris.

I push the soup away. I feel terrible.

"So, what does all this mean to you, darling?" I may as well ask, despite the rage firing in my core, the pain in my stomach. "That you, in fact, did marry me for Esther's money?"

"No, Paul, of course not," Cecilia's face softens into a look I'd call love. "Sure, at first I wanted to get close to you, sit near you, because you were the best person to learn all about Esther from. But then I fell in love with you."

Well, yes, of course she did. That much I know is true. "Go on," I say.

"I mean, how could I not fall madly in love with you? I thought you were the perfect man. Handsome, successful and so generous with your newfound fortune. And the sex, well, stupendous, in the beginning," she says. "By that point it was too late for me to tell you who I really was. I didn't want to scare you away or freak you out. I mean, I didn't know what bad things Esther had told you about her secret daughter. I didn't want anything to taint our blossoming love." Cecilia pauses, tilts her head, and leans forward. "Wow. I mean, your first wife was such a fool to leave you, wasn't she? But it was lucky for me. I was blessed when you dropped into my life. I hope you feel the same."

I stare at my wife. She thinks I'm handsome, successful, worldly. Good in bed. Does she really? Still? Now? I want to believe her, I do. I decide I won't ask any further questions about why she sought me out in the first place. I note she's cleaned her bowl of soup. Not a drop left.

But still, if I'm so perfect then who is she texting all the time? I can't imagine it would be workout buddy Christopher, I scared him. It must be food server Evan. I really need to take care of him.

"Well, my dear, I do feel the same. That's why I'm so excited for our future, our children, our happy life in Malibu," I say, although I am lying. Does she know that? Does she care?

The waiter appears. "And how was your soup?"

My stomach twists thinking about it. "A little bitter for my taste," I say.

"Oh, Paul. It was perfect, *merci*," she says. "He's a little crabby tonight, that's all."

Crabby? The waiter nods, his lips curl with a smile. Now they both are laughing at me.

And I must find the bathroom. Beads of sweat break out on my forehead.

"Paul, are you feeling OK?" Cecilia asks.

"Excuse me," I say as I hurry from the table. I feel the stare of the waiter, Cecilia and patrons at the other tables as I rush from the room. I can't be bothered to care what any of them think now. This is self-preservation time.

Cecilia

He isn't home again tonight. He said he would be. He lied again. I look around the kitchen at the elaborate meal I made for us to share. I spent hours chopping vegetables and marinating the beef tenderloin. I got a blowout, and a new outfit, just for tonight. I wanted to see if we could get back to where we were when we first married. I wanted to find out if the sparks, any of them, could still ignite. I wanted to see if he would pick me over her. Once again, he hasn't.

I walk into the dining room, a table elegantly set for two. The white taper candles remain unlit.

Some spouses put up with this type of behavior in their relationship, I suppose. Some wives are grateful, I guess, for a roof over their head and attention when it's given. But that's not me. *But not us*, our catchphrase, runs through my mind. I fear that we already are turning into an old married couple, or worse.

I turn off the chandelier and make my way upstairs to my art studio. I'll paint for a bit to take my mind off the fact that he's not here, he's not what he seemed to be when we married. I realize I need a plan. Even though this is a beautiful home, in one of the most beautiful places in the world, it is a home without love.

I can't live like that, not ever again.

Paul

Let's just say, things are not going to plan.

Fortunately, I knew where the toilet was located. Unfortunately, the French onion soup has wreaked havoc on my system. It's a terrible turn of events. Yet time is of the essence, no matter how much I'd prefer to stay locked away in the men's room. I know I must rejoin Cecilia as quickly as possible. I also know she's likely on the phone again, chatting with whoever she finds more interesting than her current company.

As I compose myself, I also remember I must reach out to Seymour Lynch, my private banker, to fire him, but all in due time.

When I finally return to my seat, facing embarrassing glances from the diners at tables close to ours, which I meet with a deathlike narrow-eyed stare, I notice Cecilia's lips glisten bright red and our next course, which appears to be a salad, has been placed on the table. Can these people not wait for me to be here before serving? *Mon dieu.*

"Welcome back. I was about to send a search party to look for you," she says. "Are you OK?"

No. My wife is a gold digger, French food kills my stomach, and I need to be in charge of this evening, which is hard to do from the toilet.

"I've felt better, but I'll be fine," I say, sitting down. "What do we have for our next course?"

"It's salade de chèvre chaud, with Parma ham, white wine vinegar, honey, and Dijon mustard," Cecilia explains. "A simple, elegant salad."

"It's amazing how much you've learned about French food during the week." Despite everything, I am actually impressed.

"I studied up on it, Paul. I didn't want to be a typical ignorant American when we arrived," she says. Big smile. She's indicating I am that.

She's gotten too big for her britches, as my mom would say. She's overconfident. Too empowered. Sure, I'm all for female empowerment, to a degree. There is a limit to what I can tolerate, even an enlightened, evolved man like me. Actually, who am I kidding? I want Cecilia barefoot and pregnant, at home, not speaking to anyone about working out, or event planning with some pinch-faced caterer, or really anything else. Just there, waiting for me to come home from a hard day of Hollywood hustle. Is that too much to ask? Susan wouldn't put up such a fuss, ever. Where's the gratitude? The love?

"Well, nice that you studied up on French cuisine, so you aren't ignorant, even though your letter to Esther would indicate otherwise. You should be sure to distance yourself from that debacle, darling. Typos do not become you," I say. Back in charge. Back on top. I take a bite of salad while she ponders how I've just checkmated her. "No one knocked on Esther's door, just to be clear. It seems it was swept under seventeenth-century rugs across West Palm, if you even sent that embarrassing letter to her neighbors. No one said a peep to your biological mother."

Cecilia smiles. "I sent out fifty copies, just so you know. It was worth a shot. The salad is good, right?"

Across from me, my wife has a tiny piece of lettuce glued to her red lips. Will I tell her that? No, I will not. She is poking a tiger tonight, this one. But I will keep her in line from here on out.

"It's good," I say. "You don't find it to be too tart, like it leaves a burning sensation in your mouth?"

"No, not at all. You and French food are just trouble together, I think," Cecilia says. "As for children, well, it just wasn't on the cards for us, at least not yet. Maybe never."

Yes, maybe never, I've come to realize. "Do you think it's some sort of fertility issue, darling? I mean, it does happen," I say.

"You're the old man here," she says. It's sharp and sudden, like when you're happily petting a cat and it turns on you, hissing and swatting at you with its claws sharp and menacing. It's why I don't like cats. I especially didn't like Mrs. Dosier's cat, Tyson. But I handled him when I was ten. I can handle this now.

"Excuse me. I'm the father of two, I'll remind you," I say. "Clearly the infertility is not my issue. I'm quite virile."

She smiles again. I'm so tired of her smile-laughing at me. "You were, but maybe things have changed. Maybe it is you?"

"Impossible," I say. Another wave of nausea sweeps through me. I'm unsure whether I can make it through even half of my salad. This is a costly problem. All of this.

"No, it's not. Men's sperm counts fluctuate over time, with age, with all sorts of reasons," she says.

I see she's somehow removed the green piece of lettuce from her lip. The dagger diamond glistens at her cleavage. She really is stunning. A gorgeous mistake. You really can't fault me for believing this was real. Not when you look at her, am I right?

Is she right about the sperm count? Could this lack of a child be my fault? My stomach stabs at me again as I mull the thought over. I'd hate to believe that it could be me, but she has a point.

"I didn't know that. I just assumed because, well, I have Sam and Mikey," I say. I don't like to be wrong, and as soon as I get home, I will have this checked out. I mean, Susan and I would make beautiful babies together. Will make beautiful babies together.

"You don't actually have Sam and Mikey anymore, do you, though?" she says.

She is chewing a big bite of lettuce. She looks a bit like a cow and that makes me happy. But she's also bringing up the past and that's not allowed.

"You kind of abandoned them, like Esther did to me," she continues. Chomp, chomp, chomp on the lettuce.

"I did no such thing. And really, Esther just never wanted a kid. Not you. Not anyone," I say. "You were a big mistake, a one-night stand with a yoga instructor, something to forget about. My boys? I'm their father. There is no comparison."

"You know my biological father got money from her when she gave me away? She paid him to sign away his rights to me. So ridiculous. He never reached out to me either, just cashed Esther's big check and travelled to yoga retreats around the world. She was an idiot to pay him, but not ever think about me," Cecilia says.

"She had so much, it really didn't matter," I say. "And you didn't exist to her. Do you get that now?" Yes, that's cruel and to the point. On the nose, as they say. I can't help it. She is pushing me so hard, too hard.

"Yes, just like you don't to your sons," she says quietly. "It's sad you don't even know where they live, isn't it?"

I feel my cheeks flush and, on my lap, my hands clench into fists.

Dear Diary,

I'm so ready for him to come home tomorrow. It's been awful since he left. I haven't had a single audition, and I can't shake the feeling that someone tried to kill me. I'm certain now that the driver of the white car tried to run me over. I'm shaking as I run through a list of people who might hate me enough to do that. Who would want to kill me? I know it wasn't an accident. The way the car mounted the pavement and came straight for me. There's only one person, really, that comes to mind. But she wouldn't dare, would she? Although the more I think about it, the more I remember the brief glance at the beautiful angry face behind the wheel, the more I come to a conclusion. I think it was my sister. I mean, yes, I have a vivid imagination. I'm an artist, an actor, I must. But it's just a feeling. If she's found out I'm here in Southern California, and she's discovered who my lover is, well, that could make her a bit angry. I realize my heart is pounding in my chest. It could make her furious to say the least.

I promised not to text or call him while he was away, but I think I need to warn him, tell him what's happening. He'd want to know I'm in danger, wouldn't he?

I text him to call me. He doesn't. He hasn't answered his phone all week. I've left so many voicemails. I'm afraid he's forgotten all about me.

He's finally texted me back!!! He's said he can't wait to see me, and that he wants to take me for a romantic escape to Santa

Barbara as soon as he's back. I've told him that I'd love that, but that he needs to call me, that it's urgent.

I'm watching my phone. I can tell he's silenced notifications from me again.

OK, diary. I will wait until tomorrow. Nothing bad will happen to me tonight, she's in Paris, too, after all. And soon he'll be on a plane on his way back to me.

I'll dream about Santa Barbara. I'll find out what the best resort is and suggest we stay there. Oooh, I really cannot wait. And when I tell him all I know, he'll be relieved he has me. And we'll be together forever.

FORTY-SIX
PARIS, 11:00 P.M.

Paul

I push my salad away from me, hoping the waiter will be by soon. It tastes awful, worse with each bite.

"You should eat that, Paul. It's delicious," Cecilia says. If she's aware of how angry her words are making me, she's good at pretending she doesn't see it. Maybe my wife is good at pretending, period.

"I'm full at the moment. What is our next course?" I ask. And now I know she'll rattle something off in French just to prove she is sophisticated.

She does.

"I don't know what that means," I say. I'm fuming, my stomach hurts and I'm still an idiot when it comes to French, even after a week here in Paris.

"It means we will be eating line-caught pollack with fresh tomatoes, chive butter, cream and crumbled thyme. Sounds marvelous, yes?" she says.

Actually, it sounds like another bathroom trip, but I am sort of hungry, in between bouts of nausea, sweating and a strange acidic taste in my mouth. "Yes, it will be good."

"You know, another issue with us getting pregnant could be that each time you ejaculate, you have a lower sperm count with each successive time, and given your age, well, you might just be running out of juice," she says as if it's perfectly normal to talk about this sort of thing in a fancy restaurant.

The waiter appears. "All finished, monsieur?"

"Oui," I say, and I don't care if I sound terrible. What is she talking about? Why is she talking about my sperm count at our romantic Eiffel Tower dinner? I stare at Cecilia, and I know I must look shocked.

"Lifestyle choices can lower sperm numbers, Paul, it's a fact," she says. She's still chomping on salad. She has no manners, no couth. "Smoking, drinking alcohol, taking certain medications can do it, too. Oh, and low testosterone."

"I do not have low testosterone." I fold my arms across my chest.

"Well, it's a fact that male fertility generally starts to decrease around age forty, and you are well past that," she says. "It's just a fact."

"I don't know who is putting all of these ideas in your head," I say.

"It's just a few internet searches, Paul. But if you want to know what I really think it is, well, you're spreading yourself too thin," she says. She's finally finished shoveling salad into her mouth and has placed her fork and knife, appropriately, at four o'clock on the plate. At least she's finally learned that from me. Esther would have croaked over her lack of manners, lack of a proper upbringing. Well, I guess it's actually Esther's fault. She could have at least checked on the poor wretch.

I realize now that I need to find my boys. I don't want them to end up not knowing about proper fork and knife placement, not at all. Maybe they should come live with me? I have three extra bedrooms, a swimming pool and tennis court. They'll probably be handsome and not as much work by now. Yes, this could be the answer. An instant family, so to speak. Credibility. Perhaps Sam will want to become an actor. Mikey could be a producer like me. They will marry California girls, with blonde hair and killer beach volleyball skills. Yes, this is a great solution.

Why does Cecilia think I'm spreading myself too thin? A ping of warning has gone off in my brain, replacing the fond thoughts of my boys living under my gilded roof.

"Oh, darling, you think I'm working too hard?" I ask. "I promise I'm not. Hollywood is invigorating, and I've made such headway."

"I'm not talking about Hollywood. I'm talking about your little love nest in Brentwood," she hisses.

Oh no. A smile dies on my lips as my stomach lurches. She knows about Susan. How? I was so careful. But from the way she's staring at me, it's true. She knows.

"Why would you talk about Brentwood?" I ask, hoping beyond hope she's clueless.

"Because that's where your mistress is, the one you have coffee with at a trendy shop, the one you go on walks around the block with, the one you have spread yourself too thin with," Cecilia says. "It's your fault we aren't pregnant. No one else is to blame. I followed you to your little love nest. How could you think I wouldn't find out about her?"

I look out the window to our spectacular view of Paris sparkling below us. Behind Cecilia, a couple share a romantic kiss at their table. Things at our table are not going that well, not at all. I don't have an answer for Susan, and I don't need one, although I am a bit surprised with the level of detail my wife is using to describe something that is none of her business. Susan doesn't need to be discussed over our last meal. Not at all.

"I guess you could be right. Maybe my sperm are tired," I say, although I cannot possibly imagine that to be the case. My mind is spinning. I still can't work out how she knows about Susan. I need to deflect. "But it could still be you."

"Maybe it is. How long have you been cheating on me, Paul?" she asks, and a silence descends on our table. I imagine the couples at the adjoining tables are leaning in, ready for a show.

"I'm not cheating on you, darling," I say.

"You are. And it's disgusting," Cecilia says. "I've followed you, and I've followed her. When you started having business at night, and overnight, I knew something was up. I'm not stupid, Paul. I know her type well, let's just say. But it's all good, I suppose, I've come to terms with the situation, although I'm not sure how to handle it all. Should I file for divorce?"

"Sir, can I bring you a different salad?" The waiter has appeared as if from nowhere. "You've barely touched this."

"I know, and it was so good. Just saving myself for the main course," I say.

The waiter looks at me suspiciously, mirroring how Cecilia is looking at me. Deny, deny, deny.

Paul

"I mean, I don't understand why I wasn't enough for you. We're newlyweds. Did you think I wouldn't notice the lipstick on your collar, on your handkerchief? You force me to help with your precious laundry. Did you leave clues on purpose?" Cecilia is asking me now. "This is a lovely dinner, though, despite everything."

Everything. Does that encompass the fact that she married me to snatch away half of Esther's estate, or the fact I apparently have a low sperm count, a mistress, a very sour stomach, and that my hands are now trembling no matter how much I try to hold them still? Or is there something else?

"Lovely," I agree. "It's nice to spend some time alone together, without all of your male admirers."

"Don't even start with that when you have Susan," she says. As if it's fact. "She's very young, Paul, eight years younger than me, and I'm too young for you."

How the heck does she know how old my paramour is? Lucky guess, I suppose. Again, deny. Pivot. "I don't know who you're referring to, but you certainly have a full dance card, don't you, darling?" I say. "You're like Aphrodite, the Greek goddess of sexual love and beauty. I love Greek mythology."

"Aphrodite, am I? That's great," Cecilia says. "I always wanted to be considered a goddess. So Paul, now we're really talking, being honest with each other, did you get Esther's estate all as a lump sum, or are your payouts over time?"

None of your business, I want to say. But here's an opportunity for me, should I choose to take it. If I make her think that, say, only a quarter of the estate is mine now, she'll expect to receive half of that quarter, should she somehow negate the prenup. It won't come to that, but it's a fun game to be playing with her right now. I mean, we still haven't had our main course. Speaking of, this is the longest dinner in history. Where is the main course? My stomach lurches at the thought of food, but I will attempt to at least have a couple of bites. I paid up front for this evening's adventure, so I intend to make the most of it.

"I've only been gifted a quarter of the estate," I say. "And that may be all I get. Probate is a long process, assets must be liquidated and sold to pay off any debts, but I'm just blessed with whatever comes my way. Just so lucky."

"I wouldn't call it luck," she says. "You're an opportunist, Paul. Some would say worse, that you're like a predator. You found an old, lonely woman who wanted to feel sexy and desired again, and you preyed on her. You are an expert."

I thought she'd said I was her sexy, handsome husband earlier. "I am not a predator. Don't be ridiculous. Where is the waiter? I need to order another drink."

"Did you ever feel guilty, I mean for pretending that Esther was everything and then having one-night stands behind her back? Yes, I know the truth. The staff talk, darling," Cecilia says. She's twisting the diamond around her neck like she's spinning a top.

"I don't know what you're talking about," I say as my stomach churns.

"Yes, you do, Paul. I know you, what you've done."

"Of course, you know me. You're my wife. But I don't understand why you're being so mean, insinuating I'm not who I seem. I am a man of good character." I take a big gulp of my vodka. I'm restless. I want to eat whatever she ordered us for our main course and then I want to go up to the second platform. I literally can't think of anything else right now as the fire rages inside me.

"What about me? How do you think I feel?" Cecilia abruptly stops talking as our long-lost waiter finally appears. For once, I am grateful for his appearance, and also for once I'm here when the food arrives.

"*Le poisson,*" he says and places our plates in front of us, Cecilia's first. Although it looks appetizing, my stomach twists at the sight of more food. But I need my strength. The waiter nods. "Anything else?"

"Another Chardonnay," says Cecilia. "*Merci.*"

"Nothing for me right now," I say. I've decided not to order another drink because I need to keep my wits about me. There will be time for that later. I take a bite. The fish is cooked to perfection and tastes buttery, with hints of herbs. *Good choice, Cecilia.*

Too bad I made a terrible choice by picking her in the first place. Such an unfortunate development. But it is what it is. And I have my plans.

Cecilia stares at me. "I said, what about me? How do you think I feel?"

"About what?" I ask. Why are women so confusing sometimes?

"About the fact you have Susan, that you set her up in a bungalow in Brentwood. That you have a fucking lover when we are newlyweds?" Her voice has dropped to a dark, quiet level. Her face has formed a frown. The diamond dagger glints from her neck, taunting me.

Paul

Cecilia isn't eating. She has a plate full of *poisson* something getting cold while she watches me eat. I am chewing large bites with gusto so I don't need to talk. Can't talk. We've said enough. I wish, however, that Cecilia had had more to drink by now. That would make her more likely to talk without thinking, less likely to think at all, to be frank. I just need her to stop thinking, stop watching me. Regardless, she is a woman, and therefore I am in control of this situation.

"Suddenly starving, are you?" she asks. She takes a big chug of her Chardonnay. Good girl.

"Uh-huh," I say, still chewing. "So good. Tress bean."

"Ugh, not 'tress bean.' You need to stop trying to speak French. It's embarrassing. You're embarrassing," she says. "It's *très*, pronounced like the English word tray which means very, and *bien*, like bee-an. We have been here for a week. How hard is it to say two simple words correctly?"

"Tray difficult," I say. We lock eyes.

You see, before, as in twenty-four hours ago when we were

still in love and exploring the streets of Paris, getting lost on the Left Bank, drinking rosé at random cafés, not making love, but having fun, it wasn't so hard. Sure there was tension between us, and I was worried about who Cecilia really was, but tonight there is a sharp edge to things. Cecilia has pulled a glinting blade out and we are both getting nicked. It's only a matter of time before blood is flowing.

"*Difficile*," she says. "*Très difficile*. Like you. I don't know how Esther put up with it, and now Susan too."

I check the table for drops of blood—mine—before reminding myself my lovely bride does not hold a knife. Not in actuality.

I'm chewing another large bite when my stomach spasms with pain. It's all I can do not to groan and cause a scene. I will not cause a scene at Madame Brasserie. No, I will not. I will instead focus on the city of Paris twinkling below us, all the lovers and poets and writers and thieves swirling below this very tower right now, imagining themselves dining in luxury atop the Iron Lady.

"Esther was a remarkable and generous woman who loved me as I loved her," I say. "You should order another glass of wine."

"Maybe I will," Cecilia says. "You look ill. Are you ill, Paul?"

"Stupid French food. It's all this sauce, it must be," I say, but for some reason cannot stop myself from eating it. Anger fires up a certain appetite, an appetite that is hard to satiate.

The waiter appears. "You do not like your fish, madame?"

Cecilia brightens in his presence. "Oh, *oui*, I love it. It's just that we are having a disagreement, so I've lost my appetite. Apparently, it all went to him. I'll have another glass of wine, please."

"Of course," he says and backs away. Now that he knows we're having a disagreement, he's giving me the stink eye. As if this is my fault. It's not. Cecilia is the one with the problem, trust me.

I have a feeling now that jealousy is a large part of Cecilia's foul mood this evening. Esther loved me and seems to have abandoned her, if Cecilia's little origin story is to be believed. Sure, that must be tough being abandoned and repeatedly rejected. It must mess with you. But it's life. There are winners, and losers. I need to begin my next plan. I had hoped this would be enough for me. This gorgeous young woman with the big laugh, red lips, sexy pout. I had hoped we would be parents by now, tucking our precious firstborn into an over-the-top, decorator-designed nursery that would be featured in a glossy magazine, along with Paul Jr. and his adoring parents. Or, in the case of a baby girl, Esther. Of course, her name would be Esther. But then again, now that she knows about Susan, I will need to revise my dreams considerably.

"Darling, shall we move past this little argument, at least for tonight?" I say. I've finished my fish and I'm ready to go. After she has another glass of compliance, that is. I know if she agrees to calm down, there will still be a big blow-up later. I take a deep breath. Come to think of it, I'd like a glass of wine, too.

Cecilia nods. "Sure, Paul, I can let it go."

Relief washes over me, even though I'm not certain I believe her. I shoot my hand in the air and wave the waiter over.

He is not pleased. He smiles at Cecilia and places her wine in front of her.

"Finished?" he asks, pointing to her untouched meal.

"*Oui, merci,*" she says.

"Look, I'm finished, too, and I actually cleaned my plate," I say.

The waiter looks at me like I have sprouted two heads. He grabs my plate without comment and turns to leave.

"Hey, wait, I'll have a glass of Burgundy, please," I say. I'm impressed with my pronunciation. They both should be, too.

"White or red?" the waiter says with clear distaste.

What? I look across the table at Cecilia. She's reapplied her blood-red lipstick. She's laughing at me again. I really hate that. I think I hate that more than anything in the world. I do not like to be laughed at. My father used that tactic. Humiliation. It was his way of winning the battles of my youth. But in the end, I won the war. I always win the war.

"Do you want a glass of red Burgundy or a white Burgundy?" Cecilia asks. "It's not a tough question."

I look at Cecilia, and then the waiter. "Bring a glass of each. I'll decide later. And the check." I turn away and look back out over the city. He is dismissed.

"No dessert, madame?" he asks. Why is he still at our table?

"No, thank you," Cecilia says. I see the side of her face reflected in the glass.

She turns toward the window and our reflections meet. I do not like what I see, not anymore.

FORTY-NINE

BRENTWOOD, TWO WEEKS AGO

Cecilia

I love shopping in Brentwood, this part of Brentwood, and of course, the bookstore at the Country Mart is famous. I stopped in as they opened the doors. I'm trying to read more books. It's good for you, reading, and it opens your mind. I've been studying personalities a bit. There are books that can help you figure out why you are the way you are, and why your partner is the way he is.

Books can't change things. They just help you see things more clearly. And that's important, especially if you need things to change.

Especially if you need everything to change.

I park my car in front of her neighbor's house. Most of her neighbors have gone off to work by now. She's still inside. She's likely still in bed. The house is a charming bungalow, Spanish-style, with red tile roof, and an arch over the doorway. It's romantic, cozy, and lovely, and I can just imagine how pleased she is with the place. I imagine the interior decorated in simple neutral fabrics, a lot of white linen. She likes to dress in white,

I've noticed, thin dresses that reveal her perfect figure when she stands in the sunlight.

She isn't alone, I know.

I followed him here again last night, just like I did when I discovered this little love nest for the first time. He didn't come home, so I came back.

His car, the one we laughed in, and made love in, as we drove across the country, is parked in front of her home. As if it doesn't matter, as if he doesn't care who could see him.

Does he know she's my sister of sorts? Does he know she was the baby my first parents fell in love with? The girl who had the life I should have had? The girl I've never stopped watching? She stole everything from me as a child, and now she's trying to steal Paul. Does he know who she is? Is that why he's doing this? To mock me, to taunt me with my own past?

I won't let him win.

And she will not win again.

FIFTY

Paul

Cecilia suddenly pushes away from our table and stands up. "Excuse me."

That snaps me out of my reflection trance.

"Wait. We haven't paid the check yet. I bet they charge an arm and a leg for these drinks. Where are you going?"

She smiles. It's not a friendly smile. "To powder my nose."

My nerves relax a bit. "Oh, of course." I attempt to stand as a sign of whatever it is when men stand for a woman, or hold the door open—gallantry, or something—but my stomach hurts so I just stay seated. "I'll be right here when you get back, darling."

She shakes her head and walks away. The waiter appears with three glasses of wine and his credit card reader.

"Monsieur," he says. If he thinks he's going to get a tip after how he's behaved tonight, well, he's got crazy notions. Besides, the French don't like tipping. They're weird that way. Me, I'd always want a tip, an incentive to do things better, to perform. And of course, I would always earn the maximum, if I were to ever find myself needing to be in a low-level position such as this.

I slip my platinum American Express into the reader. He pulls it out without comment, plops it on the table and flits away. I am left only with the choice of red or white wine. Well, that's not my only choice. Since moving to Malibu from Florida I've discovered the joy of hummingbirds. I know that sounds odd, but they are fascinating and beguiling little creatures. I've had the staff set up feeders throughout the property and I'm often surrounded by the little birds as I walk around the grounds.

The day that stands out the most, in regards to humming-birds and other matters, was the day Lola, one of my staff, was filling the hummingbird feeder closest to the tennis courts in the backyard. She's lovely, Lola is, and seeing her care about my hummingbirds, well, I must admit it was a fun scene to reflect upon.

Apparently she felt my gaze, as soon enough she waved and blushed, her hand with the glass pitcher of sugar water visibly shaking. Poor girl. I hurried to her side.

"Thank you for feeding these magnificent birds, Lola. They seem to like you," I said with a big smile to indicate my pleasure with her, the day, the birds. Mostly her. She is a beautiful girl with large brown eyes, shiny hair, a perfect little nose. I don't know why I hadn't noticed her before. Hummingbirds buzzed all around us. It was like we were in a Disney movie or some-thing. Everything was too perfect.

"My pleasure, sir, I love them, too," Lola said. "Did you know, back in Mexico, where I come from, my people call them *chuparosas?*"

I moved closer and took the pitcher of water from her hand so she could screw the feeder back together. Our hands brushed lightly, and I felt it. The telltale zing of attraction. She was flirting with me, of course. While Cecilia was the lady of the house, and clearly, the man of the house wasn't interested in anything so close to home as of yet, the notion was rather thrilling. A love nest within a love nest, perhaps?

"What does *chuparosas* mean?" I asked, leaning forward ever so slightly. I resisted the urge to tuck a stray wisp of hair behind her ear. Too much, I decided, too soon.

"It means rose-sucker," she said. "Some believe they are magical when it comes to love. They catch them, kill them and package their dried remains with a prayer."

"How barbaric," I said, staring into her intense brown eyes. "Poor little creatures."

"*Si*," she said. "The *chuparosa* charms are not good for the hummingbirds. But the people think the hummingbirds are good for them. For love."

Well, there you had it. "Let's not believe any of that nonsense, shall we?"

"Oh, I don't, sir. Do you want to know what the prayer says, the one they put inside the *chuparosa* charm?" she asked. The sun was getting quite warm on my back, and I'd had enough of this, but she was lovely and she was feeding my birds, not dehydrating them, so I had to be thankful for that.

"Tell me. What is the prayer?" I asked.

"The prayer calls on the bird to give the owner the powers to possess and enjoy any woman he wants, whether she be a maiden, married or a widow." She kept her eyes fixed on something on the lawn.

Well, some of us didn't need a dead hummingbird to have these powers, thank goodness. I handed her the pitcher.

"But that's absurd. A bird can't do that. You know that, right? These people should be ashamed of themselves. What idiots!"

"Yes, sir," she said. "Excuse me."

I watched her walk down the path through the garden in search of the next feeder. For the time being, the spell she'd cast over me had been broken. But here, alone at my fancy dinner, my last night in Paris, Lola's dazzling brown eyes are welcome company.

I look across the room and spot Cecilia walking back to our table. I guess I should be happy she didn't vanish, call a cab and disappear completely. She could have done that, I suppose.

I did google the whole hummingbird situation, just to be sure Lola wasn't telling me a tall tale. She was, in fact, correct. The most common presentation of a love charm is for the dried body of the hummingbird to be enclosed in a red paper tube surrounded by red satin thread, and with the head and beak exposed. A "Made in Mexico" sticker is often attached to the outside of the packet.

The typical breed used in the charms is the ruby-throated hummingbird, which nests exclusively in the US and visits Mexico only in the breeding season, poor things. They are on vacation to mate, and they're caught and killed in the name of love.

Cecilia's red dress catches my eye, wrapped tightly around her like red satin thread. There really is such little space between love and hate, life and death, for all of us.

FIFTY-ONE

MALIBU, CALIFORNIA, TWO MONTHS AGO

Cecilia

I arrive at Mr. Seymour Lynch's office in downtown LA early. I want to be sure I impress him with my professionalism. I already know Paul's banker likes me. Every time I've been around him, he flirts with me and hangs on my every word. He's one of the guys at the parties who I make a hasty escape from as soon as I can.

Seymour even purchased one of my seascapes the last time he was a guest at our home. He has a crush on me. I know it.

"Cecilia, so good to see you," he greets me, throwing open the door to his grand office and taking both of my hands in his. "Come right in!" Seymour turns back to his assistant. "Please do not disturb us. Hold all calls."

"Yes, Mr. Lynch, of course," the assistant says.

I'm important because of all the money Paul has parked with this particular bank. Our money. I'm not certain how much, but enough that we are VIPs.

"Please take a seat. What can I do for you?" he asks.

"I'd like to open my own bank account with a credit card to

go with it. I need to build up my credit," I explain. I've dressed in a Chanel suit and I'm literally dripping in jewelry. I find I don't dress for men, especially not my husband, not anymore. Lately I've been dressing for revenge. "I mean, Paul and I share everything and we're so in love, but because the house and all our bank accounts are just in his name, it's all on his credit report. It's very 1970s, don't you agree?"

"Yes, I do, in fact. Women need to build up their own credit. Let me just get you all set up here. I'll transfer a million into your account to start. Sound good?"

"Sure, great," I say. I really want to know the overall amount Paul received from Esther. I need to find out. "Can you tell me the balance in the primary account?"

Seymour clicks his keyboard a few more times. "This account, and I'm not privy to your overall net worth statement, but we manage more than eighty million dollars for your family, you and your husband."

"Fantastic," I say. I can't believe Paul only spent one year with Esther and got such a huge windfall. It's incredible, in so many ways.

"Here are your temporary checks. Your credit card will arrive in the next couple of days. The name on the account is Cecilia Strom," he says.

"Oh, actually, could you add my maiden name, please? For my credit card and bank account?" I say. "It's Babcock. Cecilia Babcock Strom."

"Of course." A few clicks of the keyboard. "All set."

I thank him profusely and head to my next LA errand, one that has become a regular mission for me since the first time, months ago, when I followed Paul after he said he was going to his office, and instead I tailed him while he drove to his lover's house. I watched them embrace for the first time a month ago. And since then, I've discovered who she is.

And now she's my new obsession. My favorite activity.

Following Susan.

Paul's lover.

The conniving Susan Sinclair. The taker. Everything Susan wants, Susan gets. First my adoptive parents and their loving home, and now Paul. She must be stopped.

It's a regular pastime for me these days, stalking her, so to speak. I get in my car, drive from Malibu after the morning rush hour, and follow Susan around. I know where she gets her lattes, I know where she takes acting classes. She likes to window-shop on Melrose Avenue on occasion, but can't afford to buy anything. She's always home when he arrives, anxious to greet him at the door.

Usually wearing nothing but a smile.

Paul

Cecilia slips into her seat. "Which one are you going to have, Paul?"

She's thrown me off with her questions again. What is she talking about?

"I know you're used to having anything you want, anyone you want, whenever you want it. Like me and Susan, at the same time," she says. She reaches across the table and grabs my glass of red Burgundy. Next, she seizes my white. I watch as she pours some of the red wine into the white wine crystal glass.

"What are you doing?" I ask.

"Making it so you don't have to choose," she says. She is very pleased with herself. I am not.

"Give me my wine. You're ruining both glasses," I say. I grab the now pink-colored white. She is acting like a spoiled child. I feel the flicker of rage ignite into a burning torch.

"You ruin everything you touch," she says.

My stomach clenches and I feel as if I may be sick. No one, no woman, speaks to me like this. Especially not my wife.

"Let's go." I stand up. I know my command is abrupt, but she needs to know where we both stand. One of us is in charge. The other is under my control. "Now."

I am aware the diners seated closest to us are at once staring and not, ignoring us with disgust.

"Oh, of course, whatever you say, dear." She smiles at me, the menacing smile, as she stands up.

Who is this creature? I have built everything we have for her. She owes me her entire life. *You ruin everything you touch.*

I reach for Cecilia, grab her, gently of course, by her upper arm. We manage an awkward but hasty exit, and before long we're outside on platform one. It's time to take the lift to platform two. It will be more private up there.

"Let go of my arm, Paul," Cecilia says. "You're hurting me."

I'm not, I am certain of that, but I release my grip and instead wrap my arm around her waist. "It's such a perfect evening, isn't it?"

"Where do you think you're going? The lift down is right there," she says, pointing.

"We are going up, my darling. We still haven't seen the view from the next platform up. It's supposed to be spectacular, and it's our last night together," I say as I hustle toward the lift line, arm around Cecilia like a lasso on a bull.

She starts digging her heels in, hitting my arm like an untamed creature. I see people turn to stare at us. I cannot have a scene. I let her go.

"Stop it already. It's supposed to be great up there. You're acting like I'm being unkind, when I'm just trying to salvage our best night ever." I know my teeth are ground down tight and my jaw is twitching.

"I am not going up there with you." She folds her arms across her chest, and the diamond dagger glares at me. "I am going back to the hotel. Now."

"But darling." I reach out and touch her shoulder. She takes a step back.

I feel a hand on my shoulder. "Is there a problem here, ma'am?"

I turn around. A huge man, from the sounds of it from Kentucky or somewhere similar, stares down at me. He looks like he should be wearing a muscle shirt, but he's not.

"Mind your own business, dickhead," I say, shoving his paw off my shoulder.

"No, we're fine," Cecilia says. "Thank you, though. I appreciate it."

Whatever. "Please, darling, lead the way to the lift," I say, tossing a final stink eye toward the redneck.

I follow behind Cecilia, noticing how the crowd parts for her, how men stare at her, women, too. I watch her power in the world, as if for the first time.

For a moment, as I watch Cecilia part the crowd, I consider turning around. I think about letting her go. I could fly home in the morning, drive to Brentwood, have a lovely afternoon with Susan. I could forget all about this grand mistake I have made. And I would do that, forget all about her, if it weren't for the money.

My money. She will not get her hands on any more of it, I assure you. I can hear the words of the song "She Works Hard For The Money" in my mind. I mentioned that since Mia threatened me, forced a divorce, and took my boys away, I had to hurry out of Ohio. I may have had to take menial jobs just to pay my bills. I'll never admit it publicly, of course, but until I could acquire the right clothes, the right address, the right peripheral friends, I could not attract my prey at the clubs—yacht, golf, tennis or otherwise. I needed to watch and study my prey. I needed to look the part. I needed to take my time. And I did. Once I was in the orbit of the rich widows, I would not be ousted. I worked my way up until I found my Esther. My happily ever after. My huge inheritance. My freedom. My new start. No one will come between the money and me.

Yes, at the moment it does seem as if she has the upper hand. *Perhaps that's by design, ma cherie.*

Perhaps the night, as they say, is still young. There is much more to be done.

FIFTY-THREE

PARIS, 12:15 A.M.

Paul

The lift line moves swiftly and we stand side by side, not touching, ignoring each other really, each lost in our own thoughts, until we're safely back on terra firma.

"I'm not walking back," Cecilia announces. "The taxi is waiting just over there."

Well, that's some progress. She didn't just ditch me. "Thank you for including me."

Cecilia rolls her eyes before plunging into the still robust crowd circling below the Eiffel Tower. These people probably shouldn't feel comfortable standing so close to the tower, not anymore, because this is the number one terrorist target in Europe. We made it down unscathed, well, almost.

I help Cecilia into the black car and slide in after her. We speed away through the streets of the city, closing in on our hotel in no time. Up ahead, though, on our now all-too-familiar Avenue Kléber, there is a police blockade.

"Nous ne pouvons pas conduire dans la rue," the taxi driver says.

"What? What's going on?" I ask.

"He says we can't drive any further. We're going to need to walk the rest of the way," Cecilia says. "Nous sortirons ici!"

The driver pulls to the curb. I realize we're only a block from the hotel. We've passed this way so many times before, without incident. And now, tonight, when I'm expecting our quiet, elegant street, there is a police presence. Of course. Best night ever.

"Paul, can you pay him?" Cecilia says as she slips out of the car.

Crap. I don't have any small euros. I read the meter. Eleven euros. I have a fifty. I like big bills, they look impressive. Until you're in a hurry with a taxi guy. Wait, why isn't Cecilia paying if this is a taxi she called?

"Um, darling, you ordered this car. Just pay online." I smile as I slide out of the back seat and join her on the sidewalk.

"Pardon?" the driver yells from the car. "The fare? The meter?"

For the first time I notice him. He turns around in the front seat to face me as I lean in through the back door. He's acting rather menacingly, really, for such a small number of euros.

"Paul, pay him," Cecilia says.

I reach into my pocket, grab my wallet, extract a fifty and hand it to him. His eyes are dark, with some sort of edge I can't explain.

"I do not have change for this," the driver says.

Just then, my stomach twists and it's all I can do to stand straight.

"Keep the change," Cecilia says over my shoulder. "Come, Paul. Let's go see what's going on down the street. Big fun."

Fine. He can keep the change. I have more than enough where that came from. And soon, once Cecilia and I are through, I will have control of it all. I will not make the mistake of sharing any of my fortune with another bride. No, this will be my final marriage, final mistake.

"Look. Am I hallucinating or is that a bunch of Nazis over there?" Cecilia says, pointing to a group of men very clearly dressed in German military uniforms from World War Two.

"How odd," I say as we walk closer. The street in front of our hotel is aglow with lights. Just in front of us, a German tank sits on the sidewalk. The hotel across the street from ours is the focus of the movie set. It has been renamed "The Majestic" with a big banner. Nazi guards stand on either side of the hotel's entrance. The entire scene is eerie and exhilarating at the same time.

"Keep moving, this is a closed set," a guy with a clipboard says to Cecilia and I as he walks by.

"This is, in fact, a street in front of our hotel," I say. *One you would never be able to afford to stay in*, I almost add.

"In France, we can close the streets for filming. And we did. So, bye-bye," smug movie guy says. Hollywood people for you.

"What are you filming? Just tell us and we'll move along," Cecilia says. She's giving him her best flirty look.

"It's the story of Coco Chanel. She stayed here at The Majestic, during the occupation, with her Nazi lover," he says.

"Coco Chanel? She was a spy? A double agent?" Cecilia asks. She has recently become a big fan of the beauty brand. I say recently because we all know she wouldn't have been able to afford to even look at anything but a Chanel knockoff before we married. Now, her closet is filled with authentic Chanel bags in a rainbow of colors and styles. Isn't she lucky?

Smug movie guy chuckles. "No, she was a Nazi sympathizer. You and your dad have a good night."

Cecilia looks at me and I know she knows I'm about to explode. For her part, she's trying to keep from laughing. If she laughs, I will erupt.

"Come on, let's go have a nightcap. I just cannot believe that about Coco," she says, pulling me by the hand.

As much as I'd like to pummel smug movie guy, I need to keep my eye on the goal. Tonight is not about him. If he's still around in the morning, perhaps it can be about him then. I give him my famous stare.

He drops his smug grin and finds something interesting on the clipboard. He saw me, I allowed him to see me. I smile as he turns away. He's the one hanging out with Nazis. What? I'm harmless. I'm just a guy on a date with a beautiful young woman who happens to be my wife in the City of Light.

"Paul, come on," Cecilia says. "Stop being menacing."

Menacing? Moi?

FIFTY-FOUR

PARIS, 1:00 A.M.

Paul

When I was making my way from Ohio to Florida, I spent some time in Savannah, Georgia. Among the spirits and moss, among the dead and the living. I blended in somehow in that damp Southern place. I could have stayed, actually, if my needs hadn't pulled me away.

There was no way I'd have found what I needed in Savannah. But for a bit, I found my Eden. Do you remember *Midnight in the Garden of Good and Evil?* True story, set right there in Savannah. But I like the older South—the Savannah of the slave trades, and metal spiked fences to keep people from running away. The dark evil comes out there in the evenings; it's a shared memory the place holds into itself like a humid, cloudless night. Heavy, oppressive. But bigger than any one person's troubles, that's for sure.

But I digress. It is after midnight, but it's Paris. The sky is clear, the air is crisp and Cecilia wants a nightcap. Aside from the Nazis milling about on the street, everything is, finally, as it should be.

We walk inside the lobby of our luxurious hotel, greeted as always by the crisply uniformed doorman. The concierge team and registration staff greet us by name and welcome us back.

"How was your evening, Mr. and Mrs. Strom?" one of the hotel clerks asks with a smile.

"Perfect," I say.

"How long is the movie shoot going to last?" Cecilia asks, hustling up to the staff to get the gossip. "And was it common knowledge that Coco Chanel was a Nazi sympathizer?"

"*Non, madame*, that was kept from us French people. She was sent to Switzerland after the war and returned with her reputation untarnished. She stayed here, at this hotel, you know, during that time," the clerk says.

"What? I thought she was at The Majestic," Cecilia says. I'm fascinated by her fascination with the story, I must admit. I'm in a hurry, but this is amusing.

"Madame, this was The Majestic. Here. The Peninsula Hotel. Where you stand. It was the Nazi headquarters during the occupation," the clerk says.

Wow. I can't help but look around, try to imagine if these walls could talk. So much evil transpired here, I imagine.

"Did you hear that?" Cecilia says. "I can't believe it. I don't think we should have stayed here."

OK, now she's losing it. "That's ancient history, darling. Let's go have a drink. Calm your nerves." She's almost more rattled about Coco and the Nazis than she is about me and Susan. And that's just fine, for me at least. Maybe I'm just wishful thinking, though.

"*Oui*, madame, that is the past. We are living now, in this beautiful hotel, on this beautiful spring night," the clerk says.

I don't point out there are Nazi troops right outside the door. Seems we are all in a little bit of denial about a lot of things, *n'est-ce pas?*

"Come, darling," I say, and wrap my arm around Cecilia's

waist. This time, she seems to enjoy the support. This Coco Chanel betrayal is really devastating to her. I mean, she only learned about high fashion a year ago. From me. And I'm not mourning the loss of my Chanel vision, not at all. I like it when I find out the truth about people, celebrities or otherwise. We're all human, after all. Everyone has his or her dark side. Everyone. Some just have much more of the darkness than others.

Some are made of the darkness.

The elevator doors open and we step inside. I push the button for the rooftop bar. The lift is small and private, unlike the Eiffel Tower's crowded ones. Here it's just me and Cecilia and our secrets. Our darkness.

She looks at me. "I really can't believe it."

She's referring to Coco Chanel.

I look at her. "Neither can I."

I'm referring to Cecilia.

The elevator doors open and we step into a narrow hall with an aviation theme, French-style. I don't know why it's decorated this way and, at the moment, don't care.

"Oh, sorry, we are about to close," a young woman says, appearing at the end of the hall.

Behind her I can see the Michelin two-star restaurant is filled with happy diners. No one is going anywhere anytime soon.

"We're here for a nightcap. We won't be long," I say as we brush past her and turn left, heading away from the restaurant and toward the outdoor deck. I take a deep breath, relieved to find it open.

"Where would you like to sit?" I ask. "I know from the website there is a special table up there." I point to a trellised area accessible by a winding, spiral staircase. A special spot I learned about during a Google search in the taxi leaving the Eiffel Tower.

"That looks magical, but it seems a bit high," Cecilia says.

But then she turns to me. "But why not? It's our last night together. I'll be brave."

She smiles and I return it. "Why don't you go have a seat, enjoy the view, and I'll order drinks? I'll be right up." I'm pleased we are back on solid ground, although I am wondering why she's dropped the Susan discussion. Perhaps she's saving it for later, but for now I'll enjoy the kind version of my wife while keeping my guard up in case the vicious version returns.

"Thank you, I'll do that," she says.

I make my way back inside and wave to a young man who seems to be working here, albeit reluctantly. "Son, we'd like a nightcap. Two glasses of your finest champagne will do the trick."

He takes a deep inhale. "The terrace closed at one a.m., sir."

"Oh, that's funny, because we're sitting out there right now. My wife is loving the view," I say. "Look, I'll make it worth your while. Pour a couple glasses and pretend we aren't out there. Close the terrace. Just keep the door ajar so I can leave. Deal?" I slip a couple of crisp 100-euro notes into his hand.

He considers his options, his future employment, too, no doubt.

"*Bien.* Let me just get those poured for you," he says, hurrying behind the bar. He's clearly hoping none of the rest of the staff see him breaking the rules, encouraging a guest to stay beyond midnight when they're all ready to leave for the evening. "Here you go."

He places two champagne flutes on the bar and shoves a couple napkins my way.

"Mercy," I say and follow him to the now shut door to the terrace. He slips a key in the lock and allows me to pass outside. "Remember, don't lock us out there."

He nods and then pulls a matchbook out of his pocket. I watch as he inserts it into where the door's lock is, blocking its ability to close. "It's not my first rodeo, sir."

"Of course not," I say, pleased with my choice. He'll deny he ever saw us here, like he has done every other time he's allowed a couple to stay past midnight outside on the romantic terrace.

He's a lover sympathizer, *oui*?

I chuckle as I hurry across to the back of the terrace. Cecilia sits at a table for two just above me. This corner of the terrace is private. It overlooks homes, not businesses. There are no CCTV cameras, no film crews, nothing but silence. The sound of French people sleeping.

I place both champagne flutes in my left hand and climb the spiral stairs up to where Cecilia waits. It's like a movie, this night, so perfect in every way.

I'm kidding.

FIFTY-FIVE

WEST PALM BEACH, FLORIDA, NINETEEN MONTHS AGO

Cecilia

Nothing works with Esther, nothing will soften her heart toward me. It's like I never existed. The letter to her neighbors didn't have any effect; my repeated outreaches to her over the years never opened her to me, to my existence.

The closest I could get to her is through designing invitations for her parties. Julio was such a great friend, paying me to create that art. I couldn't believe my luck, hitting it off as we did at yoga class. He asked to see my work and hired me. Working on invitations for Esther's parties made me feel one step closer to my mom, the mom who never wanted me. Ever.

Maybe it was that, the realization that I needed to find another way. That it was only fair. So I started watching her from afar, and him, her escort. They were very touchy-feely, always holding hands when out and about. Paul lies when he says they were just friends. I could tell. Anyone who watched them closely, like I did, would know.

One night, Julio called me after work quite upset. He told

me, confidentially, that Esther was dying of congestive heart failure. Her heart was giving out and there was nothing to be done to stop it, just medicines and treatments to prolong the inevitable. Julio worried about the staff, the team he'd built. I worried about how to get my hands on her inheritance.

But then, almost like Julio had been mistaken about her health, Esther and Paul were seen out and about in Palm Beach, and I was asked to design invitations for a pink party they'd be hosting soon. I was furious. I'd settled into the notion of her dying without ever acknowledging me, but now to see her still out there enjoying life while I was not, well, it wasn't acceptable.

When was she going to die already? It was then that I decided I would be the one to decide just when and how the great Esther Wilmot would die. It was after yoga that Julio gave me the idea. We were walking out of the studio and Julio was complaining about the pink party theme.

"Do you know what she wants? Candy and sweets everywhere, like a confectioner's dream, all pink. Pink champagne and rosé, pink donuts, pink cookies, pink cakes, and even pink crème brûlée, her favorite dessert," Julio said. "Esther has a raging sweet tooth but never gains a pound. It's not fair! I simply think about this party and gain weight."

"I didn't know Esther had a sweet tooth?" My heart was thumping as my plan took shape. "Look, I have to go, but I'll drop the invitations off soon. They're going to be round like a pink cupcake. To die for, darling."

I designed the invitations in a day and sent them off to be printed. It took a couple weeks of full-time effort but I learned how to make a sensational crème brûlée. I knew it was Esther's favorite dessert and I knew it had to taste exactly like it would if a fine French restaurant made it for her. And, finally, it did.

I delivered the invitations for the pink party, along with

special gifts, two crème brûlées, a chocolate one for Esther and a
vanilla one for Julio. Julio explained that he would deliver it to
Esther personally. I told him not to mention my name, but that I
was grateful for all the work she'd given me, and it was the least
I could do.

I got my thanks to her just in time. She died the next day.

FIFTY-SIX
PARIS, 1:17 A.M.

Paul

As soon as I appear on the stairs, Cecilia spots me. The entire balcony is tiny, only big enough to fit a metal table and two small Parisian café chairs. It's perched at the very top of the hotel, a little platform in the sky. Cecilia stands next to the table, her arms crossed in front of her chest, her scarf wrapped around her.

"You're right. It's a very special spot up here, even though it's making my fear of heights fire up again," she says. "Trying to be brave tonight, I suppose." Behind her, in the distance, the Eiffel Tower glows, the through-line to our evening.

"Very brave, darling. I decided champagne was in order, for our last night," I say. I am testing her. Will she connect the dots?

"Just like at Esther's celebration of life," Cecilia says. "Fitting. Cheers!"

We clink glasses. "Do you really believe I ruin everything I touch?" I can't help but ask.

Cecilia settles into a seat at the table for two. I remain standing. I notice she has kicked off the ridiculous high heels. "I do, actually."

"Well, then you're ruined, I guess. I've touched you, very well," I say.

"This is not the time for sexual innuendo, Paul," Cecilia says, taking a big sip of champagne. I had, of course, considered lacing it with something. Just to make this easier, just to take the edge off. But I didn't. She doesn't deserve it. Not anymore.

"What is it the time for, then?" I ask. I walk to the table and pull out the other chair.

"The truth, I suppose," Cecilia says. She is a remarkably beautiful woman. In the moonlit glow of our last night in Paris, I can almost see a future. With rules, perhaps. New parameters on money, on behavior, on expectations. On duty to one's husband.

"The truth will set you free." I chuckle, a low rumble, as my stomach emits a horrible sound. "Pardon."

Cecilia smiles. If she heard my stomach erupting, she doesn't say anything.

"The truth is it wasn't a coincidence we met at Esther's memorial service," she says. I notice she's spinning the diamond at her neck again. "I knew who you were. I sat next to you on purpose."

"Aha! I knew it," I say. Although the revelation isn't a surprise, it is nice to have a confession of sorts. I didn't want to believe she targeted me, but now, well, I must. The truth is a tough pill to swallow. I stare at my wife.

"Paul, you didn't know I targeted you. You thought it was fate. Love at first sight," she says.

I will not admit I was an idiot. Oh... whatever.

"Fine. I didn't realize you'd targeted me at the time." I fold my arms across my chest. So what if she tricked me for a moment?

Cecilia laughs. "Of course you didn't know you were my

mark. You fell for me right away. Love at first sight, as you always say."

"You say that, too," I remind her. My stomach clenches. I need to burp, but I don't. I am looking forward to eating normal food beginning tomorrow. Getting back to normal, that will be the goal.

"I lied."

I look at Cecilia and then to the sparkling tower in the distance. "You what?"

"I lied, Paul. I didn't love you. I don't love you. I wanted what was mine, my inheritance," she says. "And I got it."

I take a sip of champagne. It doesn't help quell the fire. There will be no more normal with us. That is clear.

"Nothing is yours, darling. You must be drunk," I say. "You signed a prenup. You will have nothing. But you're used to that, so there's that. Esther didn't want or love you. And now, neither do I." I stand up and walk to the railing. It's wrought iron, low, below my waist. It's dangerous up here, my brain warns.

Cecilia moves to my side. If someone were to see us just now, in the moonlight, side by side, they'd think we were so lucky. That we have it all. We could have, but she has ruined it. I am not the one who ruins things, it seems.

"The prenup won't hold. It was rushed. Signed under duress, and you didn't declare all your assets, all of Esther's assets she gave you, but that doesn't matter, not anymore, darling," she says. She finishes her champagne.

"Why wouldn't a legal document matter, darling?" I ask. She is pushing all my buttons at the same time. I cannot believe her. I used to think what we had was special. She does not realize I control everything. I have all the power in this relationship. She is nothing, a nobody, without me, Paul Strom.

"Paul, do you think I've enjoyed playing Stepford wife to a middle-aged narcissist?" she asks. "I mean, when we met, I felt a real attraction to you and that turned into actual love. I thought you were handsome and caring, and that you'd look after me. Treat me well. I was so excited to begin my life with the man I thought you were. But you are not that man. You never were. You are a monster. When I look at you now, I see a sinister old man. I mean, look at us. It is obvious to everyone—besides you, I guess. I would never have children with you. I never went off birth control, but you didn't notice. You only see yourself. Oh, and Susan, your lover. You see her, don't you. Did you know I almost ran her over? But then why put myself in jeopardy over your stupid choices, am I right?"

Oh, no, I see you, Cecilia. "What do you mean by all of this hate speech you're spewing?"

"I deserve more than half of Esther's estate. I am her only rightful heir," she says. "How's your stomach? You look sweaty, damp, and sort of ill."

Now that she mentions it, I realize sweat has drenched the shirt under my jacket and is pooling around my waist. I wipe my brow. I am sick. What do I have?

"You see, I don't want a divorce, Paul," she says. I watch as she begins to pace back and forth on the tiny platform. Four steps in one direction, right up to the edge, and four steps back.

My heart races in my chest. Am I having a heart attack? I grip the railing and lean forward. It wobbles under my weight. "You don't want a divorce?"

"No," Cecilia says. "Why would I settle for divorcing you and taking half of your money when I can play the role of grieving widow and take it all?"

FIFTY-SEVEN

PARIS, 1:45 A.M.

Paul

It's too hot for my jacket. I yank it off and toss it onto the chair. Did my wife just claim to be a widow? Has she lost her mind? I am right here, standing next to her, watching her pace like a restless stallion.

"Can you stop moving?" I ask. Her motion is making me dizzy. Everything is making me dizzy. She must have her words confused. That's all. Cecilia is my soulmate. I told her so, I convinced her so. Oh, well, who am I kidding? I saw a hot young thing I could groom into the soulmate I needed, the wife I needed, and I pounced. I had the money, she had the looks. All I wanted were babies and credibility. The envy of others. And a fabulous life.

Cecilia finally stops next to me on the railing. Good girl. I can control certain women. I can smell them, feel them the moment we run into each other. They are a type. I know what they want before they know it. I know how to get under their skin and make them mine.

I notice my hands have clenched into fists by my side.

"Take it all, you say?" I see my hand grab her arm. It's almost like it isn't me doing it. I stretch a smile across my perfect veneers.

"Yes," she says. "Let go. You're hurting me. From the moment I met you I knew something was really wrong with you. You're off. You're so self-centered you don't even realize how horrible you are to everyone around you. Especially me."

I need her to be quiet. "Shut up, Cecilia."

"No, I won't. You can't tell me what to do. This past year has been like living hell for me, so you shut up," she says.

I stare at her aghast, squeezing the soft flesh of her bicep. "Stop it."

"You wouldn't believe how hard it was to pretend to enjoy sex with you. And you didn't even notice. I faked every orgasm. Well, OK, a couple of times I didn't, but I mean, how gross is it that I had to sleep with a guy my mom had slept with? And all that talk about having kids. As if I'd bring another one of you into this world. Never. And then you started an affair with my former sister? You're disgusting."

I swallow and stare at the creature next to me. I'm both shocked and livid. They aren't sisters, not real sisters, they can't be. The fire rages. "Stop talking. I didn't know you were sisters. Nobody told me. But that's not what matters now. All of this, all of this is nonsense. You need to shut up. You aren't real sisters, you can't be." I put my hands over my ears, trying to calm my pounding heart and dull the fiery inferno inside me. I stare at Cecilia.

"We were sisters, I was her older sister for a time, living with her birth parents, the Sinclairs. So yes, we are related. Take your hands off your ears, now," she says coldly.

I do what she says, because I can still hear her anyway, even though I tried not to. I glare at her.

"You can't control me, Paul. You should realize that by now. I know you don't like to hear the truth," she says. "Here's what I think. I wouldn't be surprised if you killed my mom to get her money."

"Don't be absurd," I bark. I really need her to shut up. My stomach lurches.

"You're sick, Paul, and it's more than physical. You're likely a psychopath. You only care about yourself."

Well, at least we see each other clearly. I know who I am. I'm special. She is just a pretty face. She's nothing without me.

"Let me get this straight, darling. You never loved me. It was all fake. Nothing between us was real. And now you think you can leave me and take it all? My inheritance?" I realize my other hand is on her other arm and I may be shaking her with all my might. I need to remember not to apply too much pressure. We wouldn't want to leave bruises on her lovely arms.

"The money is mine," Cecilia says, defiant even in this moment. I am impressed, surprised. "Let go of me, Paul. I'll scream."

In a quick move, almost like I'm watching myself in a movie, I've spun her around until her back is pressed against me. I've cupped my hand over her duplicitous mouth, and my other arm anchors her body against me. Her struggles are fruitless. Despite my illness, I am in control.

It seems I have her attention now, though. I feel her body shaking under my control. I imagine the tears running down her cheeks, ruining her makeup. See, she's the one ruining things again. Her future, her face, her life of luxury. *No more Chanel for you, darling.*

It's sad, though, because I do still love her. How can I not? She's my wife. Sure, she thought she could outsmart me. Sure, she says she never had feelings for me but I know lust when I see it. She was so into me. And now she's trying to deny it all. Ridiculous. No woman will ever get the upper hand, never. Not Mia, not Cecilia, not even Susan, should things turn sour. I still can't believe Cecilia and Susan know each other, that Cecilia considers her a sister. Ugh. Of all the women in LA. What bad luck. But it doesn't matter, not anymore.

Cecilia's quivering body tight against mine is stirring those feelings I've had since we first met. I remind myself she's a beautiful traitor. My very own little Coco Chanel.

Cecilia flings her head from side to side in an effort to escape my grasp, moaning, trying to bite my fingers. It's amateur hour, folks. She cannot escape me. She will not. She's my little love charm, my hummingbird in a little red bag.

"Shhh, darling, relax," I murmur into her ear. "I'm so glad we had this little trip together, to really get to know each other. It's surprising what comes up during couple quality time."

"Mmmm," Cecilia says. Of course, she agrees.

"You know, darling, the truth is, I brought you here, to Paris, not for a romantic vacation. No, I was on to you and your thieving schemes. I simply needed to confirm that my suspicions about you were correct, Lila, and you admitted it," I say. "So you see, I was a step ahead, all along. And darling, the dinner at the Eiffel Tower, well, my plan was to either solidify our love, or end things there. And thanks to your revelations, and your behavior, well, I knew we were finished. I mean, I've moved on, with your sister of all people. Stunning development, but not a game changer. I guess I have a type. Anyway, back to the matter at hand." I squeeze her tighter and she moans. "Unfortunately, I hadn't realized all the security measures at the world's most targeted monument. As you noticed, it was hard to have any privacy there. A small miscalculation, although I had dreamed of watching you fall from the tower, a little red dot landing on the plaza below. So dramatic. Of course, it would have been a tragic suicide. I would have tried to stop you, but to no avail."

"Mmmm," Cecilia groans and tries to bite my hand. Futile effort.

"But I always have a Plan B, darling, and I'm always the one in control. So here we are, on this lovely private balcony, just the two of us. No one else around. You cannot possibly think you were one step ahead of me. You?"

Cecilia kicks back at me, trying to hurt my privates. I squeeze her tighter.

"No woman will ever double-cross me again. Do you understand?" I move her head up and down. "Good girl."

My stomach coils with another spasm but I keep my grip on my wife. I am finished with this charade, this farce of a relationship. Susan's lovely face pops into my mind. I will not be alone, no, far from it.

Truth is, I don't like to be alone. Without a woman by my side, reflecting how wonderful I am, well, sometimes I don't feel so wonderful. Strange, isn't it?

"Goodbye, Cecilia. I did love you," I say. And then, in a swift move, I've lifted her off her feet. I wonder how long it will take her to hit the ground once I decide her time is up. Not as visually satisfying as the Iron Lady fall, but still impactful.

She stops struggling and turns toward me. I lighten the grip on her mouth, and she says, "I'm so glad I poisoned you."

I gasp. Suddenly it all makes sense. Oh my god. I need help. The food all week. The stomach cramps. How long has this been going on? Oh my god. I need to get rid of her. I need medical help. I see the fear in her face, the darkness in her eyes. She grabs onto the railing but she's no match for me and my strength. I peel her fingers off one by one, and as she thrashes at me with her arms, I push her hard and she soars over the railing.

As she begins her fall to her death she yells, "You'll never get away with this. You don't know what's going to happen next."

I clutch my stomach, suddenly aware that I feel truly terrible. That this is her fault. That she has tried to kill me, too.

I race down the stairs, across the terrace to the closed door. Thankfully, when I yank on it, it opens. The reluctant waiter has saved my life. I rush down the hall of the oddly shaped, airplane-themed space and push the elevator button wildly. It opens finally and I duck inside, doubling over in pain.

Once downstairs, I jog to the lobby where one helpful front desk staff says, "Sir, can I help?"

"Please call an ambulance. I've been poisoned!"

And I feel my legs buckle as everything goes dark.

Dear Diary,

My sister Cecilia isn't what she seems to be. I know it was hard for her growing up. First she was a replacement for my parents' first daughter who died. But then I came along when Cecilia was seven years old. Surprise. Special Susan, the apple of their eye, arrived. That's me. Pretty soon they saw that she was too jealous of me, my beauty, my place in the family, and my parents told me they had to do the right thing and send her back to where they got her. It was for the good of the family, the Sinclair family: me, Mom and Dad. Mommy said she was worried Cecilia would hurt me, her precious child. I guess she did drop me once, or let me roll off the couch. And another time, Mommy caught her standing over my cot, a pillow in her hand. Was she going to suffocate me? They didn't know, but it scared them enough that off she went. Bye, big sister. Hello, only beloved child status for me. Special Susan, that's me.

That had to be hard on Cecilia. I mean, she was eight or nine at the time she was sent back, old enough to know what that meant: that she wasn't wanted. It could damage a person, I'd imagine. But the thing is, despite the fact nobody in our family really loved her all that much, Cecilia got a lot of attention elsewhere. As soon as I was old enough to be at the same school, I watched her. I was in kindergarten and she was in middle school, and the school was small enough that we'd run into each other for all those years until she graduated high school. She was popular, and pretty, and, well, I suppose if she had gone to college, if she'd had parents who supported her dreams, she'd be in a different place in her life. Rumor was that the Babcocks took her in, like they did the other kids they adopted, just for the money. That's sad, I suppose.

So I felt sorry for her when she didn't get to go to college like her hunky boyfriend, and pretty soon she left town. I knew he married somebody else because he's back in my hometown with his wife, but I didn't give much thought to Cecilia. It was good riddance, truth be told. It was only when I read the news of her marriage to the uber-wealthy Paul Strom that I focused my attention on her.

I mean sure, I had everything a person could want growing up: two parents who loved me, a roof over my head, but we didn't have extra. No, we didn't live high on the hog at all. So I devoured every bit of news and gossip about the fabulous Paul and Cecilia Strom. He'd inherited a fortune from some old lady and together, he and my sister were living the life of my dreams. Especially Cecilia. I saw her engagement ring when she posted it on social media. It was enough to make my head spin.

How could I get a little piece of all that money, I wondered? Well, I'd go after her husband, that's how. He wanted to be a producer, and I wanted to be an actress, so we have everything in common.

I know, that's not very Christian, and neither is it that it worked, the little romp on the casting couch, and now I'm regularly sleeping with her husband. But let's face it, Cecilia had a tough life, and she's got issues to work through. She shouldn't be married to a great guy like Paul. I knew he was attracted to me the moment he saw me in the waiting room during the casting call. I felt the same way. It was electric, and just like a Hollywood love story.

As for Cecilia, she should be in counseling or something. So really, I'm helping her out by stealing him away.

And I can feel it. He's all mine. Whatever happened in Paris, she showed her true colors and he wants out. I know it.

I'll be the next Mrs. Strom. I'll live in a mansion by the sea. Oh, and if he finds out somehow Cecilia and I knew each other in the past, that we should have been sisters, that we once lived under the same roof, who can explain the way fate works?

Nothing can stand in the way of true love. Cecilia better not try to scare me again like she did when she almost ran me over. There are cameras all over LA, and I just installed two on my front and back doors. I know how to deal with her.

I wonder why Cecilia never got pregnant? I know Paul wanted to have kids with Cecilia, he told me as much early on. I'm sure she figured out how not to make that dream come true, but that seems stupid. She could have locked him in if she had his child. But like I said, she isn't that smart.

As for me, I'll have as many babies as he wants.

As for Cecilia, she'll go away, get help or something, and I'll be walking down the aisle.

I love it.

Paul

I wake up in a hospital room. I am alive. Thank goodness.

I try to move but my head hurts. My whole body hurts. A nurse appears. She smiles.

"Bonjour, Monsieur Strom," she says. She is so cute. She saved my life. I love her. "How are you feeling?"

She is so caring, with wide brown eyes, a concerned look on her lovely face.

"Not well. My wife tried to kill me," I say.

She fiddles with some sort of IV line. "Oh, sorry. That is why we pumped your stomach, *n'est-ce pas?*"

Is this something she hears every day? Her lack of surprise surprises me. "Yes, thank you, you saved my life."

"*Mais oui*, actually, though, your vitals are still not good. Understand? You rest, *s'il vous plaît.*"

Cecilia. What a little cunning bitch. How dare she poison me? Who would do that to their own spouse? It's absurd.

Someone knocks on the door but enters without giving me a chance to tell them to go away.

"Monsieur Paul Strom?" asks a man in a uniform. A police uniform. I think they're called *gendarmes*, but I'm not going to try to pronounce that. See, I've learned so much from Cecilia. But I digress.

I consider the policeman. He is large for a French man. His arms are big, built, with huge biceps, and his eyes are shrouded by dark bushy eyebrows. He wears a scowl on his lightly bearded face. He looks American, actually, and very mean. And that gives me some comfort. Perhaps we will be able to understand each other, man to man.

"Good to see you finally. Together we can get to the bottom of this," I say. "Have a seat. Thank you for coming."

The big officer looks confused and side-eyes the smaller, more French-looking and mustachioed officer who walked in behind him.

"You are glad to see us?" big guy asks.

"Yes. My wife poisoned me. She tried to kill me. I barely survived. I may still pass away. I don't know what poison she used but I'm sure we can do tests. I want to press charges. Immediately," I say. My throat is raw, it hurts to talk but I try to sound as powerful, as righteous, as I feel.

The police officers look at each other and begin to laugh. I don't think anything is funny, but I paste a smile on my face.

Oh, now I know what is funny. How can I press charges against Cecilia? That would be ridiculous. She's dead. I change my approach. "Of course, I don't need to press charges against my poor wife. She felt so guilty she jumped to her death just after telling me she poisoned me."

"Oh really? That's what happened here?" the little French cop says. He has a smirk on his face. I don't like smirks. I'm about to tell him he should mind his manners. I'm the victim here.

"Look, officers—" I begin.

Big cop holds up a big hand and stops me. "You, Paul Strom,

are under arrest for the attempted murder of your wife, Cecilia Strom."

Attempted murder? So she's not dead? But that's impossible. There's no way she survived that fall.

"You look surprised, Mr. Strom. You thought you'd killed her but fortunately for Madame Strom, an awning broke her fall. She is injured, but very much alive," the big guy says. The little French weasel next to him laughs. "And we checked your toxicology report. There is no trace of any known poisons. It must be the rich French food, too sophisticated for a simple American palate like yours."

I cannot breathe. I cannot escape. I cannot believe this. "She told me she poisoned me. I've been sick all week. Test things again."

"There was no poison." The big French man shakes his head. "But you, sir, are in big trouble. There are witnesses. Who pushes his wife off a rooftop?"

A man who is tired of his wife. That's who. I cannot believe this is happening to me. Cecilia will not win. She should know that by now. Who would have witnessed her fall? No one. That's not possible. The movie set was across the street, on the other side of the hotel. I checked for CCTV cameras, I scanned all the balconies and all the apartments around us. They were all dark, everyone was asleep. The bar was closed for the night. There are no witnesses. None. They are bluffing.

I make eye contact with the big fella, trying to make my eyes neutral, friendly even.

"Seems a guy you met, a guy named Christopher, was watching you all night, Mr. Strom," the officer says. He's beginning to get on my nerves. "And a young man named Theo was worried about how you were treating your wife. He also followed you all night. Together, they gave us a robust view of your evening in Paris."

"Don't forget that other guy. The one at the bar?" small cop with odd French mustache says. "Theo and Christopher saw your wife talking to a man at the bar where you stopped for a drink. He's been helpful, too. Says you were an, what did he call you? Oh yes, 'an odd duck.'"

Big man opens a notepad. "Yes, Randy. He lost his wife recently. Says Cecilia reminded him of her. Thought you were acting strange."

I swallow. Was Cecilia sleeping with everyone in town?

"What do they all know? Nothing! All lies," I say. "My wife was trying to kill me. She poisoned me. It could be arsenic, perhaps, or hemlock. Both don't show up in tests."

I know I should be quiet. I really do know that. It's just that I need to find the proof.

"Mr. Strom, please," the big officer says. "We know what you did."

"I demand more testing," I say. And then I realize I may need to pivot. So I do. "And besides, it was an accident. She fell because she attacked me when she could see the poison wasn't working. She tried to push me over the balcony. It was self-defense."

Small officer with annoying mustache laughs. "Oh really? It was an accident. Your wife was trying to overpower you, sir?"

"Yes. And she poisoned me. This is all her fault. Go interrogate her, prosecute her," I say. Even though it hurts to talk, I am glad we are making some progress here.

"Did you forbid your wife from accepting a job with someone named Evan Dorsey?" he asks.

"What the hell does that have to do with anything? My wife is rich, she doesn't need a job," I say. "Why are you talking to a caterer instead of finding the source of my poisoning?"

"Mr. Dorsey says you're dangerous. That your wife was leaving you, and that they are in love," officer dickhead says.

"Impossible," I say. I need to stop talking.

"Your wife told us the same thing, Mr. Strom," huge blabbing officer says. "Oh, and a Mr. Seymour Lynch?"

The traitorous banker, yes? Of course, he wants to be part of the story. Cecilia's men all lined up to lie for her, to make me the bad guy instead of her. She's the mastermind of all this. I stare at the big officer, watching his lip twitch.

"He says you were trying to control all the money. That you sent him a text from Paris, irate that your wife had a credit card you didn't know about. You forbade him from funding anything else for your wife. He said that you were finished with her and her spending." The officer closes the notebook, as if he's had an aha moment.

He's no match for me. No one is. "My wife was sneaking around, draining my bank accounts, having an affair. I was protecting my inheritance," I say. "I demand to talk to my attorney. Call Joseph Grant immediately."

The officers laugh.

Small French guys says, "You're not in charge here, Mr. Strom. This is France. As soon as you're released, you'll be transferred to prison where you will stay until you stand trial. You have the right to either an appointed or retained legal counsel, but the majority of your trial is conducted by the judge. Your lawyer will have a limited role."

"Your prison cell, well, it will feel, let's say, the opposite of The Peninsula Hotel," big man says.

I watch in horror as they walk toward me. They pull out handcuffs and attach each of my wrists to the hospital bed. Then they do the same to my ankles.

"I'm innocent. I'm sick. My wife tried to kill me. I demand a call to my attorney! I am getting out of here, you just watch me!" I yell. My throat hurts.

I cannot believe Cecilia survived that fall. I cannot believe I'm trapped here like an animal. I rattle my arms against the restraints.

"You aren't going anywhere, not for a very long time, Mr. Strom. We'll be back to take you to prison as soon as you are medically cleared. It shouldn't be long since you weren't poisoned." The officer chuckles.

"I don't care if you don't believe me. It's the truth," I say.

Big guy stops in the doorway before leaving my room. "Our fine French food is wasted on your basic palate. That is all it is," he repeats. And then, he's gone.

I look at my wrists cuffed to the bed. I will do everything possible not to be here by the time they return. You know me, I'll get out of this situation. Stay tuned. You can't look away now, not when I need you.

But please don't worry. I'm always fine.

I control the narrative, even when I can't pronounce the language.

Until we meet again.

Adieu.

EPILOGUE

MALIBU, ONE YEAR LATER

Cecilia

I make my way slowly to the backyard, using the walker my physical therapist insists on when he isn't around. I lower myself slowly onto the lounge chair, soaking up the Southern California sunshine. I love my new home. There are gates and safety, neighbors close by in case I need help. I still have nightmares from that night in Paris, of course. Imagine falling backward into space, staring into the eyes of the monster who was killing you.

Who tried to kill you.

I landed on a retractable awning a few floors down, crashed through it, ended up sprawled on a Parisian family's deck. I don't remember much, except a scream—probably mine—the eerie blue lights flashing, the familiar faces looking down at me as the stretcher wheeled me into the ambulance. They were looking out for me, those guys, even though I hadn't asked them to.

Evan had asked Theo and his mom to watch over me. Phoebe and Evan were in culinary school together. She didn't know I'd added hemlock to the meal we cooked together in her lovely restaurant. And of course, I made certain not a drop was spilled outside of Paul's dish. It's the same method I used to kill Esther, of course, mixing it into her crème brûlée, and I've perfected my handling of the toxic plant since then. Poison hemlock is a native of Europe, if you didn't know, and quite common in French gardens. I researched that in case my stash of flowers and seeds was discovered in my suitcase, hidden in medicine vials, an empty jar of night cream and an empty bottle of Aleve. It wasn't discovered, but I had a Plan B, just in case.

And Paul thought he was the only one with devious, deadly plans.

Christopher was a lovely surprise on our last night, turning up as he did as a welcome distraction, getting Paul jealous and agitated, distracted. Christopher got such a kick out of the photos I texted him from that happy hour. He was less happy about the photos I sent him during the rest of our last night in Paris. If the police hadn't called him and told him I was fine, he was about to sound the alarm.

You could see what was going to happen, he said, by the look in Paul's eyes. The hatred. The fury.

As for my clumsiness, tripping and falling in front of the café, of course I did that on purpose. I needed a break from being alone with Paul. I needed time to think before that dinner at the Eiffel Tower. Randy, though, that was happenstance. A fortunate coincidence that Paul decided meant much more. Sometimes things are just that. Coincidence. But, of course, sometimes things are planned out to the minute. Like what I did when I implemented my plan to lure Paul to me. It all worked so well. And now here I am. The winner.

I simply couldn't take him anymore. Sure, when we first met and I lured him to me for the money, I thought, why not stick it out? I loved everything about my life in Malibu at first, including Paul. I thought we had a fairy-tale relationship. But over time, I realized everything about my new life was great—except my husband. He is just impossible to live with. I mean, listening to the way he talks about himself is enough to drive a person crazy. And then, he has the nerve to start sleeping around. On me? We were newlyweds, after all. Ridiculous. But honestly, I couldn't think of a better woman to stick him with than my former sister, my nemesis Splendid Susan. As if. They deserve each other. When I first discovered their affair, when I first figured out there was something going on and followed him, I was angry, as anyone would be. I admit I thought about running her over one night as she crossed the street. I was that furious. But then, after some thought, I realized that they deserve each other. She's a horrible person, too. And it's not like I want to sleep with the man anymore. Not now that I know who he is. Good riddance. And good luck, Susan, there's a special place in hell for women who sleep with their former sister's husband, I'm sure of it. It's ironic I was jealous of the life she lived as a child, the life I wanted. And I guess she wanted my life as an adult. Well, she could have it for a little while, I decided.

When Paul proposed the romantic trip to Paris to celebrate our anniversary, I jumped at the chance. I was so sick of him and looking for a way out that wasn't divorce. I couldn't risk having him get more of Esther's estate—he didn't deserve any of Esther's estate, quite frankly. So, he needed to die. And I decided to use the same method I used to speed up Esther's demise.

Anyway, what better place to kill someone than abroad, in Paris, where the food was foreign to his limited palate and he wouldn't suspect a thing until it was too late? I got the idea by listening to one of those murder podcasts where a creepy guy killed his wife by harvesting the weeds in his garden. I loved the idea of using a flower to kill. It just seemed so right, and the added benefit is it's undetectable unless a test is run right away for the presence of coniine. But no one would suspect it. It worked so well on good old Esther, after all.

Once I'd decided on my plan for dealing with Paul, I innocently involved Evan, who contacted Phoebe, who unknowingly provided me with the perfect poisonous lunch spot. Christopher was bummed I was going away with Paul. He knew I was unhappy in the marriage. We talked about it every morning at the gym. When he decided to come and make sure I was OK, well, that was just about the nicest thing anyone has ever done for me. And to follow me all night. So kind. Theo, too. Without them, things could have turned out a lot different.

I have the money, and the freedom. Paul has no money, no freedom. He's got nothing but time. Ha! A long prison sentence awaits him unless, well, the choice is his. He can give me all the inheritance, and I will refuse to testify against him. He'll likely get off with time served.

Or he can continue to try to convince people I was poisoning him – no proof, hemlock is undetectable – and try to plead his innocence in front of a jury. He's super lucky they pumped his stomach when they did. Me and my big mouth for warning him as I was falling. But still, his defense is ridiculous. How does one accidentally toss his wife from a rooftop, Mr. Strom? That's what we all would like to know.

I'll get all the money. He'll get a lighter sentence. He'll also be ordered to stay far away from me, I'm sure of that. Because I will ruin his reputation in LA and beyond. I've already begun that process, trust me. It takes a long time to work your way into Hollywood. It takes one bad rumor to make sure you're never welcome there again. Cancel culture. *Bye-bye, Paul.*

But no, I haven't married Evan. Or Christopher.

I know you may have been expecting that, especially if you consider the trail of destruction Paul causes everyone he gets close to, everywhere he goes. His behavior can leave you lonely, and stunned, especially if you're a nice person. I mean, it was natural for his first wife to fall into the arms of someone strong and caring and normal when she figured out who and what Paul was. She was married to a malignant narcissist for a long time, too long.

As for me, it was only a year. A horrible, long, terrible year. But I knew going in what I was getting into and what I wanted in the end. And I won. I'm free!

Just for the record, I'm not marrying anyone again.

Ever.

Evan's a nice guy and we're having fun with the event planning company, but come on, think about it. I'm still young, rich beyond my wildest dreams, and divorced from Paul. Thanks to the strong awning that cushioned my fall on the way down, I have my health and I've almost fully recovered. I still have nightmares about falling, but they'll dim over time, I'm sure.

I should never have agreed to go up on that rooftop. I thought I'd give him the final dose of hemlock in his drink, and I'd watch him die up there. I couldn't believe he was still alive after all the poison I'd given him all day and night. But before I could sprinkle anything in his champagne, he grabbed me, the jerk.

The only other regret I have is threatening a lawsuit to get my inheritance and using a second-rate lawyer who started spreading my name all around West Palm Beach. Of course, Paul heard about Lila Wilmot Babcock. My idiot attorney was supposed to keep my name confidential, but instead blabbered about my pending lawsuit to a bunch of buddies at a bar, and the next thing you know, Paul's attorney sent him that email. My one big mistake. But lesson learned: never talk to slimeball attorneys. I was too trusting. Now I am the opposite. I haven't forgotten what he did. And I will make him pay, someday.

It's taken me a bit of ingenuity, luck and strategy to get here. To get free. Do you see me clearly now? I hope so. I can be anyone I want to be, get anything I want.

I look at my phone. Evan is texting me again. He really wants to take our relationship to the next level, whatever that means. He says he loves me, but I'm not sure how I feel about him. I guess I could give it a try. You know, the whole dating thing is just like playing the lottery. Most of the time, you lose. But I suppose if he and I don't work out, I know how to extricate myself from the situation.

Susan wasn't so lucky, of course. Someone tipped off the authorities that she should be interviewed in connection with Paul, that she was having an affair with him, a married man – and not just that, but her former sister's husband. I wonder who leaked the story? She was finished in Hollywood then. And I've heard she couldn't afford to keep the bungalow Paul bought her and scampered back to the Florida swamps she came from. Karma. And good riddance. If she ever comes near me again, I know how to handle her.

I've done it before. I can do it again. I'm gorgeous, rich, and I've only just begun.

A LETTER FROM KAIRA

Dear Reader,

Thank you so much for reading *The Second Mrs Strom*. I truly hope you enjoyed it. If you did and want to keep up to date with all my latest releases, just sign up at the following link. Your email address will never be shared, and you can unsubscribe at any time.

www.bookouture.com/kaira-rouda

Writing this story was a blast because I had the chance to bring back one of my most notorious characters, Paul Strom. He's not a nice guy, but ever since his debut in *Best Day Ever*, he's been in the back of my mind, begging for a sequel. Now, perhaps, he's happy. Only problem is, Cecilia Strom isn't finished with her story yet. I hope you'll preorder my next book, *Only the Nanny*, and come along for the ride. If you enjoyed this novel, perhaps you'd like to check out my backlist of *USA Today*, Amazon Charts and internationally bestselling psychological suspense including *Best Day Ever*, *The Favorite Daughter*, *The Next Wife*, *The Widow*, *Somebody's Home*, *Beneath the Surface* and *Under the Palms*.

Thank you again for reading! If you'd like to keep in touch, I'm active on social media and would love for you to join me there! I also have a newsletter, and I'd love for you to sign up. I promise not to overwhelm your inbox, and I do have special, subscriber-only benefits.

Oh, and since you're a crime fiction fan, please tune in to the Killer Author Club, www.killerauthorclub.com, where we interview bestselling authors every other Tuesday. Join us for the fun.

Your support means the world to me. Thank you!

Kaira

www.kairarouda.com

facebook.com/KairaRoudaBooks

instagram.com/KairaRouda

tiktok.com/@KairaRoudaBooks

READING GROUP GUIDE

1. What did you think of Paul Strom at the beginning of the story? How did that opinion change by the end?
2. What role does a diary play in the story, and what does it reveal as the story progresses?
3. When did you realize who Cecilia truly was?
4. The City of Light is more than a setting in the story. How do the city itself, its amazing sites, history and the Parisian people play a role in the plot?
5. When did you realize that perhaps Paul had met his match?
6. Do you think Cecilia was justified in her feelings toward Paul by the end of the story? Do you think she loved him, ever?
7. This story is packed with twists and turns. Which of them was the most surprising?
8. Who is Susan, and why was she more important to the story than it seemed?
9. Discuss the climax of the story, and the ending. Did it surprise you? What did you think was going to happen?

ACKNOWLEDGEMENTS

This story wouldn't be possible without my brilliant editor, Lydia Vassar-Smith, who had read my story *The Next Wife* and approached my agents wondering if there was more to come from me. There was! Thank you, Lydia, for helping me make this book the best it could be and for seeing the potential. I'm excited to be working with the entire Bookouture team. Thank you, too, to my literary agents Meg Ruley and Annelise Robey, for cheering me on and being my partners in crime fiction.

Family is everything to me, and I can't thank my husband and kids enough for their support. And to you, the reader, I wouldn't be living the life of my dreams without you. Thank you from the bottom of my heart.

PUBLISHING TEAM

Turning a manuscript into a book requires the efforts of many people. The publishing team at Bookouture would like to acknowledge everyone who contributed to this publication.

Audio
Alba Proko
Sinead O'Connor
Melissa Tran

Commercial
Lauren Morrissette
Jil Thielen
Imogen Allport

Contracts
Peta Nightingale

Cover design
Eileen Carey

Data and analysis
Mark Alder
Mohamed Bussuri

Made in the USA
Columbia, SC
04 September 2024

41640508R00169